Glowgems for Profit

Profit Logbook Series
Book One

Bruce C. Davis

Brick Cave Media
brickcavebooks.com

2018

Brick Cave Media
brickcavebooks.com
2018

Acknowledgements

Thanks to Al Kalar, for giving the books their first life, and Brick Cave, especially Bob, for seeing their potential and giving them a second incarnation.

Glowgems for Profit

Profit Logbook Series
Book One

Bruce Davis

Brick Cave Media
brickcavebooks.com

CHAPTER ONE

"Highpoint Control, this is VC-334 *Profit* requesting final vector and approach clearance." Sylvia's voice was a soft, musical contralto.

I smiled in spite of a jolt hangover that made my head feel like it was on fire. The traffic officer had been flirting with Sylvia since we entered Highpoint Arcology's zone of control. He was going to be heartbroken when he found out she was the ship's Artificial Intelligence.

"You're clear for approach, *Profit*—Bay 42 spinward. Vector download on my mark—mark."

"Thank you, Highpoint. Vectored and locked," said Sylvia. "You've been so helpful."

"You're welcome, Miss," answered the traffic officer. "I get off shift in a few hours. Maybe I could show you some of the sights, seeing as how you're new here and all."

"Why, that's so sweet of you," cooed Sylvia. "Let me ask my husband how long it will take to clear customs. I'm sure he'll be as thrilled as I am to have a guide to show us around."

"Uh, well, sure...glad to, Ma'am. I'll look you up at your berth when I get off, unless the boss needs me to work a double shift." You could feel the word 'husband' filtering thru his cognitive system.

"Oh, you poor dear," Sylvia purred. "Does that happen often?"

"Oh, yeah, all the time," he answered, sounding relieved.

"Well, I hope they don't work you to death. And I intend to tell the Port Authorities how wonderful you've been. Thank you, again. *Profit* out."

As soon as she signed off, I laughed out loud, making my head hurt even more. "You're cruel, Sylvia."

"He started it," she protested. "I was just protecting the ship's good name. We can't have the whole system thinking we're easy."

I shook my head, still chuckling. "I'd better get down to the forward hold. We can't afford to have Deuce rough up a customs inspector."

I swung through the hatch at the rear of the cockpit and crossed the catwalk above the cargo hold. Deuce was just squeezing his bulk through the passageway from the aft hold. I waved him back and he nodded. I slid down the ladder to the main deck. Muted thumps outside the hull announced our docking in Bay 42 spinward. Indicator lights next to the forward lock changed from red to green as the outer bay sealed and pressurized.

Five minutes later, I cycled the forward lock and lowered the cargo ramp. It touched down near the feet of a small, officious looking man in a Highpoint customs uniform who stood waiting on the steel deck of the docking bay. His trouser creases were sharp enough to cut hull metal and his boots gleamed like mirrors.

I shivered involuntarily and wished I'd taken the time to down some analgesics before docking. The nanofibers bonded to my central nervous system made my hands tingle as my fists clenched. I forced them open and took a couple of deep breaths. Uniforms triggered that involuntary response and took me back to Bruneault Prison—the Bear—a place I'd been trying to forget for the last two years. Might as well try to forget my own name. The nanos were a gift from the Bear, but I'd have gladly ripped them out of my nerves if I could.

"Permission to come aboard, Captain?" asked the customs man. He snapped a brisk salute as he started up the cargo ramp. We both knew the request was a joke. He was coming aboard no matter what I said. Still, this was Highpoint, and the forms of protocol would be preserved.

"Welcome aboard the *Profit*," I said, keeping all but a trace of sarcasm out of my voice. The nanos retracted into their sheaths in my nervous system. I could feel a trickle of sweat run down my back as a wave of nausea swept over me. I wasn't sure if it was from the jolt I'd finished the night before or my proximity to this asshole in his crisp uniform.

The customs man flipped open a polished synthetic leather case and extracted a silver-plated datapad. He held it out and I pressed my thumb to the print reader. He glanced at the pad. "Captain Zachariah Mbele," he read. "Cargo manifest and customs declaration, please."

"My AI will download it to your link. Sylvia?"

"Done, Zack," she answered crisply, the seductive voice gone without a trace.

"Data cubes and DNA biochips for Iwamoto Artificial Intelligence Arts," he read sourly. He looked at me as if I'd just insulted his sister.

"High value and time sensitive. *Profit* specializes in priority cargo and rapid delivery," I said brightly, hoping to dispel the sinking feeling in my gut.

The inspector smiled thinly. "Good for you. But I'm impounding your cargo. Please certify the bill of lading with a finger or voice print and the stevedores will offload you immediately."

"Whoa, wait a minute. What the hell do you mean,

'impounding my cargo.' There's a heavy penalty for late delivery on this stuff. The manifest and declaration are accurate. What gives you the right to impound it?'

"This does." He shoved the datapad under my nose. "Iwamoto Arts was shut down by a bankruptcy court order sixteen hours ago. All company assets are impounded pending liquidation."

I read the notice, my gut feeling confirmed. I had to have the money from this job. We operated on a slim margin as it was and I had a loan payment coming up in five days.

"So who's going to pay the shipping fee on this stuff," I demanded. "This is an F.O.B. shipment and we're on time and still under contract."

The customs man shrugged. "Take it up with a Magistrate. You can file a claim along with the rest of the creditors."

"And wait months before I see a single yuan. Look, you've got to give me a break here. This is a premium cargo. Maybe it technically belongs to Iwamoto, but it's F.O.B. and they owe me my fee." I lowered my voice. "Why don't you let my AI make a few adjustments to that manifest? Leave me a couple of cases of chips and you can impound the rest. I'll make it worth your while. You're just doing your job, but I really need to cover my expenses."

"I missed the part where that was my problem." He didn't look up from his datapad. "Now give me your print before I charge you with attempting to bribe a customs officer."

He finally looked at me. He gave me a hard stare as he held out the datapad. The station's stevedore 'bots were already starting up the ramp. I thought about telling him where to shove his datapad, but decided he might enjoy it, so I gritted my teeth and thumbed the pad.

The 'bots loaded up our cargo, rolled down the ramp, and turned right toward the customs yard, all under the watchful eye of the inspector. The last stevedore hoisted the final two cases of biochips and followed the others. At the base of the ramp, it turned left instead of right. The inspector glanced at me with a faint smile, then touched his forehead in a mock salute.

"Welcome to Highpoint." He turned and followed the last 'bot.

"Son of bitch." I slammed my fist into the nearby bulkhead.

"Everything Jake, LT?" asked Deuce from behind me. He pronounced each letter, El Tee, a holdover from our military days.

"Golden," I snarled. "Except we just got taken for two cases of biochips by that ferret in a customs uniform. Our client is bankrupt and can't pay our fee, and there's a mortgage payment due on the Profit next week. Add to that a killer hangover, and yep, everything's golden."

Deuce leaned against the hatch coaming, arms crossed, his solid bulk nearly filling the hatchway. Sven Gulbrandsen the second (Deuce to everyone except our former commanders in the Martian Special Operations Corps) was hard, bearded, and blond. He was also the best top sergeant I had ever served with. Deuce had been with me since Basic, watching my back. He'd managed to escape the purges that had condemned me to Bruneault Prison as the Martian Revolution descended into madness and suspicion. And his was the first friendly face I saw when I walked out of that hellhole two years later.

He looked at me impassively. "You through?"

"Yeah, I'm through."

"Good. Then what's our next move?" Deuce didn't mention the hangover. He wasn't happy about my jolt habit, but we'd come to an understanding. He didn't bug me about quitting and I didn't use the drug outside of my own cabin. Besides, there was none left. No more bliss for me until I could hook up with my dealer back in Tycho City.

I sighed. "We head back to Tycho and try to find another job before the bank forecloses on us. If we have to, we'll head for the Belt and lay low until we can scrape up some cash..."

"Uh, Zack," Sylvia interrupted. "You may have to rethink the back to Tycho option. Highpoint Customs just slapped a ten percent import duty on us for the cargo they confiscated. We're under launch hold until we pay it."

"Bullshit! That's ridiculous. It's not our cargo."

"I know, but Highpoint's customs regulations say that if the recipient defaults on the duties, the freight carrier can be liable for the tariff up to ten percent of the total value."

"And that's legal?"

"This is Highpoint," said Sylvia. "Under the Unity Convention, they have carte blanche within their own zone of control. Yeah, it's legal."

"I don't suppose they'll take a marker?" I was only half joking. We were truly tapped out.

"Not a chance. This is serious, Zack. We've got seventy-two hours to pay up or they'll take the ship and auction it off to pay the tariff."

"I'll blow her up right here in the bay before that happens."

"Y'know, LT." Deuce tugged at his beard. "I've got a bit of construction grade Selenite in my kit. I maybe could make a hole in the outer bulkhead of the docking bay. Maybe big enough for us to squeeze through."

I shook my head. A sabotage rap wouldn't solve our financial problems and I didn't want to know why Deuce had that much high explosive aboard. Still, I liked the way he thought. A year ago I would have taken him up on the idea. Maybe I was mellowing. Or maybe I was just tired.

"No, Deuce. We wouldn't get a hundred kilometers before they blew us away. Highpoint has its own defense forces and they're damned good."

Deuce shrugged. "Just a suggestion."

"Exactly how much do these pirates want from us, Sylvia?" I asked.

"Five-thousand, six-hundred and twenty-seven yuan."

That plus the thirty-five hundred I needed for the loan

payment came to a little more than nine thousand *New Yuan*. All in less than five days.

I had no doubt that the Highpoint authorities would take the ship if I couldn't come up with the cash.

I turned to Deuce. "Keep your Selenite handy. It may be our last option. Meanwhile, see if there are any spare parts or fuel cells we can hock to raise cash. Maybe we can buy some time if we make a down payment on the tariff."

Deuce nodded. "I've got a couple of plasma batteries for the pulse rifle. They should fetch a hundred yuan each if I can find a buyer. I'll get 'em and try at a bar I know in the lower decks."

On Highpoint, status and class determined where one lived. The arcology was a huge cylinder, thirty kilometers long and almost six in diameter. The outer shell was two hundred meters thick and housed all of the life support, reactors, utilities, and service personnel that allowed the elite class to live in the tall fairy towers and manicured parklands of the open central core. Bars in the lower decks catered to the working class. They were also the likely spots to find buyers for unauthorized merchandise.

I nodded to Deuce and he ducked back into the passageway that led to his workshop. Somehow, I didn't think that a few hundred yuan would be enough to hold the customs collector at bay. But given what I'd just seen with the inspector, it might be enough for a bribe.

"Sylvia, any word from Rabbit?"

"Not yet, Zack. Edward Conejo is registered in the Highpoint database as a transient worker, but there is no contact information available."

Edward Conejo, alias "Eddie the Rabbit," was a freelance computer analyst, a top programmer and slicer who knew everything about every operating system on three worlds. He was the reason Sylvia's personality program could make you believe she was human. He was also a friend. We'd been cellmates in the Bear during the Revolution and had both done time as human guinea pigs in Hans Metternich's biotanks.

Rabbit had contacted me a few days ago and asked if he could hitch a ride home to Tycho with us. I was mildly surprised. Rabbit was paranoid, had been since the Bear. He would occasionally hire out for a consulting job if the price was right, but he'd be nervous about commercial transport. It was natural for him to beg a ride.

How he knew we'd be at Highpoint was another matter. I hadn't told him, not that that made any difference. Rabbit was the best data slicer in the system and had probably accessed my contract and delivery schedule the minute I'd signed it.

I didn't know anything about his job here on Highpoint, but knew the price had to be high to get him to come in person. I hoped he was flush enough to float me a loan. Otherwise we'd all be walking home.

"What's the plan, Boss?"

"No plan. I'm just trying to stay a jump ahead. How much can you access on the arcology database?"

"Only the public net. What are we looking for?"

"Work. Anything that can raise some cash quickly. And see what you can find out about that inspector who just raped us. If he's crooked, maybe his bosses are too. We need to find someone we can bribe or lean on for more time."

"Okay, Zack," Sylvia sounded skeptical. "But this is Highpoint. Graft and corruption are art forms here."

"I swear, Sylvia, if I hear 'This is Highpoint' one more time, I'm going to disable your voice programming. Just get me something I can use."

"Yes, Boss."

Deuce stepped through the aft hatch, a small canvas bag slung over his shoulder. "I found a couple extra coils of platinum monofilament. Should fetch a thousand or so from the chandler, maybe more below decks if the buyer ain't particular about purity."

"We'll sell them at the chandler's. We'll take a discount, but the sale will be quick and legal. It'll look better when we suddenly have some ready cash."

"Whatever you say, LT," Deuce shrugged. "But I could get more down below."

"I know. But we'll do it this way. Fewer questions. And don't get caught pushing those batteries. I don't want to have to bust you out of a Highpoint brig."

"No fear, LT."

"Never," I grinned.

"Sylvia, are we cleared to leave the ship yet?"

"Yes, Boss. You and Deuce are registered as business travelers with access to all public areas."

"I'm going as far as the chandler's with Deuce, then I'm going to see if I can find Rabbit. I'll be on my link. Put him through if he makes contact."

"Sure, Boss."

Deuce opened the weapons locker and drew out a blunt nosed pneumatic pistol. I slid a short-bladed sheath knife into the top of my boot and a slim Huang needler into the inner pocket of my jacket. I didn't know what the local laws on concealed weapons were, but I never left the ship unarmed. Needlers and pneumatics could be deadly to flesh and bone but wouldn't breach a pressure hull, so it wasn't like I was placing the whole arcology at risk. Besides, I was packing a sleeper magazine in the needler. I doubted that would carry much weight if the local cops frowned on citizens bearing arms, but I didn't much care, either. Deuce secured the locker and we walked out through the starboard sally port.

"Lock down, Sylvia," I said as we descended the boarding ladder. "Release code: 'Tharsis seventeen'."

She'd button the ship up tight as a vacuum bottle until I gave her the release code. I hate people snooping about when I'm not home.

Our footsteps echoed in the cavernous docking bay. I glanced back at the ship. She always took my breath away; a slim cylinder with her cockpit perched high on the bow. She had a pronounced bulge amidships where the gravity drive and reactor were housed. Her paint job was gleaming black with gold trim around the cockpit, cargo doors, and sally ports. Gold lettering spelled out her name and registration number on the nose and the impulse engine nacelles. At 60 meters overall length and four thousand metric tons of capacity, she was small for a freighter, occupying only a quarter of the bay. She'd started her life as an interceptor for the Martian navy. Property often went missing in a war zone and it hadn't been too hard to sneak past the Feddie blockade. The bribes for forged ownership papers and the conversion from warship to freighter had cost me plenty, though. I'd been struggling with debts ever since. Still, her drive and inertial dampers could push her at thirty G's for short bursts and she could maintain ten G's until her reactor ran down. With her, I could run far and fast.

The ship chandler was two decks up, near the main spaceport at the 'north' end of the cylinder. Right next to the spaceport were the tube and lift stations that led to the rest of the arcology. The lifts gave vertical access to the various decks of the main hull and tubes ran lengthwise along the main axis. By convention, locations were designated 'spinward' or 'antispin' for their direction away from the arbitrary baseline running through the main cargo terminal. The designations were artificial now that gravity grids provided a uniform Earth standard G throughout the arcology. The station turned once in twenty-four hours to simulate a day/night cycle rather than to simulate gravity.

The chandler occupied a space three bulkheads spinward of the centerline. Large holotanks displayed wares ranging from biochip processors to whole ships. Here they bought and sold anything and everything a ship captain needed to keep his vessel flying.

Deuce and I found an open sales window and keyed up the AI. We dropped the coils in the analyzer and after a second or two a quote flashed in the matrix. Eight hundred and twenty-seven yuan. Less than I'd hoped, but clean and legal. And more than I'd had when we'd docked less than an hour ago.

"Do you wish to confirm this sale?" the AI asked. Its tinny vocal synthesizer wasn't nearly as smooth as Sylvia's. I couldn't tell if it was supposed to be male or female.

"Confirm," I said.

"Eight-hundred twenty-seven yuan will be credited to any business account with the Highpoint Security and Trust Bank, unless you prefer a cash payout."

I didn't have a business account. "Cash."

"There is a ten percent charge for issuing Federal scrip. Highpoint scrip can be issued for a three percent charge. Would you prefer Federal or Highpoint scrip?"

I had to admire the AI's masters. They knew how to run a tight scam. They'd also make sure their own scrip was marked and tracked.

"Federal." I'd take the seven percent hit.

The cash slid out through a slot next to the analyzer. I scooped it up and we walked away as the AI thanked us for our business.

"Could have gotten a lot more down below," muttered Deuce.

I ignored him. "Sylvia," I said over the link implanted in my right mastoid. "How does someone get a business account with the local bank?"

"It's not hard, Zack. Any registered visitor can open a temporary account with the government-run bank. A lot of businesses will only accept a direct debit from a registered account. There's no service charge and the temporary accounts don't earn any interest. It's mainly a convenience service."

"Which lets Highpoint track everyone by the way they

spend their yuan." I shook my head. "No thanks. We'll deal in cash or not at all."

Deuce was muttering again. I turned to him. "You got something to say, Deuce?"

"We don't belong here, LT. Too much damn government. Sooner we can raise some cash and get back to Tycho, the better."

"Yeah, I'm working on that. Try to get what you can for the plasma batteries, but be careful. We don't need to attract any more trouble. I'll meet you back at the ship."

"You worry too much, LT." He grinned. "I'm just gonna hoist a few in a working man's bar. What could go wrong?"

"Right."

He punched my arm and turned away, heading toward the lift for the lower decks.

I called up a map on my link and found the lift for the upper decks. A few minutes later, I stood on a balcony near the lift station and looked out over the open parklands of the arcology central core. Tall, spindly buildings with outsized cantilevers and balconies lined a broad tree-lined avenue that stretched thirty kilometers to the opposite end. Green parklands sloped up the sides of the cylindrical space covering almost half of the circumference. The green ended abruptly at a five-hundred meter wide stretch of transparent glass that penetrated the cylinder, clear out to space. High overhead, the central spine was packed with mirrors to reflect sunlight throughout the interior. Beyond the central core, on the opposite surface of the arcology was a mirror image of the greenery that stretched out in front of me.

I shuddered inwardly. Wide-open spaces gave me the shakes. Raised underground in the cities of Mars, I had the tunnel rat's mistrust of open sky. Duraglass and viewports were for the Earthbound or the very rich. Tunnel dwellers preferred a few tons of friendly rock overhead. I had thought to look around and play the tourist until I heard from

Rabbit, but hadn't counted on this much open air. Now I felt like running back to the ship and putting plenty of hull metal between me and the great black beyond on the other side of all that glass.

As I gripped the railing of the balcony and struggled to settle my nerves, my link chimed. Sylvia was calling. I ground my teeth to activate the connection.

"Yes?"

"Hello, Zack. You said to call if Edward Conejo checked in."

"Good. I need to speak to him."

"Are you all right? You sound strange."

"I'm fine," I said through gritted teeth. "Where is Rabbit? Did he say?"

"He left a comm locus. He wants you to call him back at 1600 local time. That's about fifteen minutes from now. He said he wanted you to meet someone who may have a job for us, but didn't give me any details."

"Why can't I call him right now?"

"You could try. But he was very specific about the time."

I thought for a second. Rabbit had been paranoid about maintaining security since we got out of the Bear. This was probably just another of his neurotic fantasies, but it would freak him out if I tried to call early. I decided to wait.

"Okay, Sylvia. Any luck with that other matter?"

"No. There's not much personal data on the public net. Highpoint has pretty strict privacy laws."

I slammed my palm into the railing in frustration. It had been a long shot, but I seriously wanted to get something on that inspector. I hated being manipulated, and this was now personal.

"Zack? Any other instructions?"

"Not right now." I sighed and broke the connection.

I turned my back on the greenery and headed toward the lift with a feeling of relief. I told myself it wasn't fear, just sensible precaution. Whatever lies you have to tell yourself to get through the day, right?

CHAPTER TWO

I felt better as soon as the lift doors closed. I rode back down to the spaceport and found a coffee bar a couple of bulkheads spinward of the ship chandler. I used a little of the cash in my pocket to buy an espresso. Caffeine was supposed to be good for a jolt hangover. The barista eyed the Fed scrip suspiciously for a second, but took it and gave me change—in Highpoint currency.

I found a table where I could see the door and keep my back to a wall. I sipped the hot coffee and waited until 16:00, then called up the locus Sylvia had downloaded to the link. Rabbit answered on the first chime.

"Zack?" he said in his high-pitched, breathless way. "You're late. I've been waiting for almost a whole day for you to get here. This place isn't safe, you know. They think they know about security, but their systems are hopeless. Did you know that they're still running Vigilant 3.2? Three point two for God's sake! It's like two years old and so full of holes a three-year-old could slice it. They hired me to update their face recognition protocols but what good is that if they haven't updated the root code in over twenty-four months? Of course, I took their money and did the job. Even gave them a free update, but it's like patching a sieve. And did they thank me? No! Bunch of arrogant bastards. By the way, what kept you?"

"Nice to hear from you too, Rabbit." I knew the sarcasm would be lost on him. "Sylvia said you had a line on a job."

"Huh? Oh, yeah." His voice became hushed. "I met a guy here. He needs a ride out. Says it doesn't matter where, as long as the Feds and the local law don't know he's gone. He can pay, Zack. I think he's legit, or at least he's got the cash. I checked that out first thing."

"Okay. Who is this 'guy' and why is he on the run from the Feds?"

"Who said anything about being on the run? He's just in a jam and needs to get back to the Belt in a hurry."

I thought about that for a second. Rabbit might be paranoid, but he didn't know shit about people. Still, I couldn't afford to turn away from a paying job.

"So how do we play this?"

"There's a food court in the FashionMaxx shopping arcade on deck three." Rabbit paused for a second, probably consulting a link. "It's ring seven, frame 33 spinward. Not real secure, but Marco wants to be in a public place. That's the guy's name, Marco. He thinks it's safer in public. I tried to tell him it's not. A meeting in my hotel room or better yet, aboard the Profit, would be a lot more secure. He says he doesn't trust you. Wants to meet you first. I told him..."

"Rabbit, enough! When?"

"Oh, um, is half an hour okay? He's waiting for me to call and tell him it's on."

"Fine. Tell him I'll be there." I logged off and called up the map again. In a few seconds, it showed me the best route to the shopping arcade. I dropped some of the Highpoint money on the table as a tip for the barista and walked out.

The FashionMaxx arcade didn't look very fashionable to

me, but then, I don't keep up on the latest trends. The food court was one of those pretentious spots that seemed to be cropping up in middle-class areas all over Tycho. Here, too, apparently. No AI operated food stalls; real people manned the food vendors and waited on tables, just like in the old days. At premium prices, of course.

I sat at a table near a bulkhead and ordered some orange juice. Vitamin C is supposed to help jolt hangovers, too. I desperately wanted something stronger, but didn't want to spook a potential client. I was watching the door, looking for Rabbit, when the waitress arrived with my juice.

She set it on the table and asked, "Will that be all, sir?"

I glanced up at her—and stared in spite of myself. She was stunning. Short black hair framed her heart-shaped face. Her skin was smooth and brown, the color of Saigon cinnamon. Her lips were painted a brilliant red. Not overly tall, she was trim but not thin with a full bust and hard, cordlike muscles on her bare shoulders and forearms. She obviously worked at staying in shape. But it was her eyes that grabbed me. They were emerald green, flecked with gold and silver, like moonlight on a tropical sea.

"No...no," I stammered. "Nothing else." *Smooth. You really impressed her, sport.*

She smiled, enjoying herself. She held my eye for another second before she turned and walked away. I gazed after her.

"Zack?" Rabbit brought me back to the moment. I hadn't heard him approach. "You okay?"

I nodded as I turned his way. "Fine, Rabbit. Is this your friend?" A short, lumpy looking man stood behind Rabbit's power chair.

Rabbit rolled closer to the table and waved his hand to the man. "Come on, Marco. This is Zack Mbele, the ship captain I told you about. Zack, this is Marco Scalzi. Marco needs a ship."

Scalzi approached slowly, looking around as he pulled

out a chair across from me and sat down. He didn't offer his hand, just nodded my way as he settled into the chair. His eyes never stopped moving as he continuously scanned the food court.

I looked him over. He was short and overweight, soft around the middle and thin in the legs. His suit might have been stylish once. On him it looked shapeless and rumpled. His scalp was dark, with black stubble, three or four day's growth at least. He smelled faintly of garlic.

"Nice to meet you, Mr. Scalzi," I said.

"Yeah, likewise." His voice was thin and reedy. He nodded again, only briefly looking me in the eye before resuming his scan of the room.

The guy was obviously a twitch, and a skittish one at that. Still, Rabbit said he had ready cash, so I decided to play it light until he was ready to do business.

"New chair, Rabbit?"

"Yeah." He smiled. "The latest DeCastro. Cost me all of my fee, but it's worth it. Shiny, isn't it. You can't get one of these on the Moon. The only distributor off Earth is right here in Highpoint. 'Course, I modified its root code to accept my nanos. The interface is kind of wonky, and it makes my left leg hurt like hell, but that'll pass as the nanos adapt."

I knew what he meant. Rabbit and I shared a bond born in the biotanks of Bruneault prison. Rabbit was luckier than most. Nine out of ten who went into the 'tanks died in agony as the nanofibers ripped their nerves to shreds. A lucky few, like Rabbit, emerged with a partial bond, crippled but alive and maybe even sane. He was paralyzed from the waist down, but he could use the nanos to control a power chair.

My bond was different, unique as far as I knew. The nanofibers were there, stable but dormant. When I needed them, they could augment my own nerves, speeding my reactions, increasing my sight and hearing, even making me stronger for short bursts. The price was pain—searing heat like I had felt when they first invaded my nerves, deep aching as my tortured muscles recovered after each use, and blinding headaches as my brain burned with sensory overload.

I shook my head, coming back to the present. I was getting careless, losing focus twice in one day. *Some hotshot operator I am.* I glanced at Scalzi. He had stopped studying the room and was now studying me.

"What can I do for you, Mr. Scalzi?"

"Conejo tells me you can get me out of Highpoint." He resumed his scan of the room. It was getting on my nerves.

"We do take passengers on the *Profit* occasionally. We have a standard charter package. Where do you want to go?"

He stopped looking around and leaned toward me, lowering his voice. "I'll tell you once we're outside the zone of control. I'll pay well as long as it's soon and quietly. No customs or immigration. And no cops. The authorities can't know I'm gone until we're clear. Can you do that?"

"Yes." I gave him a reassuring smile, one of my best. "But that sort of service is more expensive."

He nodded and scanned the room again. "I'll pay you ten thousand yuan."

"Cash," I said. "Fed scrip, none of that Highpoint crap. Five now, five once we're clear."

He shook his head. "Three now, the rest when we're outside the zone." He touched my hand. "And you take me where I want to go once we're in the clear."

"Four thousand now." I kept my tone even. "Or you can find another ship."

He sat back in his chair and rubbed his upper lip. His hand shook, only a little but I noticed. *Gotcha.*

"But you'll take me where I want to go once we're outside the zone of control?"

"Sure. For ten thousand, we'll take you all the way to the Belt if that's what you want."

"When can we leave?"

"Whoa, spaceman." I held up a hand. "There are some things we need to cover first. If I'm going to run interference for you, I need to know why you need to stay invisible. What sort of heat should I be looking for?"

"No heat. I just want to leave quietly."

"Then book a commercial flight. You don't need me." I pushed my chair back and started to stand up. "Good bye, Mr. Scalzi."

"Wait." He grabbed my arm. "I'll tell you. Just sit down."

I settled into my chair again, feeling smug. I'd read him right. "Go on."

"I have an ex-wife," he said. "We were married here, but lived in Gagarin Center most of the time. I should have suspected something when she insisted on coming back here for our fifth anniversary. She filed for divorce the day after we docked."

"So, she's your ex now. Why should you care if she knows you're gone?"

"Zack," said Rabbit. "It's Highpoint. Community property."

"I don't understand."

"The court gave her half of everything," said Scalzi. "Because we were married here, the divorce Magistrate claimed jurisdiction. She gets half of the savings, the flat in Gagarin, half of my pension. And I'm supposed to pay the court costs, which amount to ten percent of the settlement." His eyes hardened. "They won't get it. I converted whatever I could to cash. She doesn't know and once I'm outside of Highpoint's jurisdiction, these bastards can't touch me."

"Hard luck." I nodded. "Okay, so it's not a criminal jam you're in. That's good. I think we can help you."

"So, when do we leave?" he repeated.

"I'll need a few hours to arrange our departure. Rabbit, are you ready to go?"

Rabbit nodded. "I just need to pick up my gear. I can

meet you at the ship whenever you say. How's Sylvia? I haven't been able to update her personality routines for a while. Maybe I can do that while we're traveling, okay?""

"Sure. We'll meet at the ship as soon as I get in touch with Deuce." I gave Scalzi a hard look. "And as soon as I see some cash."

"Oh, yes," he stammered. He reached into his pocket and pulled out a wad of bills. At least he had enough sense to keep it hidden under the table. He peeled off four notes and handed them to me.

"Go with Rabbit to his hotel. Deuce will pick you up there and see that you get to the ship. Don't worry, Rabbit knows Deuce. He'll vouch for him." I pushed back my chair to leave. "And Scalzi, stay with that story if anyone else asks. It's a little rough, but believable."

He opened his mouth to protest, but I shut him up with a wave of my hand. "Calm down. I didn't believe a word you said, but you offered more money than you needed to for a charter, and enough more to make it okay. Don't worry. I'll get you off Highpoint. Then we can discuss your real story."

I started to stand up but froze as I caught a glimpse of movement to my left. It was the goddess who had brought me my drink. Only now she held a long black needler in a shooter's stance. She was pointing it at my new client.

"Marco Scalzi," she said. "You are lawfully detained to answer charges filed with the Highpoint Judicial Magistrate. Don't move. I am authorized to use force to detain you."

She looked even better with a weapon in her hand.

CHAPTER THREE

She kept the needler trained on Scalzi. She didn't seem to notice me as I drew my own weapon.

"Not gonna happen," I said. "Drop the needler."

She was fast. Scary fast. She pumped two needles into Scalzi, then swung toward me.

I was faster. My first needle took her in the neck. The second stuck in her left arm. Her first shot whizzed by my ear. She managed to fire a second time before her eyes glazed over and she sagged to the deck. Her needle embedded itself in the table in front of me, just above my crotch.

"Rabbit, check Scalzi."

"Already did," Rabbit squeaked. "He's okay. She was shooting sleepers. Who the hell is she? Geez, Zack, she's fast. Almost as fast as you."

"Not a waitress, that's for sure. Local law or freelance bounty hunter would be my guess. Damn good, too." I stepped over to her and kicked her needler out of reach. She was still the most beautiful woman I'd ever seen. I was glad I'd loaded sleepers as well.

"Zack, we gotta go," said Rabbit. " The Law will be here soon and I can't move Marco. You'll have to do it."

I considered for half a second. This was more trouble that I needed right now.

"Get out of here. Pick up your gear from the hotel and get down to the ship as fast as you can. I'll deal with Scalzi."

Rabbit nodded, spun his chair around, and rolled away. I watched until he turned the corner into the main arcade. Then I stepped over to Scalzi and heaved him onto his back. I knelt at his side and quickly checked his pockets. The wad of cash went into my own jacket. He had a Fed identity card with his name and hologram on the front. I flipped it over. The tracker had been scraped off the back. That would get him arrested and slapped with a heavy fine if a cop checked his card. This guy was trying to duck a lot more than a greedy ex-wife.

I stood up and turned toward the exit. I took half a step and stopped, sighed, and turned back. I had made a deal with the man. That still counted for something with me.

I bent over him and pulled him into a sitting position. The nanos extended into my arms and legs and I hoisted him easily into a fireman's carry across my back and shoulders.

The small crowd that had gathered when the shooting stopped backed away. I lifted my head as they parted in front of me. I was sure that by now, my face and all the action had been recorded on a dozen eye cameras, not to mention the arcade's security cams. Hiding my face was a waste of time.

A rapid blink of my left eye opened the visual interface of my link. I checked the clock and was surprised to see that less than two minutes had passed since the shooting started. If Highpoint cops were at least as good as Tycho cops, I only had another minute or so to get Scalzi and myself out of sight.

I scooped up a couple of bottles of fish sauce from a

tabletop as we passed. Ahead, between a falafel stand and a place selling Martian-style noodle bowls, was a service corridor. I kicked the swinging door open slamming a busbot into the wall in the process. There was a lift at the far end of the corridor and I ran toward it.

The lift door opened as I approached and another busbot carrying a load of clean dishes rolled out. I stepped in as it passed and the doors hissed shut. I eased Scalzi to the floor as the lift started down. There was a security cam in the rear upper corner of the lift. A few squirts from the squeeze bottle of fish sauce covered its lens with sticky brown liquid and blanked out any view of my new friend or me. He moaned softly, then started to snore.

The lift dropped rapidly, three decks according to the counter near the door, before stopping again. The doors hissed open. Another couple of squirts from the fish sauce bottle took out the security cam on the outside of the lift. I hoisted Scalzi onto my shoulders and stepped out of the lift into clouds of steam.

Rows of busbots stretched in front of me. All were busily engaged in cleaning plates and cutlery in oversized ultrasonic dishwashers, loading and emptying linens from huge centrifugal cleaners, and pressing and folding lengths of cloth in giant steam presses. A continuous line of heavy plastic bins slung from an overhead track moved slowly around the perimeter of the compartment. 'Bots moved back and forth, emptying the incoming bins and loading the outgoing ones. There wasn't a human being in sight.

I walked quickly to the left where the outgoing bins were moving into a long tunnel. I dumped Scalzi into a partially empty bin and climbed in after him. The bin entered the tunnel and picked up speed.

I called up a map on my link but this level wasn't on it. The entire deck was apparently dedicated to automated services. Good for avoiding other people but not much help in find my way back to the ship. I activated my link and called Sylvia on a scrambled frequency.

"Zack, where are you? The cops are looking for you. There was a shooting at the FashionMaxx Arcade and they say you were involved."

"Yeah, I seem to attract the wrong type of women. Can you track my signal and tell me where I am?"

"Sure." She paused for a half-second. "You're on deck six, about five bulkheads away from the spaceport and moving toward the opposite end of the arcology. Deck six is a service deck, almost all automated."

"How do I get out of here and back to the ship?"

"Searching," she said in that computer voice she used when she was accessing information. "Okay, in about thirty seconds you'll come to a junction. There's an access ladder that will take you down three decks to a residential area. Just 'north' of there, that is toward the spaceport, you'll come to a tube station. You can catch a pod there for the freight terminals."

"Any open paths that I can walk on this level? The cops are sure to monitor the tubes."

"There's an access tunnel leading away from the junction. But it's only 150 centimeters in diameter. You won't be able to stand upright and it's almost a kilometer to the terminal."

"Okay, thanks Sylvia. The junction's coming up. I'll call back in a few minutes. Keep tracking me and watch the news services for any information about the search area."

"Yes, Boss."

The tunnel ended in a wide space with a low overhead. I rolled out of the bin and dragged Scalzi after me. There was a circular track for the bins and tunnels leading off in three directions. Bins entered and circled the junction before being shunted off to one of the other tracks. On my right, curving back the way we had come was the access tunnel Sylvia had told me about.

I scanned the space around me. There were no cameras in sight and no people or 'bots. I sat on the floor next to

Scalzi. Most standard sleeper needles would put a 70-kilo man down for about two hours. Scalzi weighed more than that, but he'd taken two shots. He'd be out for a while yet.

I called Deuce.

"Hey, LT. Why the scrambler? We in trouble again?"

"Just a little," I said. "Where are you?"

"Just left a bar on deck eighteen. Got a little more than three hundred for the batteries."

"Good work." I grinned thinking of the wad of scrip in my pocket. "I need you pick up a special package and bring it to the ship."

"Sure, LT. What kind of package?"

"Human."

"Alive or dead?" Deuce's voice was flat, as if he were asking the time of day.

"Alive. Client, actually. He took a couple of sleeper needles in a fight. The law is looking for him. We need to get him to the ship without being seen and I can't do it. The cops are looking for me, too."

"Everything Jake with you?"

"I'm golden. The shooter was a tad slower than I was. I think I can convince the cops I was a bystander, just trying to help out. But that won't wash if I'm hauling this guy around."

"Understood," he said. "Where do I pick up the package?"

"Deck six, about five bulkheads south of the spaceport. Sylvia has the location."

"Time limit?"

I looked at Scalzi. He lay on his back, snoring softly. "Probably no more than four hours. Hard to say for sure. She hit him with two needles, but I don't know if she was using standard loads."

"She?"

"I'll fill you in later."

Deuce logged off. I pulled a dirty tablecloth from one of the passing bins and wadded it up as a pillow for Scalzi's head. He didn't move as I positioned it behind his neck.

The access tunnel was as cramped as Sylvia had said. My back was aching before I had traveled a hundred meters.

I pressed on.

Occasionally, side tunnels opened off to the right or left, but the main passage led straight ahead, angling upwards. I figured I climbed one deck for every hundred and fifty meters, which would make it just under a kilometer to get back to deck one.

I called Sylvia again when I figured I was getting close to deck two.

"Sylvia, where am I?"

"About eighty meters south of the spaceport and between decks two and three. The tunnel you're in ends in a right angle turn twenty meters ahead. That'll be deck two. You'll find a ladder going up from there. The exit is on deck one in a 'bot service area. I don't have access to the security net, but there are probably cameras there. You'll have to move fast."

"Will do. Deuce will be checking with you for directions to the junction I just left. He's picking up a package for me. And get in touch with Rabbit if you can. Tell him to get to the ship ASAP."

"Yes, Boss. Good luck."

I quickened my steps, at least as much as running while bent almost double allowed. The tunnel ended abruptly in a cylindrical void that stretched high above me. It seemed to be a vertical access shaft that went all the way to the opposite side of the arcology. A ladder to my right clung to the wall and led upward. I climbed up one deck and found an access hatch about a meter and a half in diameter with a center wheel to release the dogs that held it sealed to the cylinder wall. The wheel spun easily and the hatch swung outward. I crawled through.

I stood up in a long narrow compartment. Service 'bots lined the walls, their recharge cable plugged into power outlets. There was a hatch to my left, man-sized this time. I swung it open and stepped out into a crowded public walkway. A few people glanced at me as I closed the hatch, but no one said anything as I joined the flow of foot traffic headed toward the tube station.

CHAPTER FOUR

I walked purposefully, but not too rapidly, toward the station, hoping to blend into the crowd of people going about their business. No one stopped me as I walked past the tube station and turned right into the spaceport entry. Of course, the cops already knew who I was and where I'd likely be going. Two uniforms stood next to the security checkpoint and I saw a couple of plainclothes types circulating around behind me. No matter how they dressed themselves up, I could always pick them out.

I paused for half a second, then walked straight toward the uniforms. One of them stepped forward. The other hung back but I heard the snap as he unbuckled the flap of his sidearm holster.

"Zachariah Mbele," said the cop who stepped toward me. It wasn't a question. He was shorter than I, broad in the shoulders and narrow in the waist. His black hair was cut close to the scalp. His almond shaped eyes bored into mine.

"That's me," I tried to look casual. "What can I do for you officer?"

"Come with us, sir." His tone was courteous but firm. "We'd like to ask you a few questions."

"Do I have a choice?" I carefully kept my hands in view as I turned to face him.

The cop actually smiled. "Not really."

I shrugged and he gestured toward a small alcove to my right. I turned and walked that way as he fell in next to my right arm, his hand hovering at my elbow. His partner followed a step behind, still fondling his sidearm.

A discreetly placed door opened as we entered the alcove and my escort steered me into a small office. He waved me into a chair as he stepped around a chipped and stained metal desk and took a seat in the only other chair in the room. The second cop closed the door behind us and leaned against it.

"I'm Senior Inspector Akira Kensai," said the cop who had first approached me. "I must ask you to place your weapons on the desk top."

"Me? What weapons?"

He smiled again. "The Huang needler in your right jacket pocket and the knife you have concealed in your left boot."

I laughed. This guy was good. And more human than the average cop. I liked him. I carefully laid the Huang and the knife on the desk.

"May I?" He asked as he reached for the needler.

"Suit yourself."

He picked it up, popped out the magazine, and cleared the pneumatic chamber. He held up the mag and nodded. "Nice weapon. Built in pneumatic boost, self-priming gas cylinder, fifteen shot magazine. I prefer a Steinbauer, but Huang has a reputation for ruggedness. You're only packing fourteen rounds, by the way."

"Oh?"

He nodded. "A guy like you, I figure you don't go anywhere unarmed, no matter what the local weapons laws say. You'd go out with a full mag and one in the pipe."

"So?" I said, letting him have his fun.

"So, somehow two of your needles found their way into a young woman at the FashionMaxx arcade today. Want to tell me what the fight was about?"

"Honest officer," I held up my hands. "I was just an innocent bystander." He gave me a sour look and I shrugged. "Too much, eh?"

He nodded, waiting.

"Okay, I went there to meet a friend, Eddie the...Eddie Conejo." The cop was good enough to have cross-referenced the security cam images with Rabbit's visa picture, so there was no harm in giving his name. "He had a guy with him. We sat at a table in the food court and talked for a bit. Rabbit, that is Conejo, needed transportation back to Tycho, and I agreed to take him. Next thing I know, this waitress is drawing down on Rabbit's friend with a needler. So I drew mine. I was just faster than she was."

"Had you ever seen this woman before?"

"Huh? No, not until she served me a fruit juice. That was just before Rabbit and his friend showed up."

"How do you know Marco Scalzi?" Kensai set my needler back on the desk.

"I don't. I just met him when he showed up with Rabbit."

"So you drew your weapon in defense of a complete stranger? Why?"

"He was unarmed," I said, suddenly not liking Kensai as much. "I'd have done the same for anyone. Even a cop."

He smiled at that and nodded. "And then you hoisted him onto your shoulder and left through the service lift, disabling the surveillance cameras along the way. A lot of trouble for a guy you just met. Where is Mr. Scalzi, by the way?"

"I don't know." I did my best to look him in the eye. People tend to believe you if you look them in the eye when you lie. "I didn't want to leave him in the middle of the food court where that gun-toting waitress might get him. I left him in the lift. If he's not there now, then maybe he woke up and went home."

His forced smile told me he wasn't buying it, but he didn't push it. Instead he asked, "What's your connection to Cleopatra Lee?"

"Who?"

"The 'gun-toting waitress' you shot."

"Never saw her before. Who is she?"

"She's registered as a transient worker," Kensai said. "Her visa lists Tharsis as her home of origin, but we have reason to believe she's actually from Singapore, on Earth. She's been linked to several bail bond recovery operations here and on the L4 arcology."

"Bounty hunter." I had figured as much. "She working for you?"

"No." He looked surprised. "We have our own people for that sort of thing. We don't hire freelancers."

"How about Scalzi?" I asked. "Were you looking for him?"

He didn't answer for a second. Then he shook his head. "Again, no, although it's not policy to discuss cases with civilians. But, since we weren't looking for him, there's no harm in saying so."

"Interesting," I said, remembering what Lee, or whoever she was, had said about a Highpoint arrest warrant when she drew on Scalzi.

"Meaning what?"

"Nothing. Just interesting. Why was Lee after Scalzi?"

"That's one reason why we're having this talk. I was hoping you could tell me."

I laughed at that. "Why don't you ask her?"

He looked away and fidgeted with his badge.

"Oh ho," I said softly. "You don't have her, do you?"

"No," he sighed. "Just after you hauled Scalzi out, a couple of paramedics showed up with a transport litter. The patrol officers arrived a few seconds later and she was already on the litter. They checked her, saw no other weapons, and cleared the medics to leave the scene. None of them were seen after that."

I laughed again, longer and louder. "That's rich. Look, things went down just like I said. She drew on Scalzi, I drew on her. I was faster, but not by much. I dragged Scalzi into the lift and left him there. I made my way back here."

"So that's your story and you're sticking to it," Kensai said with a wry smile.

"Yes, sir, officer. Can I go now?"

He nodded.

I retrieved my knife and needler. I was mildly surprised when he didn't stop me. He kept the magazine, though.

"I can't prevent you from leaving Highpoint once you pay your customs duty." I noticed he didn't seem to doubt that I would come up with the cash. "But," he went on. "I would ask that you let me know if you plan to leave. Call it a professional courtesy."

"Sure," I said. "And, Inspector Kensai, if you go after Cleopatra Lee, take a full combat team. She'll eat your normal patrol officers alive." I touched two fingers to my forehead in a mock salute. "Professional courtesy."

CHAPTER FIVE

I keyed my link and spun up the scrambler as soon as I cleared the security zone and was safely out of Inspector Kensai's sight.

"Talk to me, Deuce."

"Just picked up the package, LT. I'm on the service deck headed for the main tube station. I found a big toolbox that wasn't locked up so well. It's just big enough to hold your friend, so there won't be any nosey questions when I come out of the service lift."

I knew how Deuce "found" useful things he needed for jobs like this. I only hoped the box didn't have some kind of security tag on it.

"Good work. Check with Sylvia when you're close to the freight terminal. We'll need to work up some sort of dodge to get you past security." Deuce just grunted in reply and I logged off. Deuce could take care of himself until he got closer to the security checkpoint. I called Sylvia next.

"Sylvia, has Rabbit shown up yet?"

"Yes, Boss. He arrived a few minutes ago."

"Okay, let him in and get him settled in the charter cabin. I'll be there shortly."

"He's already in the cabin, Zack," she said meekly. "I couldn't stop him."

I sighed. I should have known that my lockdown wouldn't keep Rabbit out. He'd programmed most of Sylvia's higher functions in the first place.

"I'll be there in a few minutes." I logged off and quickened my pace through the freight terminal. There were a few other spacers and service personnel in the bays as I strode past, but no uniforms. I reached our bay and palmed the lock. It opened immediately. So far, my little gunfight hadn't attracted much official attention beyond Inspector Kensai.

"Release code, Sylvia," I said as I approached the ship. "Tharsis seventeen."

"Yes, Boss." The starboard sally port opened and a short ladder unfolded from the hull. I climbed the ladder two steps at a time and closed the port behind me as I entered the forward hold.

"Rabbit!" I shouted. "Get out here."

A few seconds later, he rolled out onto the catwalk above the hold. He'd been in the salon on the second deck. I didn't ask how he got his chair up there.

"Hello, Zack. Where's Marco? I've been here for almost an hour. How did you get him out of the food court? Sylvia tells me Deuce is bringing him, but I expected one of you to be here by now. By the way, you're out of coffee." He held up an empty mug.

I had long ago gotten used to Rabbits disjointed speech pattern. The coffee would wait.

"Deuce is going to need help. How fast can you slice the Highpoint security grid?"

He laughed derisively. "They're using Vigilant 3.2. Even if I hadn't left a backdoor when I updated their software, I could slice it in under two minutes."

"Do it. Patch Sylvia into the grid with as much access as

you can get. Deuce will need to get past Port security with your buddy Scalzi in a box. It'll be hard to explain if the authorities stop him."

"Time me," said Rabbit. "I'll bet I can do it in less than 90 seconds."

"I don't care as long as you get Deuce and Scalzi past security."

Rabbit rolled across the catwalk to the cockpit. "Sylvia, I need a keyboard and access to the public net. We've got some slicing to do."

By the time I joined him in the cockpit, he had finished. He looked up and grinned crookedly as I stepped through the hatch.

"Told you. Took me just over a minute. Where's Deuce now?"

"Sylvia?"

"He's just approaching the tube station on deck one, Boss. I've got him on visual."

The forward view screen lit up with a wide angle overhead view of a broad passageway. Traffic was sparse, only little knots of people hurrying to and fro. Deuce walked slowly but steadily near one bulkhead, pushing a large metal box that rolled on heavy casters. Somewhere along the way, he'd picked up a gray coverall. It was a few sizes too small for his bulk and the fabric strained dangerously across his chest, but it did give him an official appearance. Most of the people in the corridor brushed past without a second look.

"Deuce?" Rabbit said over the link. "It's me, Eddie the Rabbit, you know, Eddie Conejo. I'm here on the ship with Zack and Sylvia. We've got you on visual."

"Ain't that grand," muttered Deuce. "What do you want? I'm busy here. No time for your crap."

"Can it, Deuce. Rabbit's going to get you around security. Do what he says."

"Aye aye, LT. But if that freak gets me pinched, I'm gonna rip out his spleen."

"Uh, Okay, Deuce," said Rabbit. "A couple of meters ahead there's a door on your right. It has a palm lock in the frame. Stop at the door until I can tweak the security system for your palm print." He turned to me. "Do you have biometrics; palm, thumb, voice and DNA prints, on Deuce?"

"Sure. Sylvia?"

"Downloading"

After a half second and a few strokes at the virtual keyboard that hovered in the air in front of him, Rabbit said, "Okay, Deuce. Palm the lock."

Deuce placed his palm in the doorframe and the door popped open. He held up a thumb for the camera and passed through. Rabbit stroked the keyboard again and the view shifted. We now looked at the door from the other side. Deuce stood in a narrower service corridor. The lights were bright and the walls and floor were colored a flat metallic gray.

"Follow the service corridor for about thirty meters. You'll come to another door. That's the security section, so hold there until I can scan the area on the other side."

Deuce pushed the heavy box forward and made his way along the corridor. It ended at T-junction with a wider passageway that paralleled the main public corridor behind him. Directly across from him, on the far wall of the second passageway was a heavy door. On the wall next to the door was an optical scanner. Deuce looked left, then right along the passageway before looking up at the overhead camera and giving us another thumbs up.

Rabbit shifted the view through several security cameras before speaking to Deuce. "Okay, Deuce, go to the door and use the optical scanner. I've already entered your biometrics into the system. You're cleared for access to all areas of the port except the brig."

Deuce muttered something that the audio pickup didn't catch. He crossed the passageway and put his eye to the scanner. The door lock blinked from red to green. Deuce held the heavy door open with his foot as he maneuvered the toolbox through. Rabbit shifted the view to follow him. He stood in long narrow room. Lockers lined one wall and a shower stall was set into a recess at the far end.

"The locker room will take you around the security checkpoints," said Rabbit. "Be careful. There are two access doors that allow the security agents to get to their stations at the checkpoints. I'll try to give you a heads-up if one of them leaves his station, but it's only a couple of steps to where you are. There's another exit at the far end, just past the showers."

"Be careful? That's the best advice you've got? Just watch those agents. Let me worry about getting out of here."

Rabbit split the screen so we could watch Deuce and keep an eye on the security checkpoints at the same time. Deuce started across the room. The casters of the toolbox rattled on the grating that covered the floor and slowed his progress. Rabbit glanced nervously at the screen where the security agents were checking a shipment of hybrid oranges. Deuce was a little more than halfway across the room. The agents finished their inspection and waved the pallet of oranges through. Deuce neared the end of the lockers and drew even with the showers. One of the agents spoke to the other and gestured with his thumb toward the locker room. The second man nodded and waved him away. The first agent laughed and turned toward the door leading to the lockers.

Rabbit gasped and keyed Deuce's link. "Deuce, get out of there. Someone's coming."

Deuce reached the exit and pushed it open. "Don't crap in your panties, Conejo. I'm almost out of here."

Deuce wrestled the toolbox through the exit as the door from the security checkpoint swung open. He stepped through behind the toolbox and eased the exit door shut as the agent entered the locker room. The security agent looked around, then walked over to a locker and opened it.

Rabbit's voice shook as he said, "Okay, Deuce. Go right. The corridor ends at the main concourse. From there you can head straight for the ship. No one should stop you."

"Right. See you all in ten."

Rabbit shut down the main screen but kept a surveillance window open. "Keep an eye on him, please, Sylvia," he said.

"Boss?"

"Do it. Let us know if anyone seems interested. Rabbit and I will be in the salon. Call me when Deuce gets to the docking bay."

"Maybe I should stay here and watch, Zack. What if Deuce runs into a random security sweep? I can reprogram his clearance and maybe get him passed."

"Salon, now!" I barked as I stepped out onto the catwalk. Rabbit paled and rolled after me.

I crossed the catwalk to the main section of the *Profit's* upper deck. The 'salon' was the largest compartment of the ship's living area, although salon was a pretentious name for the space. The bulkheads were bare metal, painted functional gray. A large pedestal table stood in the center with four metal chairs that swung down from the underside. A food dispenser and a holomatrix occupied the bulkhead nearest the catwalk. Spare equipment was secured by cargo webbing to the others. The only concession to comfort was my chair—an overstuffed synthetic leather armchair that had once graced the outer office of the President of the Martian Republic.

I settled into the chair and sighed. Rabbit rolled in and moved over to the table, not as far from me as possible but far enough to be out of my reach.

"Stop being ridiculous, Rabbit. I'm not going to hit you."

"Okay, Zack," he said uncertainly.

"Tell me about Scalzi. And don't repeat that bullshit story about an ex-wife. Who the hell is he and who's after him?"

"He's just a guy I met, that's all." His eyes darted around the compartment, refusing to meet my hard stare.

39

"Don't give me that crap. You don't just meet people and invite them to travel on my ship. Hell, Rabbit, you're so paranoid you wouldn't talk to someone you'd just met unless you had a good reason to, never mind traveling with the guy. So who the hell is he?"

Rabbit swallowed hard. "He's the Green Lantern."

"Who?"

"Green Lantern," he said as if I should recognize the name. "The slicer who corrupted the Martian defense database during the war?"

I shrugged. If some sort of cyber attack had corrupted our database during the war, it was news to me. It might have happened during my time in the Bear. I wasn't exactly plugged into the intelligence net then.

Rabbit gave an exasperated sigh. "Don't tell me you've never heard of him. He's only the most legendary slicer in the whole system. Back during the run up to the Reunification War he played hell with all the Martian systems. He and I once fought a virus duel that lasted for thirty hours. I didn't know who he was back then, of course. Only that he was damned good."

"So you met him during the war? Or after?"

"No. I told you. I just met him a couple of days ago. I knew him, but I never met him. He was deep in the Federal intel services. Not really assigned to any agency but plugged into them all. We only knew him by his slicer name—Green Lantern. It's from an old realie character back on Earth. He came up with it himself and had the nerve to sign his dataworms and slicing viruses with it in a line of non-functional code. He's a legend in slicer circles. I thought for sure you'd have heard of him."

"If you'd never met him in person, how did you hook up with him here at Highpoint?"

"I didn't know him, but he knew me," Rabbit said. "Before the Bear, I was in cyber defense working for the Martian military. Like I said, we knew the Lantern by his signature code but we didn't know his real name or what he looked like. I must have run a dozen operations against him and the Federal database but his firewalls and traps were the best I'd ever seen. And his attacks on us were just plain nasty. Multiple nested worms, sleeper logic bombs, viral slicing programs, you name it. Did I tell you we once fought a virus duel that lasted over thirty hours? It set a record. I spent the whole time in the Bunker, thirty straight hours of entering code, Zack. Nobody's done anything like it since. In the last hour, he got through my toughest firewall and would have gotten to my AI core if I hadn't tricked him with a datatrap. It was really shiny. What I did was set up a dummy..."

"Rabbit," I interrupted. "That's not important. Just tell me how Scalzi found you."

"Oh. I thought that was obvious. He sliced the Martian military database, remember? Got through my best defenses and copied the whole thing before he shot it through with viruses and dataworms. He got my dossier; name, pictures, code signature, everything. Wasn't really my fault, you know. I warned them that cyber defense wasn't static, that I'd have to review and update the firewalls regularly, but they said they had their own people for that. Their people! Stupid incompetents if you ask me."

"So Scalzi approached you. Where?"

"In the main public passageway. Just outside the Information Ministry. I had just finished the code upgrade. I spent three days working under all kinds of restrictions with a substandard code. I left them with something truly shiny and they showed me the door like I was a common technician."

"Rabbit, tell me about Scalzi," I said, nudging him back on track.

"Oh, yeah. He knew who I was, so when he bumped into me in the passageway he recognized me. He said he was surprised to see me; didn't know I had survived the war.

He'd heard about the Bear and figured I was dead. So after a few minutes he said we should go someplace for a drink and talk about the old days. You know I don't drink, Zack. I was going to tell him no, but I was so mad about the way they treated me in the ministry that I figured 'what the hell,' one drink can't hurt me. Besides, I knew he'd understand. About the code upgrade, I mean."

Sure he would, I thought. One thing was clear to me: the meeting wasn't accidental. Scalzi was looking for Rabbit when he 'bumped into him.'

"We went to a place Marco knew on the garden level," Rabbit went on. "Real nice, pricey. Marco paid, but I just had a Martian fizz. We talked about the war, about coding, about a lot of stuff. I told him about the Bear and about you and Deuce. Then he told me he was in trouble and needed a way off Highpoint. It was perfect, Zack. He obviously had money and needed a ship. You have a ship and need money." He grinned, proud of himself for arranging the deal.

I didn't burst his bubble by pointing out that Scalzi had set the whole thing up. "If Scalzi is such a great slicer, why didn't he do the same thing you did just now? He could have sliced the security programs and canceled any official hold on his departure. Why risk hiring us to smuggle him out?"

"Huh? Well, I suppose he, I mean maybe; gosh, Zack. I don't know."

"Neither do I. But once Deuce gets here, I have a few questions for your friend Marco."

CHAPTER SIX

Deuce arrived about ten minutes later. I lowered the forward cargo ramp and helped him push the toolbox up into the hold. Deuce opened the top of the box as I raised the ramp and locked it down. I turned back toward him as Deuce reached in, hauled Scalzi out by the shoulders, and raised him in a fireman's carry.

"Where do you want him, LT?"

"Better lay him out on your bunk, Deuce. Unless you think you can get him up to the salon."

Deuce grunted. "Been pushing him around for the last hour. He's a heavy boy. I don't think I can haul him up the ladder. Hate to give up the bunk, though."

"He shouldn't sleep too much longer."

Deuce nodded. "You better come on then. I got a bunch of spare parts on the bunk that'll need moving."

I led the way down the passageway behind the ladder to the upper deck. It snaked around the bulge of the reactor and the gravity drive. Just beyond the main drive access was the hatch to Deuce's workshop and living quarters. I stepped through and swept a tangled mass of power cables and servojunctions off the bunk. Deuce tossed Scalzi onto the now empty bedding and took the cables from my arms.

Scalzi snorted and rolled onto his side. He coughed a couple of times and then raised himself up on one elbow as he rubbed his eyes. He looked slowly around the compartment but froze when he saw me.

"Mbele," he said. "What happened?"

"You took a couple of needles. I got you out of the food court. Deuce here brought you to my ship." I swept a hand in Deuce's direction.

Scalzi's eyes widened as he looked Deuce up and down. He shook his head, then sat upright and reached for his pockets.

I held up his wad of cash. "Looking for this?"

He started to his feet, but sat down when Deuce took a step forward. I placed a hand on Deuce's shoulder and he stepped back again.

Scalzi looked up at me, his face pale and sullen. "That's mine."

"And you'll get it back after we're clear of Highpoint control and I get what's owed to me."

"Why should I trust you?"

"Because I could have taken this," I held up the cash again. "And left you to that bounty hunter. If you want out of our deal, just say the word and I'll put you out in the commercial port with your money. You can try to find someone else."

"No, that won't be necessary. I suppose I should thank you for getting me out of there."

"Save it. What I want are answers. Who was that woman and why was she after you?"

"I don't know. I've never seen her before. Maybe she's working for my ex-wife."

"Bullshit!" My voice was loud enough to make him jump. "Don't try that stupid story with me. I told you I didn't believe a word of it. And don't try to blame the Highpoint police. She wasn't working for them, either."

He didn't say anything at first, just sat staring at the floor. "I don't know who she is," he said at last. "But she's probably working for Colin Jones."

Deuce whistled softly. "She's a Dragon?"

The Red Dragons got their start out in the Belt when a gang of Welsh 'roid miners caught the independence bug. They fought a low intensity rebellion against the corporate powers that dominated the mining communities. Drug running and extortion funded their military operations. After a while, the money got too big and the idealists who still wanted to fight for independence were either forced out or killed. Within a few years, the Red Dragons controlled a third of the inhabited Belt and ran most of the casinos and brothels in the Martian city of Tharsis. Colin Jones had risen through the ranks as a soldier and enforcer for the extortion business until he'd seized control of the whole organization a few years ago.

Scalzi shook his head. "No, at least I don't think so. Most of the Red Dragons are known to Highpoint security. There are only a few of them in the arcology right now and the cops keep pretty close tabs on them. If she were a Dragon, I'd have a dossier on her."

"So Rabbit was right about you," I said.

"How's that?"

"He said you were some kind of super slicer. Worked for the Feds during the war. He said you managed to slice the whole Martian defense network. How deeply have you penetrated Highpoint security?"

"I did some work for the Federal Republic during the war," he said cautiously. "I'm retired now."

"Sure you are. But you keep your hand in, don't you? Especially when you're on the run from Jones' people. Tapping into Highpoint security would let you keep track of any Dragons in the arcology's zone of control. Is that how you found Rabbit, too?"

Scalzi nodded. "I saw his name on the list of transient workers. I knew from his old dossier that he was a bit paranoid. I figured he'd have a secure way out of here, or at least a secure channel he could use to contact someone. When he told me about you, I came up with the story about a vindictive ex-wife."

"Which brings us back to my main question. Why is Colin Jones after you?"

He didn't answer right away. He looked from me to Deuce and back to me again. "I can't tell you that. Just that he wants me alive."

"Not good enough, Scalzi. I've already stuck my neck out for you with the cops. I'm not going up against Jones and the Dragons for nothing more than a few yuan and your word that he's after you."

Scalzi closed his eyes and muttered something that I didn't catch. He shrugged and said, "You won't believe me anyway. I'll pay more, if that will satisfy you." He pointed at the cash in my hand. "I have forty thousand there. Half of it's yours if you get me out of here."

"All of it's mine if I toss you out the lock and let Jones get you."

He actually smiled at that. "I don't think you will. You could have taken the money in the food court if that was all you wanted." He paused and his face grew serious. "You were willing to do the job for ten thousand. You put yourself in danger to get me here. Now, I'll pay twenty thousand if you get me out of Highpoint and take me to the Belt."

"Just like that." I made it a statement edged with sarcasm, not a question.

He sighed. "I am asking you, please, get me out of Highpoint. I guarantee, I'll make it worth your while."

I thought for a long moment. I was already involved anyway, like it or not. He was right; if I'd wanted the money, I could have taken it and left him in the food court. I had made a contract here, and I would keep my end. It wasn't the kind of contract you could get a court to enforce, but that was just the kind you need to keep. In the end all I had was the ship and my credibility as someone who'd do what he said he'd do. The kind of jobs I got depended on that reputation.

"All right," I said. He started to speak, but I held up a hand. "But, we do this my way. You will stay here on the ship. You will speak to no one, go nowhere, until we leave."

He didn't say anything, just nodded.

"Now, I think Deuce wants his bunk back. Come with me."

Scalzi got to his feet and followed me out to the cargo bay. We climbed the ladder to the upper deck and I showed him to one of the spare cabins.

"It's a bit Spartan, but it's clean and safe."

Scalzi just nodded. I left him and returned to the salon. Rabbit was still there, noodling with his virtual keyboard.

"Scalzi is awake," I said without preamble. "He's in the spare cabin. I don't want you talking to him unless I'm with you, okay?"

"Sure, Zack. But why?"

"Because I don't trust him. He didn't just run into you in the passageway, Rabbit. He found your name on the security database and arranged to meet you."

Rabbit nodded, "I kind of thought so. After you asked why he didn't just slice himself a clearance, I got to thinking about it. He's the best, Zack. He could make himself invisible to the officials here if he wanted to. He's scared of something, but it isn't an ex-wife or a divorce judgment. I think he's scared of Martian reprisals. There have been a lot of strange things going on in the Belt lately. And you know, Metternich's still out there. I'll bet he's got the Revenants looking for the Green Lantern."

"Oh, cut it out, Rabbit," I said. "I'm sick of your conspiracy theories and rants about 'Martian reprisals.' There is no secret society of Martian freedom fighters taking revenge on the Feds. And Metternich's dead. I saw what the Federal offensive did to the Presidential Palace. Nothing could have survived that explosion."

"They never found a body," Rabbit said stubbornly.

"That's because it was vaporized along with half of the compound! He's dead. Rabbit. You're wasting your time looking for him."

He didn't answer. He just folded his arms and glared at me. We had been over this ground before. The Revenants were rumored to be a secret society of Metternich loyalists dedicated to resurrecting the Revolution. Rabbit's paranoia centered on Metternich and the conviction that he was still alive. My sanity depended on the conviction that he wasn't.

Colonel Hans Metternich had been the driving force behind the Martian Revolution. For two years running, up to the overthrow of the Federal governor, I'd recruited revolutionary cells in Tharsis, supplying arms and money funneled from Metternich's Third Directorate of Martian Intelligence. Metternich had trained me, been my mentor, my friend and the closest thing to a father I had known since the age of seven. Thirteen weeks after he executed the governor and took over as Martian President, I was swept up by a Black Ops squad and dumped in Bruneault prison. I invoked his name over and over again; cursed him when he didn't save me, and purged what was left of my ideals and loyalty in the heat of his biotanks. All that was left was a hatred that someday would consume me. Jolt helped me hang on. The drug combined with a specific radiofrequency pumped through my datalink to stimulate the endorphin centers in my brain. It shut out the pain for a while. Alcohol did the same thing, but jolt was faster.

Before either of us could say anything else, my link chimed. "What is it, Sylvia?"

"There's a call for you, Zack. From a woman calling herself Cleopatra Lee. She's on a public commlocus. She says you have business with her."

"Put her through."

The contact lens camera in my right eye flickered and then she was there. In spite of myself, I gasped at the sight of her. She stood in a public link booth, still wearing the waitress uniform. Her eyes pierced me, drawing me out of myself and into a world of longing and lust. I swallowed hard.

"What can I do for you, Ms. Lee?" My voice sounded weak and tinny in my own ear.

"I need your help, Mr. Mbele. I was supposed to do a job, but because of your interference, I failed. Now I'm in trouble with the people who hired me."

I desperately wanted to help her, to do anything I could to get closer to her. Instead I said, "And how is that my problem?"

"You interrupted my play at the food court. Please, just meet me at the passenger terminal tube station. I'm desperate. I'll do anything you say."

That opened a whole new world of possibilities in my mind. I shoved them all down and considered what she might want.

"All right," I said. "I'll meet you there in fifteen minutes. Can you wait that long?"

"Yes." She glanced over her shoulder. "Yes, I think so." She reached out and broke the connection.

Rabbit looked at me quizzically. He'd only heard my side of the conversation. "Who is 'Ms. Lee'? Is she the waitress from the food court? You're not really going to meet her, are you? Are you going to sell Marco out?"

"Rabbit, shut up. I made a deal with Scalzi. I don't go back on my word."

"I know that." He looked like I had struck him. "I'm sorry."

"Don't sweat it. Just don't talk to Scalzi without me around, okay?"

He nodded, and I turned and left the salon. I stopped

by the weapons locker and took out a fresh magazine for the needler. I worked the action, loading a needle into the chamber, then flicked on the safety, and tucked the weapon into my belt.

I walked quickly through the freight terminal, turning spinward onto the public walkway. Reaching the tube station a couple of minutes early, I hung back, looking over the wide plaza that fronted the station. The crowd ebbed and flowed as the tubes emptied their riders onto the plaza. I watched for a while, getting the rhythm of the place. After a couple of minutes, small details stood out. A cluster around a holomatrix broadcasting news, a falafel stand, individual knots of people engaged in conversation. And then I saw her.

She walked slowly back and forth across the plaza, never following a set path but seeming to wander at random. I stepped out into the open and walked quickly toward her. She gave a small gasp as I fell in step beside her, but didn't slow her pace.

"You came," she said.

"I do what I say I'll do, Ms. Lee. What did you want to talk to me about?"

She glanced nervously around. "You can help me get out of Highpoint. I know you helped Scalzi get away after you shot me. I need you to help me do the same."

"Why should I do that?"

She stopped and whirled to face me, clutching my arm in an iron grip. Her deep emerald eyes filled with tears as she held my gaze. "Because you put me in this spot. The Red Dragons don't give you second chances when you screw up a job. Help me Mr. Mbele. You're my only hope."

I drank in those wonderful eyes for another second. Then I laughed. "Oh, you're good, lady. You're very good. The tears are easy. I think it's the little quaver you get in your voice when you say 'Help me, Mr. Mbele' that makes the performance so compelling."

She frowned, sudden anger darkening her eyes. Then she shrugged, with a small smile and her expression softened. She eased her grip on my arm.

"I suppose I deserved that. But it's the truth. I was supposed to deliver Scalzi to the Dragons. They got me out of the food court before the cops could question me, but unless I can get Scalzi to them in the next twenty-four hours, they'll kill me."

"What do the Dragons want with Scalzi?"

"Walk with me." She hooked her hand into the crook of my elbow. We started walking. She didn't speak immediately, but scanned the crowd as we strolled along. Finally she asked, "What do you know about Fingal Malloy?"

"Not that old legend," I scoffed. "Don't tell me you believe in that crap."

"Humor me," she said, turning those magic eyes my way once more.

I sighed. "Fingal Malloy was a 'roid miner back in the early days of the Belt settlements. One day he walked into a bar on a backwater asteroid called Delilah and plunked down a glowgem the size of his fist as payment for a round of drinks and a bed for the night. He died in that bed a few hours later with backpack full of glowgems under his head. The tales about Fingal's Cave started right after that—a hollow asteroid somewhere out in the Belt filled with glowgems, some as big as a shuttle. Since then, dreamers and fools have spent hundreds of thousands of hours scouring the Belt for it. People found glowgems, singly and in clusters, but no hollow asteroid. The story won't die, like the legend of the Lost Dutchman's Mine, or the Underground Lakes of Barsoom. It's hard to kill a good legend, especially one that promises riches beyond most people's imaginations. I don't see you or Jones believing that shit, though."

There was no question that Fingal's gems were real, even if the Cave was not. Glowgems ranged in size from a few millimeters to several centimeters. Silicate in composition, they were unremarkable rough crystals when found in the cold of space. But warm them to a temperature above twenty degrees Celsius and they would shine in a rainbow of shifting colors. Each one was unique. And if they were cut or broken they would never glow again. A five-millimeter gem could fetch several thousand yuan on the open market. One the size of a fist would have been worth millions.

"It doesn't matter what I believe," she said. "Jones paid me to bring Scalzi in, or if not Scalzi, then an antique notebook he might be carrying."

"Notebook?"

"Yes, a small leather bound book about fifteen centimeters by ten. In the old days, they used to write things down on paper and keep information in these little books."

"I know what a notebook is," I grumbled. "What I mean is, why would Jones want something like that? It can't be worth much."

"Unless it tells where Scalzi got the glowgems. About six weeks ago, he started selling gems to dealers all over the system. A few on Mars, two big ones on the Promenade in Tycho City and just last week a pair of color-matched gems here in Highpoint."

That made a bit more sense. Scalzi was clearly flush and a couple of glowgems would explain where he got the forty thousand in cash. Still, Fingal's Cave? I doubted Jones was going to buy a story like that.

"How much was the bounty on Scalzi?"

"Ten thousand for Scalzi alive." She shrugged. "Three for the notebook alone. But I don't have either one and I've already spent the advance money I got for the job. Without the notebook or Scalzi, Jones will kill me." Her grip tightened on my arm again. "I know I overplayed the girl in distress bit, but I am in trouble and it's partly your fault. I don't know anyone here I can trust. Please, I'll pay you back any way I can. Just help me get out of Highpoint alive."

All those worlds of possibilities reawakened in my head. Besides, I'd rather have her where I could keep an eye on her than worry about her coming after Scalzi from some blind spot. So what else could I do?

"Do you have any money?" I asked.

"A little. A few hundred yuan."

"Give it to me." She reached into a pouch at her belt and pulled out a pile of notes, three hundred at most. I tucked the bills into my back pocket. "We'll figure out a way to pay for the rest of your passage once we're out of here. Ever been to the Belt?"

Scalzi would shit moon rocks when I showed up with Cleopatra Lee in tow, but what did I care? It wasn't like he had any say in the matter. I held all his ready cash and he wasn't about to risk running into the Dragons if he left the ship. I didn't trust Lee any more than I would a loaded gun. But, oh those eyes!

CHAPTER SEVEN

She stopped and blinked at me. I think she expected more negotiation. "Are you serious? You'll really help me? Why?"

"What is it with you? First you beg me to help you, then you question me when I agree. Do you want to get out of here or not?"

Her eyes flashed anger again, but she dropped a veil over them quickly. "Yes," she said, her voice tight. "I just want to know what this will cost me."

"Scalzi's paying me ten thousand yuan."

"I can't afford that."

"Didn't think you could. That's why I said we'd work it out later." Her eyes flashed again. "And I don't mean by having sex with me. You have other skills I may be able to use. Are you ready to leave, or do you have clothes or gear to pick up?"

"I don't think I should go back to my room. If I start packing, they'll know I'm doing a runner. Let's go straight to your ship."

I smiled. She was smart. Even if her story was a complete lie, she was sticking to it. She took my arm again and we turned toward the entrance to the commercial port.

I scanned the crowd as we walked. Something wasn't right. The nanos were twitching. I could feel them extend into my arms and legs. My vision became sharper and shifted into the infrared so that people in the crowd glowed with a halo of body heat. I didn't exactly control the nanos. They seemed to respond to my needs, but I never knew when they would activate. If they were waking up now, my body was sensing something my brain hadn't noticed.

My eyes flicked from face to face, looking for ones that didn't fit. I passed him once, but came back. His shape was wrong. The nanos tingled and I realized what had bothered me. He was wearing an augment vest under his dark business suit. Skin tight and woven from magnetically charged microfibers, the vest would stop a needle or pneumatic round and would turn most conventional knife blades. Movement caused a small electrostatic charge to build up on the vest's surface, which made the outer clothes balloon outward ever so slightly. That's what my subconscious had noticed and the nanos had responded to.

I steered Lee to the right toward an emergency exit. "Company," I said in response to her questioning glance. She nodded and followed my lead.

I activated my link. "Rabbit, I've picked up a tail. I need an exit. I'm headed toward an emergency hatch on the main plaza outside the tube stations. Can you disable the alarm if I open it?"

"I need five seconds, Zack. Are you headed to the hatch spinward of your current position?"

I glanced around and got my bearings. The guy in the augment vest quickened his pace to close in on us. "That's the one."

"Okay, no problem. I've disabled the alarms on all the

emergency hatches on the plaza, but you could have opened that one anyway. It's showing a ground fault. The alarm's off-line."

I didn't like the sound of that, but there was nothing for it now. Our uninvited shadow was closing fast. I kicked the hatch open and steered Lee through it. I followed her and slammed the door shut. There was no lock or dog to secure it. After the brightly lit plaza, the dull red emergency lights in the escape shaft seemed dark as a lunar night. We stood on a landing in a stairwell leading up and down. Lee started down without waiting for me, her footsteps padding softly on the metal stairs.

"Wait," I called, as I started after her. She had already stopped and was backing up slowly. Approaching her from the landing below us was a large man with a drawn pneumatic. His clothes were black, but his body heat glowed dull orange in my infrared vision. The hatch behind me slammed open and our shadow stepped through, a needler in his right hand. I started to reach for my own weapon but stopped as Lee stepped up next to me and gripped my arm.

"Not yet," she whispered with a slight cock of her head toward the big man climbing the stairs from below.

"Ms. Lee," said the man with the needler. He was smaller than his companion. His suit was soft, natural wool, well tailored, and expensive looking. His narrow eyes glittered, like a rat in the dark. "Where are you going in such a hurry?"

I turned to face him. "Why do you care where she goes?"

He held up his left hand, palm out, showing me the tattoo. The red Welsh dragon reared on a green and white shield. At least part of Lee's story was true. These guys were soldiers for the Red Dragons.

"That'd be no concern of yours." He looked at Lee. "Mr. Jones wants a word with you, Ms. Lee."

She bowed her head, as if giving up. I saw her fist clench and felt her ease her weight onto the balls of her feet. Time seemed to slow as my nanos bridged the gaps between my nerve junctions, speeding my reflexes and augmenting my muscle strength.

Lee swung toward the larger man just as he reached the landing beside her. Her balled fist lashed out striking him on the bridge of the nose. I heard bones crunch as blood spurted from his nostrils. She grabbed his wrist with her other hand and twisted. The man grunted and the pneumatic fell to the deck. Before he could make a move she brought her knee up into his groin. He doubled over and she smashed the heel of her hand into the space behind his left ear, dropping him like a stone.

Before her first blow landed I had my needler out and pressed under the smaller man's chin. "Don't move," I said. He froze. "Drop the needler." He hesitated for only a half-second before the gun clattered to the deck.

Lee picked it up along with the pneumatic she had wrenched from the large man.

"You okay?" I asked her.

"Sure. I wasn't sure you got my signal."

"Loud and clear. You have anything to say to this clown?"

She shook her head. I pushed my needler hard up under his chin causing him to rise on his toes. His breath wheezed in my ear. He smelled of cologne, floral and sweet. It clashed with the cold look in his eye.

"Tell Jones if he wants to talk to Cleopatra Lee, he should come in person. Either that or send better boys." I stepped back but kept the needler leveled on his head. "Now help your friend up and get out of here."

The larger man coughed as he struggled to his feet. He stood with his shoulders hunched, his hands on his thighs. He stepped forward with a cautious shuffling gait. Lee had stepped back out of his reach and covered the both of them with the pneumatic.

"Jones will hear about this," grunted the big man as he staggered toward the hatch.

"Good. Be sure to tell him how a woman beat you up.

And get my name right. It's Mbele. I'll be aboard the *Profit*; Bay 42, spinward."

The small, rat-like man with the feminine cologne turned on his heel and strode out into the plaza without another look back. The bigger man moved slowly, easing his bulk through the hatch with his legs bowed.

Baiting the Dragons wasn't the smartest thing to do, but if I wanted to get Colin Jones' attention, reckless was better than smart. And if I hoped to cut a deal, it would be with Jones himself and not some thug out to make points with the boss. Now that both Scalzi and Lee were with me, I had a strong hand to play. The two of them had something the Dragons wanted. Something Jones would pay to obtain. This trip might turn a profit yet.

Lee regarded me with a curious look. "Was that smart? Taunting them like that."

I shrugged. "They already know you and it won't take Jones long to figure out who I am. A bit of bravado will impress him and may make his goons think twice about taking another run at us. So, yeah, it was a smart move."

I stuck my head out the open hatch and surveyed the plaza. Nothing seemed amiss and my nanos were retracting back into their resting state. A dull headache was already throbbing behind my eyes. I stepped out and Lee followed.

Lee said nothing more as we made our way to the ship. I didn't feel like talking. My head throbbed and my muscles ached with the after-burn of the nano augmentation. The confidence that I could turn the situation to my advantage was waning as well. I still didn't trust Cleopatra Lee, but at least part of her story checked out. The Dragons were after her. And that, in an oblique way, confirmed what Scalzi had said about her. Still, something told me there was more going on than I knew. I didn't believe in Fingal's Cave, but could buy Lee's story that Scalzi was selling glowgems. It explained his twitchiness and the large wad of cash. But where did a slicer with no evidence of any other skills get his hands on glowgems? If I threw Scalzi and Lee together, something would shake loose. And that might be valuable enough to sell to Jones.

By the time we reached the *Profit*, the stiffness in my muscles had eased but my head was still on fire. I palmed the lock on the starboard sally port and it opened. I gestured for Lee to climb the ladder and then followed and closed the port behind us.

She stood in the center of the forward hold and surveyed the scene. I was suddenly aware of the layer of old grease under the cargo lift, the jumble of netting and nanocord tie-down straps hanging from the bulkheads, and the chipped paint on the edges of the hatch coamings and ladders. *Why the hell should that bother me?* I wondered.

"Not much to look at, is she?" Lee smiled. "Kind of like her captain."

I flushed, which made my head hurt even more. Before I could answer, Rabbit rolled out onto the catwalk.

"Sylvia said you brought someone back with you," he said. He looked down at Lee and stopped, open-mouthed.

"Hello." She looked up at him, her head cocked. "I'm Cleo Lee. I recognize you from the food court."

Rabbit closed his mouth and nodded, looking from Lee to me, eyes wide.

"Zack has been kind enough to offer me a ride," she went on. "Will you be coming with us as well?"

I didn't like the way this was going. Bad enough she made me feel uncomfortable about the seedy look of the ship, now she was using my first name like we were old friends.

"Rabbit!" I said sharply. "Stop gawking and move your stuff into my stateroom. You'll have to bunk with me. Ms. Lee will need the charter cabin."

"Please, Zack," She gave my arm a light squeeze. "It's Cleo."

Part of me, the part that thrilled to that light touch on my arm, wanted to reach out to her and promise to protect her, no matter what happened. I knew what she was doing. I could see how she was manipulating me, which buttons she was pushing. What's more, she knew I could see through her, but she played me anyway. I didn't care. Wherever this was leading, I would go willingly.

"Cleo, then. I'll show you to the charter cabin once Rabbit gets his gear out of there."

"Rabbit." She cocked her head at me this time. "Odd name."

"His real name's Edward Conejo. He's a slicer; goes by Eddie the Rabbit. Most people who know him just call him Rabbit."

"It suits him. Tell me, have you picked up any other strays?" Her tone was playful, but I sensed an edge behind it.

"Maybe one or two. Let's go up to the salon while Rabbit clears out of the charter cabin."

She smiled enigmatically, but said nothing more. I pointed to the ladder and she walked over toward it, moving with an enticing sway that took my breath away, even though I knew it was staged for just that purpose. I shook my head and followed her.

She waited for me at the top, standing with a hand on her hip, her head cocked to the side as she watched me. Again, I felt an odd embarrassment at the run-down look of the deck and the rough unfinished salon. I pointed the way and she ducked gracefully through the hatch.

Scalzi's shot echoed through the ship.

I'd expected some reaction when he saw Cleo, but hadn't anticipated he'd be armed. Where he'd hidden the pneumatic was beyond me. Fortunately, he was a lousy shot. The slug smeared itself across the hatch coaming before falling to the floor.

Cleo dove to the left and came up with the pneumatic she'd taken from the big Dragon, leveling it at Scalzi. He turned his gun toward her. I dove at him, the nanos augmenting my speed and strength.

Cleo caught the movement and diverted her shot.

I knocked Scalzi's hand up and swept his feet out from under him. He went down on the deck and dropped the pneumatic.

"Enough of that." I picked up the pneumatic and pushed him back down when he tried to get up. I checked the weapon and flicked on the safety. It was a 5.5mm Smith and Wesson, easily concealed in the palm, or in a pocket. I mentally kicked myself for missing it when I searched Scalzi.

"What the Hell is she doing here, Mbele?" Scalzi demanded. "We had a deal."

"Our deal was to take you away from Highpoint. I said nothing about taking on other passengers."

"Nice to see you again, Marco." Cleo slid her pneumatic into a pocket and leaned against the bulkhead.

Scalzi scrambled to his feet. I let him up, but pushed him into a chair when he looked like he was going to bolt for the door.

Cleo smirked as she crossed the salon and leaned forward onto the table. "Where is it, Marco?" she asked, holding his eye.

"Not here. Why would I have it on me?"

"Well, it isn't at Tharsis, either. Jones would have it by now and wouldn't have needed to blackmail me into tracking you down. Why'd you run out on me, Marco. That wasn't smart."

"Smart like you?" Scalzi scoffed. "I'm not the one who got pinched in her room with her pants off."

Cleo whipped out the pneumatic, but I snatched it from her hand. Her eyes blazed, first at Scalzi, and then at me. "You'll regret that." Her voice was barely above a whisper.

"I already do," I said, seeing the gleeful look on Scalzi's face. "But you haven't been straight with me, so I've got no reason to trust you."

"You can't trust her," Scalzi said. "She's a liar and a whore. She'll sell out to anyone with money or a big—"

I backhanded him across the mouth. "Shut up. You've got no room to talk. From the first, you've done nothing but lie to me. What is this 'thing' both of you are talking about? The notebook?"

Scalzi stared sullenly at the tabletop rubbing his swelling lip. Cleo lifted her chin defiantly. Neither said anything.

"All right. This is my ship. While you're aboard, both of you belong to me. You do what I say, when I say, or I'll put you off. Here or out in the black, it doesn't matter to me. Clear?"

Scalzi paled. "You wouldn't really..." He stopped and nodded vigorously when I gave him a hard look.

Cleo wasn't so easily cowed. She held my eye for a long moment before smiling and nodding once.

"Go down the passageway to the right. First cabin. Rabbit should be moved out by now. Wait for me."

"Oh, Zack. A date? How exciting."

I frowned. Why couldn't she stop picking at me? "Shut up. Just get out of here while I talk to Scalzi. Then I'll want to talk to you."

She ran a finger under my chin. "I'll be looking forward to it."

I stood there for a second after she left the salon, struggling to control the anger and enticement that warred inside me. She was beautiful and mysterious, alluring and exasperating, and I wasn't sure which qualities were more frightening.

I turned back to Scalzi. He looked up at me through half squinted eyes—a shrewd, calculating look. "What are you looking at?" I asked.

He shrugged and resumed his study of the tabletop.

I stepped over and slammed my palm down on it. He only jumped slightly and hardly moved his eyes. *Not the timid twitch he makes out to be.* "Talk. What's the connection between the two of you?"

He looked up with that same calculating look. "Why should I say anything. You've got the hots for her so bad, you won't believe a thing I say anyway."

"Try me."

He sat still, looking up at me.

I folded my arms.

"What do you want to know?"

"Why did she draw on you in the food court? Is she the reason you want get away from Highpoint?"

He laughed. "I didn't even know she was here until she shot me with that needler. Last I saw of her, she was taking one of Jones' boys up to her room at the Regent Hotel in Tharsis. I figured she meant to sell me out, so I left the hotel and went straight to the spaceport. Caught the first shuttle here."

"What were you doing in Tharsis?"

"Same thing I'm doing here. Selling gems. I know she must have told you about that, so there's no sense in trying to keep it secret. You have all the money I made from them. I left Tharsis with nothing but the gems and my overcoat. I sold the last of them here on Highpoint."

"Where do you get the gems? You don't look like a dealer to me, more like a grifter."

"That's my business," His face hardened. "Nothing to do with you or our deal."

"I could make it my business."

His jaw clenched, but he said nothing, just shook his head. Wherever he got the gems, he'd rather take his chances on his own than tell me.

I changed the subject. "How did you get mixed up with Cleo Lee?"

"I met her in a bar on Delilah. She needed a job and I needed a bodyguard for this trip. A mutual acquaintance vouched for her skills, and he didn't lie. She is good. We traveled from Delilah to the Moon. I did business on the Promenade and in Gagarin Station. She took care of the rooms, local transportation, and handled the travel bookings. I thought we worked pretty well together.

"Then we got to Tharsis and all of sudden she goes all twitchy. Starts changing our hotels in the middle of the night, seeing muggers in every shadow. Then she takes up with this guy with a Dragon tattoo on his hand. I thought she was setting me up, like I said. So I got out of there fast and came here."

"So why the secrecy about leaving Highpoint?"

He got that hard look on his face for a second, then shrugged. "The Dragons. I sold my last two gems to a dealer here. I went back after converting his bank draft to cash. I was going to try to negotiate a deal for platinum wire to sell on Delilah. There were a couple of goons in expensive suits there. I didn't go in. Instead I took a room in a lower deck hotel and looked for a way out. When I came across Conejo's name I saw my chance and arranged to run into him."

I didn't ask more questions after that. Most of his story was at least consistent, but I was sure that a good bit of it was a lie.

CHAPTER EIGHT

I left Scalzi in the spare cabin with a warning to stay put unless he wanted to deal with Cleo on his own. I made my way aft to the charter cabin. It was by far the cleanest and best-furnished space on the ship. Sylvia had chosen the colors for the fabric that covered the bulkheads—teal and deep purple—and I'd sprung for some decent deck-mounted furniture. Still, with Cleo in it, it seemed drab and pedestrian.

She sat in a teal colored armchair, smoking and reading from a datapad set into the chair's arm. I knocked on the hatch coaming even though the hatch was open.

"So, what did Marco tell you?" she asked with an air of amusement.

"That you sold him out to the Dragons and he barely escaped with his skin."

She laughed. "I expected it would be something like that."

"Want to tell me your side of it?"

She drew deeply on her cigarette and let the smoke out slowly. "There's not much to tell. I was stuck on a backwater asteroid after a client welshed on a job offer. An acquaintance arranged the meeting with Marco. He wanted some discreet muscle and I needed the work.

"He had two tickets for the Moon, but no cash. He showed me a handful of gems and offered a share of the profits on spec if I'd help him. We struck a deal. It went well at first. He paid out my share, as agreed, after each sale. I watched his back, handled travel and hotels, and generally made sure no one bothered him. He could have done it without me, but he seemed, I don't know, twitchy somehow. It was like he expected trouble, only he wouldn't tell me what to watch for."

She paused and took another drag on the cigarette. She looked at me through the smoke, a small smile on her face.

I didn't take the bait. My head still hurt and I didn't feel like playing games. I crossed my arms and glared at her.

She smiled more broadly and continued. "By the time we got to Tharsis, he was really nervous. He made me change hotels three times and refused to leave the room except when he met with dealers. Even then, he convinced two of them to come to the room to do business. He had me standing guard outside the door. I told him that wasn't smart. The quickest way to advertise that you have something worth stealing is to let everyone know you have a bodyguard.

"Sure enough, later that same day as we were getting ready to check out, I noticed a couple of goons in high-priced suits with tailored vests; the kind that hide shoulder holsters. They were in the hotel bar, but they weren't drinking. I told Marco to get out of sight while I checked them out. I got close enough to see the Dragon tattoos and that's all I needed to see. I started for the lobby to warn Marco, but one of them caught up with me and flashed a needler. He told me to be a 'good girl' and take him up to Scalzi's room. Either they hadn't seen Marco, or didn't know what he looked like. I got in the elevator with him just as Marco ran out the front."

This was basically the same story Scalzi had told me, with a few differences. That could be put down to point of view and motive. The bottom line was that Cleo had been hired to watch Marco's back and had done just that. It still didn't explain how she ended up working for the Dragons by the time she found Scalzi here in Highpoint.

"So Scalzi ran out on you in Tharsis and you decided to work for Colin Jones instead."

She snubbed out her cigarette. "It's not that simple. I saw Marco get away and figured he'd wait for me at the spaceport. He had the tickets, but I knew we had a couple of hours before the ship was due to lift. The goon with the needler wasn't a problem. After that 'good girl' crack, he deserved what he got."

I'd seen her in action and didn't doubt that she could handle a lone gangster, even with a needler in her back.

"I got out through the service entrance and made it to the spaceport with almost an hour to spare. Marco wasn't there. I checked with the ticketing AI and found out that he'd canceled our reservations for the Belt and booked himself on a ship to Highpoint instead. He left me stuck with a little cash, a Dragon's needler and no ticket out."

"So, when did you make the deal with Jones?" I repeated.

"They caught up with me at the spaceport. I didn't have too many options and they weren't happy about the guy I'd left in the elevator. When the other guy from the hotel showed up with reinforcements, I thought they'd just kill me. Instead, they took me to a warehouse near the port. Patel was there, the rat-faced guy you met earlier today. He's Jones' main enforcer. He made me an offer: find Scalzi and the notebook and he'd pay me ten thousand yuan. He'd even pony up a few thousand in expense money against the fee. Fail, and I'd be outside the nearest lock wearing nothing but my birthday suit." She paused and looked up at me. "So I ask you, what was a girl to do?"

"And did he say why this notebook was so valuable to

them?"

She shook her head. "No. But I gather it has something to do with where Scalzi has been getting the gems. He may be a lying scumbag, but the gems are real. And they're not tagged. They're brand new on the market. They don't come from any known source."

Once again, a lot of her story squared with Scalzi's, but something wasn't right. There was a lie buried in all those words. I just didn't know where.

"How much of this tale is actually true?" I asked.

"Oh, every word. I swear," she said with an amused grin on her face.

"Okay. We've got all night. I'll get the galley to make us some coffee and we'll go over it again."

She laughed again, a soft throaty sound. "Make mine black. It's going to be a long night if you're going to make me tell it over and over."

We went over it again. And again, but the changes she made were minor. By the last telling she was getting sullen, no longer amused at my questioning.

"Tell me again about the notebook. When did you see it last?"

"I told you, I never saw it. Patel told me about it. The whole time I traveled with Marco, I never saw it."

"And he never told you where the gems came from?"

"No." She crossed her arms and looked down and to the right, as if there were something very interesting on the deck in front of her.

"So, where did the story of Fingal's Cave get started?"

She shrugged. "On Delilah. It's part of the local folklore. That's where Malloy died and left the first big cache of glowgems. Scalzi caused a sensation when he offered a small gem for his room and board at the same tavern where Fingal Malloy had stayed."

She was looking to her right again. My instructors in the Special Forces had emphasized that when people lie they tend to look to the right. Something about the right side of the brain being used for creativity. True memory resided in the left side of the brain, so when someone was remembering details of true events they glanced left.

"Why would he do that?" I was not accusing her of lying, not yet. "Was he looking for trouble?"

She shook her head, looking me square in the eyes now. "More like attention. He had no contacts in the jewelry markets. No buyer is going to meet with a guy selling unmarked gems unless they have some assurance that his gems are real. The attention he got in the tavern was enough to buy an audience with the dealers guild on the Moon. Once they vetted the gems, he had dealers calling him to try to buy more. When asked where he got them, he'd just smile and say 'Fingal's Cave.'"

It was late by the time I was satisfied that she wouldn't let me pry any more information out of her. I left her with the same speech I'd given Scalzi. She just nodded and said she'd stay in the cabin. She closed the hatch behind me as I left and I heard the inner lock click. She didn't want any company, either.

I made my way forward to the cockpit and sat in the command seat. "Did you get all that, Sylvia?"

"Yes, Boss. What do you want me to do with it?"

"Just make a file, cross reference it to Scalzi's story and mark the places where the stories don't match. I'll review it later if I need to."

"When do we leave, Boss? There's been nothing but trouble since we got here."

"Soon, Sylvia. I need to check out a few things." I looked into one of her cameras. "Did you find out any more about our friendly customs inspector?"

"Yes, thanks to Edward's slicing into the security net. His name is Levi Zink. He's been a full inspector for three years. Pay grade six out of twelve, middle level civil service, yet he lives in an upper deck flat with a view of the central parkland. The flat alone costs more than his official salary for the past five years."

"So he's thrifty," I played devil's advocate.

"Maybe, but he's also part owner of a restaurant in a high priced shopping arcade, has a lifetime membership at the Highpoint Athletic Club, and owns at least three rental flats below decks. Rough estimate, he's worth half a million yuan."

I whistled softly. "All on a civil servant's salary. I know this is Highpoint, but is everyone on the take?"

"Just about. He's covered his tracks well enough. I can't access his full financial statements. Even on Highpoint, the privacy laws are taken seriously. Maybe even more so."

"What about his tax returns?" I closed my eyes, suddenly very tired.

"Public record, but he pays on his declared income, even the rental income."

"So we know he's crooked but can't do anything about it."

"That's the size of it, Boss. Unless we can prove to the law that he's taking bribes, we can't touch him."

A surge of anger made me clench my fists. *Oh, I can touch him, all right,* I thought. *Getting away afterward is the problem.*

I must have muttered something because Sylvia asked, "What was that, Boss?"

"Nothing, Sylvia. Get Rabbit to help you. See if you can slice his bank accounts. I want to nail this bastard."

"Is that smart, Boss? Maybe we should just get out of here. We have a charter. It'll pay the mortgage for a while."

I slammed my palm into the arm of the command chair. "Just do it."

I thought about going to my cabin, but remembered that Rabbit was there. The last thing I wanted right now was to deal with Rabbit. I eased the command seat back into the reclining position. "I'm going to get some sleep, Sylvia. Keep an eye on our 'guests' and let me know if either of them leaves their cabin."

"Sure, Boss. Sleep well."

I closed my eyes, but sleep didn't come immediately. I knew there was more to this than either Cleo or Scalzi were saying. I could buy that he'd hired her as a bodyguard. I could also buy her deal with the Dragons. She wouldn't have had much choice if things went down the way she said. But she'd said Scalzi was edgy before the Dragons actually showed themselves. Why?

On the other hand, Scalzi had said Cleo was the one who got twitchy at Tharsis. What was he supposed to think when she left the bar with a Dragon on her elbow. A prudent man would run, wouldn't he?

Whether I wanted to admit it or not, I was more inclined to trust Cleo because I was attracted to her. Not a good basis for making important decisions.

CHAPTER NINE

I managed to nap in the command chair for an hour or so. I awoke groggy and unsettled, but at least the headache was gone. What little sleep I got was disturbed by vague dreams of drowning. It was late evening, ship's time. Highpoint operated on GMT so the local time matched *Profit*'s. I don't usually nap in the afternoon, but the drain of using the nanos earlier in the day, combined with the residual from the jolt hangover, had left me exhausted.

"Status report, Sylvia," I said, rubbing my eyes.

"Ship's systems are nominal," she said in her officious AI voice, the one she used when she was pissed at me. "The customs duty payment was sent and the receipt is logged. Our guests are still in their cabins. Scalzi has been accessing the local newsnet but I haven't intercepted any outgoing messages from him. Ms. Lee seems to be napping."

"Has Rabbit had any luck slicing Zink's financials?"

"Some. You should probably ask him."

I scratched and stretched as I stood up. Sylvia was being difficult. Maybe it hadn't been a good idea to have her programmed with a female personality.

"Don't worry," I said. "I know what I'm doing. We'll be on our way soon."

"Okay, Boss." She didn't sound convinced.

I left the cockpit and found Rabbit in my cabin. He had his virtual keyboard and a holomonitor set up on the battered desk that folded out of the far bulkhead. He sat with his back to the door, muttering as glowing lines of code crawled across the monitor. He jumped and spun around as I entered.

"Geez, Zack. Knock or something. You startled me. Hey, I managed to slice this guy's accounts. He's either very smart or he's got a smart accountant covering for him. No question he's into something crooked, but there's a lot of cover here. Hard to trace the money to any one source. If he's taking bribes or raking off customs duties, he's hiding it well."

"I don't know," I said. "He didn't strike me as being all that smart. Just venal. Could he be part of a bigger organization?"

"Make sense. Whoever set up these accounts really knows his stuff. The encryption algorithms were top notch. I had to construct a new..." Rabbit babbled on in technogeek. I tuned him out. How he sliced the accounts wasn't important. Zink had enough cover that a simple bank statement wasn't going to hang him. Rabbit wound down and looked at me expectantly.

"Thanks, Rabbit. This is really good stuff."

"Are we going to leave soon, Zack? I'm sick of this place. I want to get home to Tycho."

"Me too. I'm going to check with Deuce. If the ship's ready, we'll leave as soon as we get clearance."

I left the cabin and ran into Scalzi in the passageway.

"What's the hold-up, Mbele? We've been sitting here for hours. I paid to get out of here, not hide out aboard your ship."

"We leave when I say so. I had some unfinished business. We'll be on our way soon."

"What business?"

"Personal, no concern of yours. If you don't like the way I run my ship, I'll refund your money and you can get off now."

He started to say something, then seemed to think better of it. He turned and walked back to the spare cabin.

I slid down the ladder to the forward hold and made my way aft to Deuce's workshop. He was stripping his pulse rifle and replacing the emitter when I knocked at the bulkhead.

"Hey, LT. We leaving soon?"

"Yeah. Rabbit sliced some info on that weasel of a customs inspector but nothing we can use. We'll have to settle accounts with him another time. Our passengers are getting twitchy again. Everything golden down here?"

He snapped the rifle's housing back into place and locked it down. "Ship's ready anytime you are."

"Okay, I'll have Sylvia get us a launch clearance and we'll get out of here."

Deuce nodded. "That customs guy really got to you, didn't he?'

"Maybe. It doesn't pay to let something like that pass. But he's got protection and I can't afford to risk more official heat just now."

Deuce shrugged and replaced the pulse rifle on the rack next to his bunk. "Like I said, LT. Too damn much government in this place."

Sylvia called on my link before I could say anything else. "Boss, we've got a visitor. A cop, Inspector Kensai, is here. He wants to talk to you."

Deuce gave me a questioning look. I shrugged. "Put him through, Sylvia."

"Mr. Mbele? Kensai here. May I come aboard?"

"Hello, Inspector Kensai. Is this an official visit?"

"In a way. I'd like to talk to you about your guest."

"Do you have a warrant?"

"Do I need one?"

"I'll be happy to come out into the bay and talk with you. Or we can go to your substation, if you want to make this really official. But I can't ask you aboard without a warrant. Principles, basic rights, all that kind of stuff."

He actually laughed at that. "Anything you say. I'll wait for you out here."

I crossed the hold and opened the starboard side sally port. "Sylvia, make a recording of this through my link."

"Recording."

I descended the ladder and found Kensai standing near the center of the cargo bay, about ten meters from the ship. I crossed the deck to him and he nodded in greeting.

"You're an interesting guy, Mbele. If I were a suspicious man, I might think you had something to hide."

"What did you want to talk to me about, Officer?"

He didn't speak right away. He seemed to be considering what he wanted to say. I folded my arms, waiting. Finally, he said, "You had a spot of trouble in the spaceport plaza earlier today."

"Is that a question?"

"It could be. We identified the guy who followed you and Ms. Lee into the emergency stairwell. His name is Patel, Ashok Patel."

"Never heard of him."

"He's a close associate of Colin Jones. He has a reputation as an enforcer for the Dragons."

"That's not news, Inspector Kensai. I got up close and personal with his palm tattoo while we were in the stairwell. Did you come all the way down here to tell me his name? Or is there something else?"

"Ms. Lee accompanied you back here. She's aboard your ship. A bit odd, considering you pumped a couple of sleeper needles into her early this morning."

"We kissed and made up. Are you here to arrest her?"

He shrugged. "Unless Marco Scalzi wants to press assault charges against her, all we have on her is a couple of misdemeanors—disturbing the peace and illegal discharge of a weapon. Not worth the trouble to book her." He looked at me closely. "And since Marco Scalzi is still missing, there's not much point in running her down."

I held his gaze but said nothing.

"Where is Scalzi? And why are the Dragons after Cleopatra Lee?"

"Can't help you there. Cleo is leaving Highpoint with us. You shouldn't have any more trouble with her. As to Scalzi, who knows? Maybe he's the one the Dragons want."

He rubbed his chin. "Yeah, I thought of that. Look, Mbele, I'm not interested in your personal business, or in whatever is going on between you and Lee. But the Dragons are a different matter. We've kept a lid on them here for the past few years. I don't want to go back to the days when they had half of the arcology on their payroll and an honest cop stood a good chance of being pushed out an airlock if he tried to do his job." His eyes flashed as he said the words. "If the Dragons are trying to make a comeback, they'll have to get through me."

His anger seemed genuine and surprised me. Maybe I'm too cynical. I assumed graft and payoffs were just a fact of life here and that Kensai was part of the same system. An honest cop in Highpoint? That was a surprise.

"Patel only seemed interested in Cleo Lee," I said after a slight pause. "I didn't hear anything to make me think they had plans for the rest of the arcology. She'd made a deal to track Scalzi for them and they weren't happy when she lost him."

He nodded. "Okay. If it's like you say, we won't try to bring her in on the misdemeanors. Just get her off my arcology and make sure she doesn't come back."

I laughed. "As if I could tell a woman like her what to do. But don't worry. We're leaving now that that bogus customs duty has been paid." His face darkened at the mention of the duty. "Something else bothering you, Kensai?"

"Damn customs service is full of snakes. They rake off billions every year in extortion and bribes. You want to file a complaint?"

"Would it do any good?"

He sighed. "No. The money goes a lot higher than my pay grade."

I reflected on that for a second, then said, "Sylvia, would you please get the financial statements that Rabbit has and download them to Inspector Kensai's link."

"Are you sure about this, Zack?" she asked. "Those records are confidential. We could get in trouble for slicing them."

"Just do as I say."

"What's this," Kensai asked.

"Check your download folder. You'll find complete financial records on a customs inspector named Levi Zink. He took us for two cases of biochips and slapped that bogus duty on us."

Kensai scanned the file on his link eyepiece. "I could arrest you right now for theft of confidential information. That's a class two felony around here. Besides, what am I supposed to do with this? I can't take illegally obtained evidence into court."

I smiled. "Probably not. But if you follow the money trail, maybe you can develop your own evidence. Zink's a small time player, but he's connected to a big organization."

"Maybe. I'm not sure I like doing business with you Mbele. Do I need to warn you about coming back to Highpoint on my watch?"

"No, sir. Can we go now?"

He nodded. "Watch your back. I don't know what game Scalzi and Lee are playing, but you seem determined to put yourself in the middle of it. No skin off my nose as long as it's not here."

CHAPTER TEN

There's a time, just before takeoff, when everything is ready. The locks are sealed and the drives are humming with pent-up energy; all the loose gear is tied down or stowed away and I'm in the command chair looking out through the thick viewport at the deep black maw of space. That's the time I feel truly free. Metternich and the Bear and the 'tanks are distant echoes of a past life. The future is waiting, out in the black, out ahead of me. All I have to do is say the word and we can leap forward to chase any dream we want. It's better than a jolt high.

"Take us out, Sylvia."

The open doors of the docking bay slid past and fell behind as Sylvia nudged us forward with the impulse engines. Good manners and practical physics dictate that we not activate the drive until we were clear of Highpoint's gravitational field. Two competing grav generators create all sorts of unpredictable tidal forces. When that happens, the object with the greater mass usually wins, but can still be damaged by flying debris as the smaller mass is torn apart. *Profit*'s mass was a fraction of the arcology's. Even I could do the math.

"Gravity in sixty seconds," Sylvia announced over the intraship link. It hadn't occurred to me to warn our passengers so that they weren't caught floating a couple of meters above the deck when the drive switched on.

I smiled at the thought of Scalzi tumbling to the deck in the forward hold. The longer I was around that weasel, the more I disliked him. Turning him over to the Dragons would be a pleasure. I might consider doing it for free if he continued to piss me off.

I had decided I would sell Scalzi to Jones, if the price was right. I didn't exactly trust Cleo, but she offered benefits that Scalzi couldn't match. Once we were free of Highpoint's zone of control, I'd have fulfilled the letter of our contract. True, I'd agreed to take him to the Belt, but if my conscience bothered me I could always refund half his fee.

The gravity drive kicked in and I felt my standard G weight settling into the chair's padding. I unstrapped and stood up. "Take us out to freefall space, then hold position." I said to Sylvia.

"Aren't we going to the Belt, Boss?"

"Maybe. I need to have another talk with Scalzi. And if he doesn't tell me what I want to know, I'll be wanting to talk to Colin Jones, so see if Rabbit can come up with a commlocus we can use to reach him."

"Yes, Boss."

I walked aft to the salon. Scalzi was there, sitting at the table with a bowl of soy noodles in front of him. He peeled back the thin plastic cover and lifted the bowl to his mouth, shoveling noodles into it with a pair of chopsticks. I stood over him until he stopped chewing and looked up at me.

"You want something, Mbele?"

I gripped the table to keep from flattening his nose. "A little civility, maybe. We're in freefall space, outside Highpoint's zone of control. No one knows you're aboard. I've kept my end of our deal."

His eyes narrowed. "You said you'd take me to the Belt."

"I said I'd take you there for twenty thousand. The original deal was ten thousand just to get you out of Highpoint. That's been done. I'm going home. If you don't want to get off here, I'll refund the other ten and you can get off when we get to Tycho City."

"Or?"

"Or you can tell me about the notebook."

He set the bowl back on the table. "She told you about that, did she?"

"She told me Jones wants it. He'll pay ten thousand for you or three thousand for the notebook alone."

"I don't have it." He said, picking up the noodle bowl again. "I wouldn't be stupid enough to carry it around with me."

"Not what I asked. What's in the notebook and why is Jones interested in it?"

"Fingal's Cave." His voice was barely above a whisper.

I scoffed. "Don't give me that crap. The cave is a myth."

"Then where did a guy like me get those gems?" His look was smug, challenging.

I didn't answer him. Instead, I said, "Sylvia, I'll be wanting that commlocus for Colin Jones."

"Okay, Zack. Edward has two potential loci. Calling the first one now."

Scalzi jumped to his feet, spilling the remnants of his snack. "Wait. You can't do that." I looked at him again but didn't answer. He licked his lips and rubbed them with the back of his hand. "All right. I'll tell you about the notebook. Just keep me away from Jones."

"Cancel the call, Sylvia." I gestured toward the chair and he sat back down. "I'm waiting."

"I'm a slicer," he said. "Best in the business. But since Reunification, I haven't had much work. What's legal in wartime is criminal once the shooting stops." He saw my impatient look and held up a hand, speaking faster. "Anyway, I was slicing bank records, looking for orphan accounts or safe deposit boxes. At first it was just small change—dead accounts, abandoned boxes full of personal papers, but nothing much of any value. Then, in Tharsis, I found an account and a box that was almost a hundred years old. No activity in all that time. The name on the account was Malloy, F.X. Malloy."

"Fingal Malloy?" I asked.

He nodded. "There was about ten thousand yuan in the account; accumulated interest piles up over the years. The box held a single glowgem and an electronic key. It took me the better part of a month to slice the key. It was for a storage facility on Delilah. I went there. The facility was abandoned, part of the old prospecting settlement. The key still worked, though. Malloy had his own storage pod there. It was full of equipment. I don't know what most of it was for. It looked like medical gear or some such. In a locked drawer at the back was the notebook and a dozen glowgems. I tried to read the notebook, but it's full of equations and columns of numbers. Nothing that makes much sense to me. But the gems, those I understood. I took the gems and locked the pod. Then I looked for a way to sell the gems."

"You still haven't told me why Jones wants the notebook."

"He thinks it has directions to Fingal's Cave. He really believes I found it and that's how I got the gems. But I swear, the only gems I found were the ones I sold. I don't know where Malloy got them."

That didn't sound like the Colin Jones who had seized control of the Red Dragons. I didn't see him buying this story about a mythical cave full of glowgems. "Where's the notebook now?"

"Back on Delilah. In Malloy's storage pod, right where I found it."

Sylvia interrupted before I could ask another question. "We're being hailed, Boss. Someone named Ashok Patel.

He says he's in a ship just outside the Highpoint zone. He claims to be calling for Colin Jones."

"Damn it, Sylvia. I told you to cancel that call."

"I did, Boss," she said, her voice frosty. "I don't know anything about this guy."

Scalzi paled at the mention of Patel. I remembered that Kensai had called him an enforcer. I also remembered his tiny rat-like eyes.

"I told you we were wasting too much time," Scalzi said. "Now, Jones is onto us."

I ignored him. "What does he want, Sylvia?"

"He wants to talk to you about Cleopatra Lee."

I turned to Scalzi. "Go to your cabin. He didn't mention you, so there's a good chance he doesn't know you're here." To Sylvia: "Give me thirty seconds, then put him through to the salon."

Scalzi hurried out and I sat down at the table, facing toward the video pickup on the nearby bulkhead. A few seconds later my eye camera flickered and I stared into Patel's narrow, dark eyes.

"What do you want, Patel. I told you, if Jones wants to talk to Ms Lee, he should call himself."

"This isn't Highpoint anymore. You should show a little respect."

I laughed. "To a second-rate enforcer like you? Don't hold your breath."

To his credit, he didn't take the bait. He stayed cool and held my gaze for a long moment. "Like I said, Mbele. We're not on Highpoint anymore. My boss wants Cleopatra Lee. Hand her over and I'll let you live a while longer."

"Come and get her, if you think you're capable."

He smiled, thin and cold. "I hoped you'd say that. She's as good as dead anyway. Payback's a bitch, isn't it." He broke the connection.

I sat back in the chair, puzzled for a second. Then it hit me and I gripped the armrests. "Sylvia! Vertical acceleration,

30G's now!"

Acceleration slammed me to the deck before the inertial dampers spun up and relieved the pressure. "Get us out of here, Sylvia. Zigzag, maximum acceleration."

"They're shooting at us, Boss. A hypervelocity missile just missed us."

"Don't talk, just get us moving." I ran for the cockpit as the inertial dampers whined again.

"Zack, what's going on?" Rabbit called on the link.

"Can't talk right now, Rabbit. Stay put and hold on." I clicked my link twice as I crossed the catwalk. I grabbed the handrail as one of Sylvia's sudden turns exceeded the damper's tolerance and almost pitched me headfirst into the hold. "Deuce," I called over the link. "We're under fire. I need some kind of countermeasure."

"On it, LT."

Profit had started her life as a warship, a fast interceptor in the Martian navy. When I'd converted her to a small freighter, her weapons and targeting systems had been torn out along with the massive generators for the particle beams. Maintaining weapons, especially particle beams and hypervelocity missiles was expensive. Most commercial ships didn't bother. Piracy was rare in the heavily traveled lanes of the inner system. Even in the Belt, pirates were interested in cargo or ransom, not random violence. If you couldn't outrun them, you could usually find a way to pay them off. If the Dragons had sent an armed ship after us, they seriously wanted us dead.

I reached the cockpit and climbed into the command chair. "Status report, Sylvia."

"I have two ships in pursuit, about 1500 kilometers astern. We're pulling ahead slightly, but with all the zigzagging we lose two kilometers for every three we gain."

"Are they both shooting at us?" I strapped myself into the couch and pulled up a three dimensional status display into the holotank.

"No. Only the trailing ship. The lead one seems to be faster. It was trying to cut us off, but I changed course and it overshot. I've dodged three missiles so far, but they're getting closer."

"Deuce, any ideas for countermeasures?" *Profit's* offensive systems had been removed, but the countermeasures tubes in the belly and stern were integral hull components. They'd been left in place. The actual decoys they were supposed to launch were long gone, but the tubes could be accessed and trash collected from the decks or spare nuts and bolts, could be flushed through them.

"I've packed the stern tubes with aluminum strips cut from the cargo boxes. Mixed 'em with a little Selenite. If one of those missiles hits a cloud of that stuff it'll be vaporized. 'Course, we don't want to be too close when that happens."

"I'll keep that in mind. Stand by." I called Rabbit. "How are you doing down there?"

"No problem, Zack. I locked my chair to the bunk and stowed my gear under the desk. What's going on? Sylvia's really stressing the damper field. I can feel it slipping around down here."

"The Dragons are on our tail. They're shooting hypervelocity missiles at us."

"Well, can't we shoot back? Or get away?"

"Working on it. I need you to help Deuce. Can you program a small transmitter with our IFF code? I need to make sure those missiles hit Deuce's countermeasures instead of us."

"Sure, piece of cake. I'll just take a..."

"Rabbit, stop talking. Just do it now." I checked the holotank. As I watched, two more missiles sped away from the trailing ship. Sylvia threw the ship into a violent corkscrew. The missiles closed with alarming speed, their oversized drives boosting their accelerations to a hundred G's or more. "Deuce, countermeasures."

"On the way."

A second later the lead missile exploded close inboard on

the starboard side. The hull rang as fragments peppered the starboard impulse nacelle. The second plowed into the expanding cloud of chaff and explosive that Deuce had flushed from the stern tube. A lucky hit.

"Damage status, Sylvia."

"A few small hull leaks, otherwise no major damage. But that was the closest yet."

This couldn't go on much longer. We could outrun them in a straight stern chase, but if we tried to run straight and fast, the missiles would catch us.

"How's it going down there, guys."

Rabbit answered. "Transmitter's done. Deuce is loading it into the tube now."

I gave them a few more seconds. "Grab something and hold on. We're going to cut the gravity in a few seconds." I checked my seat harness. "Okay, Sylvia. Cancel the zigzag course. I want a straight run, maximum acceleration away from those ships for thirty seconds. Then I want a negative z-axis translation, ten G's for two seconds, then cut the drive and shut down the gravity field."

"Do you think we can lose them by cutting off the drive?" Sylvia asked.

"At this range, the missiles are tracking our wake. If we play dead, they may fly by and miss us, especially if Deuce and Rabbit can fool them with the IFF transmitter. If we're moving away from the ecliptic, the ships behind us may lose the track once the missiles detonate."

"Whatever you say, Boss." The doubtful note in her voice did nothing for my confidence.

"Okay, Sylvia, start your run now. Thirty seconds to course change." I watched the clock and the holotank. As I expected, as soon as our course straightened out, the ship behind us launched two more missiles. We pulled away rapidly and within a couple of seconds, our pursuers were out of sensor range.

"Deuce, launch your countermeasures on my mark."

I watched the seconds tick down. Despite our speed, the missiles were faster. They popped up on the holotank and streaked toward us. "Three, two, one, mark!" I didn't need to tell Sylvia what to do. The inertial dampers howled as Sylvia dove below the ecliptic, converting thirty G's of forward acceleration to two G's of downward translation.

I kept my eyes on the holotank. The expanding wall of chaff looked like a pale green cloud. The red blips of the missiles locked on to the transmitter Deuce had packed into a ball of aluminum foil with the debris. The holotank flashed white as the missiles struck the transmitter and exploded.

"Cut the drive, Sylvia. Shut down the gravity field and all nonessential power."

The deep hum of the gravity generator cut off abruptly and the overhead lights went out. Half a second later, the battle lanterns clicked on filling the cockpit with dull red light. I kept my eyes locked on the holotank.

CHAPTER ELEVEN

"Two targets at extreme range," Sylvia said. "They're slowing."

I could see the icons in the holotank. The debris field from the exploded missiles plus our load of aluminum trash spread over several hundred cubic kilometers and slowly expanded as the ships approached. Our momentum, meanwhile, carried us farther away each second.

"They're stopping Zack. I'm not detecting any scan directed toward us."

"Keep an eye on them. Let me know if they make any move in our direction." I unstrapped and pulled myself toward the catwalk. "I'm going to check on our guests. Keep the grav generators off line until I get back."

I pushed off and slithered through the hatch without touching the coaming. I glided across the open space above the cargo hold until I could snag a stanchion and swing myself toward the salon. A quick glance through the hatch showed it to be empty. I pushed off again and drifted down the corridor to the spare cabin.

Scalzi floated upright next to the bunk, feet pointed toward the deck, steadying himself easily with one hand on the bulkhead.

"So?" he asked.

"Relax. Patel only mentioned Lee. Then he started shooting. Jones wants you alive, at least until he has his hands on the notebook. If they knew you were aboard, they wouldn't be lobbing missiles at us."

"How long am I going to have to hang here? Freefall isn't my favorite pastime."

"Get used to it. We drift until I'm certain Patel is satisfied we're dead." I left him grumbling to himself and moved on to the charter cabin.

The hatch was still locked from the inside. I banged on it and shouted, "Cleo. Unlock the door." She may have moaned.

"Sylvia, override the lock on the charter cabin please."

There was a brief whir and a click as the hatch unsealed. I pulled it open. The smell of sour vomit assaulted me. Small spheres of thick viscous liquid drifted out of the cabin on a faint air current. Cleo moaned again. She hung in midair near the center of the cabin, curled into fetal position.

"Cleo, what are you doing? Get your feet under you, pointed toward the deck."

"I can't. Make it stop spinning." Her stomach heaved, but there was nothing left to come up. The violent spasms shook her body, causing her to drift higher above the deck.

I pushed off the floor and glided up next to her. Her hair was matted with vomit and wet with the cold sweat of nausea. She jumped when I touched her, flailing about as she tried to push herself upright. I caught hold of her wrist and pulled her closer. She clung to me, wrapping me in her arms and legs. I'd seen this before, usually in newbies from Earthside. Some people could handle freefall, some couldn't. Most learned or adapted, some never did.

I managed to get a foot against the bulkhead and pushed

us toward the deck. We drifted close enough to the bunk for me to get a grip on it. I swung Cleo toward it and she clutched at the frame. I disengaged from her grip and showed her how to strap herself in.

"Sylvia, where are those Dragons?"

"They're still in the debris field. It looks like they're searching for something—quartering the area and moving in a grid."

"What's our range?"

"Sixteen thousand kilometers. We're moving away at twelve hundred meters per second."

"Give it another five minutes, then reengage the gravity field, standard one G."

"Yes, Boss."

I swung back to Cleo. "Are you going to be okay?"

She nodded, still pale and sweating. "Yes. Thank you. I never could handle freefall."

I looked around at the floating globs of vomit. "Some can't. Stay in the bunk. Gravity in a few minutes." I pulled a towel from the locker near the sink and wiped her face and hair with it. Then I opened it up and used it like a net to capture as much of the floating gunk as I could. When the liquid globs struck the towel, their surface tension broke and they soaked quickly into the fabric. The towel went into the recycler.

The cabin no longer a toxic waste zone, I pushed off toward the door. Scalzi was there, in the passageway. His nose wrinkled at the smell that followed me out of the cabin and he snickered.

"Not so tough now, is she?" he said.

"You have thirty seconds to get back to your cabin." I managed to keep my voice even, but the anger must have come through. He reddened but had enough sense to keep his mouth shut. I turned away and headed for the catwalk. The gravity reengaged as I reached the salon. I crossed the catwalk and ducked into the cockpit.

The holotank showed no ships within range of our sensors. Just because we couldn't see them, it didn't mean they couldn't see us. But I doubted that Patel's sensors were better than the *Profit*'s.

"Let's get underway, Sylvia. Standard one G acceleration."

"What course, Boss?"

I thought for a moment. If Patel really believed we were dead, we could go anywhere. But I doubted he was fooled by the debris field. There wasn't enough metal there to make a cargo box, much less a ship. I figured he knew we'd given him the slip and was looking for us. My first instinct was to head for Tycho City. It was our defacto home and we had friends there, both official and unofficial. I thought better of it. It would be the obvious choice with plenty of potential for ambush. No, I needed a safe place to lay low and try to make contact with Jones. I had both Cleo and Scalzi and that gave me leverage.

"Set a course for Delilah, out in the Belt. Keep us below the ecliptic for a while, just in case the Dragons are smart enough to think of it too."

"Delilah? Why not home?"

"Because Delilah's where this whole mess with Cleo and Scalzi started. And the Dragons will expect us to head for Tycho. They'll be waiting."

"Okay, Boss. But that last maneuver strained the induction coils. Efficiency is down thirty percent. If we burn one out on the way to the Belt, it's a long way to the nearest shipyard."

"Have to take that chance. Better a long transit than a missile up our ass." I left Sylvia to plot the course and headed aft. Rabbit was climbing the ladder from the hold. His chair latched on to the handrails and climbed using a worm gear. He rolled onto the catwalk as I approached.

"How long until we get home, Zack? I don't mind freefall, but it messes with the chair gyros. I need some tools from my workshop to recalibrate them. And what stinks? Deuce and I could smell it all the way in the aft cargo hold. He's not real happy about the drive, by the way. The coils are overionized and we can't keep straining the dampers that way unless we want to limp home on impulse power; at least that's what Deuce says. Do we even have enough fuel for that? I hope we don't have to. I don't want to be stuck aboard with Deuce for that long. He doesn't really like me, you know."

"Sorry," I said. "It may be a while before we see home. Those Dragons who jumped us as we left Highpoint were waiting for us. They knew when we'd be leaving. Your trick with the IFF code helped us give them the slip. But they'll expect us to head for Tycho. We're going to the Belt instead."

"The Belt? Don't the Dragons have a base out there?"

"More like a whole section under their control. Which is why it's the last place they'll look for us. I need some time to figure out Scalzi's game and come up with something I can deal to Jones."

Rabbit lowered his voice to a whisper. "Do you think Marco really knows where Fingal's Cave is?"

I shook my head. "Doesn't matter. He got the gems from somewhere. Maybe he knows where there are more of them. But I don't believe in Fingal's Cave."

Rabbit looked unconvinced. "What about Revenants? They're supposed to be out in the Belt, too. Some say Metternich himself is out there with them, waiting for the chance to come back. We're marked, you and me. They have us on their death list. If we run into some of them…"

Anger flared inside me. I was sick of his rumors about escaped Martian war criminals and their secret plan to resurrect the Revolution. I managed to get a grip on my temper and laid a hand on Rabbit's shoulder. "Don't worry about them. They're too busy running from the Feds to pay attention to small-timers like us."

"Sure, Zack. You're probably right."

"I know I am. Go on to the cabin and get some rest. It'll

be a while before we get to Delilah."

He turned and rolled away. I slid down the ladder to the cargo hold and headed aft to see Deuce. He was in his workshop, restowing some gear that had come loose during our escape.

"Any damage?" I asked as I stepped through the hatch.

"Nothing serious. Just wear and tear on the induction coils. They'll get us home, I'm thinking, if we don't push them too hard."

"Not going home. We're headed for Delilah. Will they hold up 'til then?"

"Probably. If you don't drive like a madman. I might could take them off line one at a time and degauss 'em. That'd extend their life a few days. Best we replace them on Delilah, though, or it'll be a long trip home."

"I hear you. We've got the cash for a change, if the chandler has the coils. Never know in these backwater shipyards."

"Why the Belt, LT? That don't sound like a smart move to me."

I repeated the reasons I had given Rabbit and Sylvia. "Plus, there's more to this than Scalzi is letting on. It all started on Delilah and he claims Malloy's stuff and the notebook are still there. I figure one way or another there's profit to be made, either by selling Scalzi to Jones or by finding the notebook ourselves."

"I don't usually hold with ratting folks out to the likes of Jones, but in this case, I can't complain too much." Deuce stroked his beard. "What do you figure on doing about the girl?"

"Too soon to tell. Jones seems to want her dead, but maybe he'll take Scalzi instead."

"You sweet on her?"

I laughed. "I'd sooner kiss a snake. She's poison. That kind of woman can take you from ecstasy to despair with a twist of her head. I don't need that kind of trouble."

Deuce's look told me he wasn't buying it.

I didn't care. I hadn't made up my own mind about her yet. But one thing was certain, I wasn't going to let Jones kill her without going through me first.

CHAPTER TWELVE

We limped along on one coil at a time as Deuce worked on them in turn. After a day and a half, he pronounced them reasonably fit.

"They'll get us to Delilah okay. They might get us home to Tycho if we take it easy. But I'd be a lot happier if we replace 'em at the next stop."

"We'll do what we can. I don't expect much from the Delilah shipyard. From what Cleo said, it's pretty primitive."

Cleo kept to herself in the charter cabin. Space sickness usually settles down after a return to gravity, but she didn't strike me as the type of woman who liked to show any weakness. She cleaned and sanitized the cabin, but stayed out of sight.

Scalzi, on the other hand, became more obnoxious than ever. Once he found out that we were bound for Delilah, he got it into his head that he had somehow forced me to take him there. He started issuing orders as if the *Profit* was his own private yacht. Deuce came close to breaking him in half on the second day, but backed down at a sign from me. I was willing to put up with Scalzi for the time being. I needed him if I wanted to have any leverage with Jones.

I was out of jolt for this trip, which made Deuce happy. But I slept in the command couch so the nightmares wouldn't wake up Rabbit. Sylvia knew about my dreams and sealed the cockpit at night. She pumped the electronic white noise that activated the jolt through my link, but without the drug, it didn't do much for me. I had a bottle of single malt in my cabin, which might have helped, but I didn't want to let Rabbit know how bad things were. I'd never hear the end of it.

* * *

The spaceport at Delilah didn't look much better than Cleo had implied. The docks were relics from the days before the Moss drive with huge blast shields covering the inside of the docking bay. The bulkheads were pitted and scarred from more than a century of use. The bay's outer doors groaned closed behind us as Sylvia brought the *Profit* to rest in our assigned berth. The docking collar extended from the nearby bulkhead and sealed itself around our portside lock.

A bored looking customs official in a coffee-stained uniform checked our registration and cleared us without a second look. Deuce followed the customs man out, heading for the ship chandler's in search of induction coils. Scalzi gathered up his small store of possessions and found me in the salon.

"You want something, Scalzi?"

"My money. The deal was twenty thousand. I had almost forty on me. You owe me the rest."

"And you owe me for two induction coils. We damn near burned them out getting you away from Patel and his missiles."

"You can't put that down to me," he blustered. "You said

yourself they were after Lee."

"Because she didn't deliver you and then made Patel look a fool when he tried to muscle her. From where I sit, it all comes back to you and the gems."

His eyes narrowed. "What do you want? I don't have any more money and I already sold all the gems I had."

"But you know where to get more, don't you? Cleo tells me you were trying to cut a deal with one of your buyers to deliver more gems." I figured the lie might shake something loose.

"She's got you whipped, Mbele. She feeds you crap and you eat it up. I'm telling you, the gems were a one-off, a lucky find. Without that cash, I'm busted."

I grabbed him by the front of his jacket and pulled his face close to mine. "What goes on between me and Cleo Lee is none of your damn business. You'd do well to remember that. You've done nothing but lie to me since I brought you on board. Now, do you want to save your sorry ass, or do I have Deuce lock you in a cargo box without a pressure suit and ship you to Jones, C.O.D."

"Why Zack, defending my honor? I'm flattered." I hadn't heard her behind me until she spoke.

"Nothing to do with you," I said, giving Scalzi a shake. "Marco here was just about to tell me where the gems really came from."

Scalzi's eyes darted from me to Cleo. "She knows. I told her before the first sale. You think you're girlfriend here is a victim? She's in this up to her neck."

"Shut up, Marco," Cleo said. "No one is buying it."

I let go of Scalzi and shoved him down into a chair before turning on Cleo. "Don't be so sure of that. I put this ship and everyone on board at risk for you. I think that earns a little truth. Sit down. We're going to settle this."

She smiled. "Whatever you say, Captain."

Why did she do that? Everything she did seemed calculated to put me off balance. I watched her slide into the chair, even that simple movement played for my benefit.

I pointed to Scalzi. "You first. Where did you get the gems?"

"I told you. I sliced some old storage container accounts and came up with Malloy's name. The storage facility was abandoned, but the seals on Malloy's space were intact. He had a bunch of old equipment, the notebook and a cache of gems in it. I took the gems to sell and left the rest there. It's not worth the trouble to clear out, even if you could sell the gear. No one on this rock has any use for it."

"Then why did tell one of your buyers you could deliver more gems?"

"I was trying to run a scam on him, get a down payment for some gems and wring a little more cash out of this trip." Scalzi kept his eyes on the tabletop, avoiding my eyes.

Cleo touched my hand. "Ask him about Art Smolensky."

Scalzi jerked as if she had struck him. He started to get up, but I shoved him back down into the chair.

"What about it, Marco? Who's Smolensky?"

"Just a business acquaintance. He put up some cash to help me get off this rock. I owe him the money and some interest for that. That's why I need the rest of that forty thousand."

It was a plausible story, but his reaction to the name made me think there was more to it. "So let's go meet Mr. Smolensky. If everything's like you say, I'll pay him off and we can discuss the rest of your story."

He shifted uncomfortably in his chair. "He won't meet with you."

"So persuade him. If he wants his money, he'll have to deal with me."

"I don't know where he is. I'm supposed to meet him at the Drill Bit. It's a bar in the mining settlement. There's a public message board there that he monitors."

I turned to Cleo. "Does that square with what he told you?"

"More or less," she said with a slight toss of her head.

"How much more or less? And stop playing stupid seduction games with me. I still haven't decided whether to help you or sell you to Jones."

She pouted. "Don't be cross with me. I'm trying to help here."

"Just answer my question."

"He told me he had a silent partner. I heard him talking on the comm to someone named "Art" just before we left here for the Moon. And I saw the name "Smolensky" on an IOU in his pocket database. There was also a lot of stuff in it about supplies he was supposed to buy on the Moon and ship back here to Delilah."

"How did you slice my PD? It's encrypted."

She smiled at him. "You really should be more careful with your password. Anyone could overhear it if you use a verbal interface."

"What kind of supplies?" I asked.

"Mostly chemicals. Boron, lithium, vanadium, hydrofluoric acid. Also some electronics and a gravitational separator."

I whistled softly. Pretty sophisticated stuff for a backwater mining 'roid. Grav separators used a controlled gravitational field to separate isotopes of gas or liquid elements on an industrial scale. Gas miners used them on Mars to tease oxygen and some noble gasses out of the ice at the poles.

"What does your partner want with that stuff?" I asked.

"How should I know? I just ordered what he told me to."

This was getting me nowhere. I knew he was still lying. Jones wouldn't want him if he didn't know anything. Time to play a different hand. I pulled my needler.

"Okay, get up. I've had enough of your crap. Jones wants you; he can have you. Move!" I gestured toward the door with the needler.

"What are you going to do, Mbele. Put me to sleep again?"

"No. I'm not packing sleepers anymore. These are cyanide

needles. You can move or I can carry your carcass out of here. Your choice."

He paled, his eyes fixed on the needler. He stood and walked stiffly to the door. I nudged him toward the spare cabin. He hesitated for a second.

"Don't be stupid, Marco," I said in his ear. "If I wanted you dead it would already have happened. Now be a good boy and get in that cabin so I can see what Cleo knows about the Dragons."

He stared at me, puzzled. I closed the door in his face.

"Sylvia, seal the door to the spare cabin. Then get Rabbit to help you slice into the local security grid. I want everything you can get on Scalzi, Cleo Lee, and a guy named Art Smolensky."

"Yes, Boss. And I have a call from Deuce. Do you want to take it now?"

"Sure." After a pause: "Hey Deuce, good news?"

"Not hardly. The chandler doesn't have coils for a Mark VI drive. He's got a couple of used Mark V's, but I wouldn't trust one of those if it was still in the packing foam."

"Can we make it back to Tycho with the ones we have?"

"Got my doubts. Maybe, maybe not. We could try to degauss 'em again."

"Can you do that? I thought it was a one-time deal."

"Yeah, technically it is. But they've got a three-gigaTesla generator here. Biggest I've ever seen. We could run the coils through it and probably wring another hundred hours out of 'em. If they don't get too brittle and shatter the first time we put a load on 'em."

That was a cheery thought. "How long to do it?"

Deuce paused and I could hear him talking to someone in the background. "Yugo says he can start any time. Twenty hours to run the degauss, another hour to install the coils and recalibrate 'em; call it a full day."

"Okay, get on it. I'll fill you in on the rest when you get back to the ship."

CHAPTER THIRTEEN

I returned to the salon and found Cleo waiting for me. "Tell me again about how you and Scalzi hooked up," I said without preamble.

"I was stranded here after another job fell through. Scalzi needed a bodyguard and a mutual acquaintance got us together."

"Who is this mutual acquaintance? Give me a name."

"What's that got to do with anything?" She turned her head and stared at a spot on the bulkhead.

I reached out and gently pulled her chin toward me forcing her to look at me. "I'm trying to help you. Jones is serious about wanting you dead. Sending an armed ship after us was expensive and dangerous. The *Federales* don't tolerate civilians with military hardware inside lunar orbit. The Dragons ran a huge risk to try to kill you. Why would they do that?"

She held my eye. "Because I took their money and didn't deliver. Because we made Patel look bad back on Highpoint. Maybe both."

I shook my head. "What you took was chump change. And making Patel look bad might buy you a knife in the ribs, but not a hypervelocity missile attack that close to the Lagrange League. They think you can hurt them. Why?"

She didn't answer right away. I let go of her chin, stood back, and folded my arms—waiting.

She took out a cigarette, flicked the tip to light it and drew in a deep draught of smoke. "I told Jones I knew where the gems came from. That he didn't need Marco. The deal was to get the notebook and kill Marco."

"Then why did you shoot him with sleepers? If the contract was to kill him, why not use a black load?"

"Because I have no idea where the notebook is or what's really in it." She took another drag on her cigarette. "I thought I could take Marco and get him to tell me what he knew."

"Torture him, you mean."

She smiled. "There are other ways to get a man to talk, Zack."

I still wasn't buying her story. It didn't answer the question: why go to such lengths to take her out? "And then you'd kill him."

She smiled again. "Do you really believe I'd do that?"

I slammed my hand on the table. "Enough! Yes, I do. I'm beginning to think Scalzi's right; you're a cold-hearted bitch who'll do anything for a price."

She leapt to her feet with the same scary speed I'd seen in the food court.

The nanos shot through my muscles, and I jumped back just in time to evade the slashing blow she aimed at my face. Before she could recover and strike again, I had the needler pointed at her head.

"Why, Cleo? If the Dragons wanted you to kill Scalzi and get the notebook, why would they try to kill you before you finished the job?"

"They think I already did it. The paramedics who got

me out of the food court were Dragons. I told them I shot Marco with cyanide before you shot me. Now Jones wants the notebook and thinks I double-crossed him because I left Highpoint with you."

Shit! That would do it. If Jones thought Cleo was trying to cross him, he'd kill her and write the notebook off. He'd kill me just for being around her.

"Sit down." I gestured toward a chair with the needler. "Convince me that I shouldn't give you to Jones and save my own skin."

Her eyes grew hard and cold. No trace of the soft seductiveness that she projected earlier. "He'd have to kill you. He couldn't be sure I hadn't told you about the notebook."

"Maybe. But Scalzi's alive. Jones doesn't know that, yet. If Jones has Marco, you're irrelevant."

She laughed. "You don't know Jones. He'll kill us all once he gets his hands on the gems, or the notebook if it tells him where the gems are."

I nodded "I figured as much. Our only leverage is the notebook. We have to find it before Jones does and figure out what it means."

"Get Marco to tell you."

"I don't think he knows. I pushed him pretty hard. I think he was just the salesman. Someone else gave him the gems to sell."

"Smolensky." Cleo nodded.

I raised the needler again. "Like I said, convince me that I need you. Scalzi and Smolensky, maybe. You're excess baggage."

"I can give you Smolensky." She held up a hand toward the needler. "He keeps in touch with Jake Tani, the owner of the Drill Bit. Jake's the one who hooked me up with Marco. I'm pretty sure Smolensky was behind it, though."

"So how will that give me Smolensky?"

"Unless Marco's been on the comm, no one knows he's

here. If I show up without him, Jake will wonder why. I may be able to convince him to get in touch with Smolensky."

I thought for a second, then put the needler away. "Okay. We'll play it that way. Marco is under lock and key for the time being. Sylvia can keep him off the comm. As soon as Deuce gets back, we'll pay this Jake a visit."

She smiled that seductive smile again. "So, I convinced you?"

I smiled back but didn't answer. I turned and left her in the salon. Let her worry for a change. We were in a precarious position, thanks to her, and I wasn't letting her off the hook yet.

As I stood on the catwalk looking down over the cargo hold, the port side lock cycled and Deuce stepped through. He waved from below and started for the ladder.

"Everything's set, LT. Yugo got the coils into the generator and started the degauss cycle before I left."

"Great, Deuce. Stay down there and break out your pulse rifle. We're going out in a few minutes."

He nodded and turned away from the ladder toward the weapons locker.

I stepped into the cockpit, mainly to be able to talk to Sylvia in private. "What did you and Rabbit find out about Art Smolensky?"

"Not too much. He's been on Delilah for the past two years. He works for the Feds as a mine inspector. That's odd, since the mines here are pretty much shut down. Only a few hundred people actually work them anymore, and most of them are salvaging equipment. Then, there's the man himself. There's no record of a family and not much of a life before he starts here."

"No data on him before Delilah?" I asked.

"Not in the local database. It may be someplace else, but usually bios are pretty complete and job history is standard. There's nothing on this guy."

"Then he's either a *Federale* on assignment or he's hiding

from them."

"Edward thinks it's the latter," Sylvia said. "He seems to think Smolensky is connected to the Martian revolution somehow."

"He would. Anything else?"

"No, Boss. But I have access to the security net. I'll cross reference him with police and BPS records and see what turns up."

"Okay. I'll take Deuce and Cleo with me and check out this bar where Smolensky stays in touch."

I left the cockpit and descended to the cargo bay where Deuce stood by the weapons locker. He pulled out my Huang pneumatic, and tossed it to me along with a sixteen round magazine and a belt holster. I slid the magazine into the grip and clicked the safety on before tucking the gun into the holster. The needler went into a jacket pocket as a back-up.

I opened the intraship link. "Cleo, come down to the cargo deck please."

She appeared at the top of the ladder and nodded to me, then favored Deuce with one of those heart-stopping smiles. She hooked her arms and heels on the ladder and slid expertly to the deck, landing lightly on her toes. "You must be Deuce. I'm Cleo."

I'd never seen Deuce look stunned before. He always had an eye for a pretty girl, but Cleo left him speechless.

She looked in the locker. "Do I get a gun, too?"

"You already have a needler. And stop messing with my crew."

"Sure, Captain. Anything you say."

We were back to that. I shook my head. "Sylvia, we're going out now. Keep Scalzi in the cabin and get Rabbit to help you with the data mining. Lock down; release code Tharsis seventeen."

We cleared the lock and passed though the docking collar into the spaceport. The place had seen better days. Deep rust stains etched the seams between the deck plates. In a few areas, the corrosion was deeper and I could look through the open holes to the decks below. The port was deserted except for an AI at the information desk. It gave us exhaustive directions to the Drill Bit Bar. I think it was lonely and wanted to talk. Too bad we left Rabbit at the ship.

CHAPTER FOURTEEN

Delilah had been settled by miners. Most of the asteroid was composed of high-grade nickel-iron ore, and for almost one hundred years the mines and smelters had turned out steel for the industries of Earth, the new colonies on Mars, and the Moon. But even a big 'roid like Delilah held only so much ore. The metals had become harder and harder to extract, until finally the cost got too high and the smelters shut down. But ninety-three years of settlement was a hard thing to abandon. Generations of spacers had been born, grown up and died in Delilah's tunnels. Many had followed their fathers into the mining and smelting trade. When the mines shut down, they faced the hard choice of moving on or staying and finding other work. There were also those who had made their living on the economy generated by the mines. Storekeepers, tunnel riggers, builders, and plumbers; all manner of construction and service trades. Many of them chose to stay on, clinging to the husk of the mined out asteroid in hopes of building a life apart from the mines.

One line of business that seemed to do well in bad times were bars like the Drill Bit. In happier times it might have been a neighborhood place, with a small cozy dining room and a much larger bar. A place where both the rough men who worked the mines and their families might gather for an evening.

By the time we walked through the old-fashioned double saloon doors, the dining room had long since been shut down, the kitchen closed and replaced by vending machines selling soy nuts and algae crisps. The bar was long and broad, made of real wood that must have cost a small fortune when it was first brought out from Earth. Now it was spotted and stained. One whole section was charred black by a long forgotten fire.

Behind the bar, bottles of expensive liquor lined a high top shelf, all covered with a thick layer of dust. The lower shelves were packed with the cheap generic alcohol that was generated as a byproduct of algae farms everywhere. Add color and a bit of flavor to generate whatever brand of booze your customers craved.

The large room was more brightly lit than most such places. The tables and booths along the wall were in good repair and reasonably clean. The rock walls had been sandblasted smooth and painted a deep green. Two large holotanks faced each other from opposite walls, both continuously broadcasting the feed from an Earthside sports network. In one corner, a public bulletin board advertised jobs, goods and services for sale, and personal messages.

There were a few men seated at the bar and an elderly couple sitting in a booth in the far corner, but otherwise the place was empty.

"Nice place," Deuce said. "Wonder what they've got on tap."

"Local brew," said Cleo. "Not bad if you like beer. Stay away from the liquor, though. Unless diarrhea and a roaring headache is your idea of a good time."

"Been here often?" I asked.

"Twice. Once when I first got here and again when I hooked up with Marco. The owner is an old contact of mine from Planetia. He set up the meeting with Marco."

"This Jake Tani character. How did he come to own this place if you knew him from Planetia?" I asked.

She smiled. "Jake wasn't popular with the Third Directorate. He never bought into Metternich's Martian Way philosophy. When the Revolution came, he had to leave Mars in a hurry."

I searched my memory for the name Tani but came up empty. When I was a sublieutenant in the Third Directorate Special Forces, I had routinely reviewed the watch lists of potential opposition leaders, but only paid attention to the names in my sector of Tharsis. Planetia was a different sector. It was possible that Tani had been on their list and I hadn't noticed.

Back before Bruneault and the 'tanks, I could still believe in the Martian Way. I could still justify what I did in the name of the Revolution as service to a greater cause. A cause that would make life better for all Martians despite the blood and pain of its birth. But everything went sideways and the new Martian Republic descended into madness and suspicion. My own imprisonment and torture had been the only things that had saved me from prosecution as a war criminal after the Feds retook Mars. Idealism was for simpletons and fanatics.

That's over. The Way is dead. I look out for myself now, I thought fiercely. But the nanos tingled under my skin, giving the lie to that thought even as it formed.

Deuce touched my shoulder and motioned with his head toward the bar. I nodded. He slung the pulse rifle over his shoulder and strolled over. The few customers at the bar eyed him cautiously, then returned to their drinks.

"A pint of the local brew," Deuce said to the barkeeper.

The man pulled the tap and dark amber beer flowed into an aluminum mug.

"Half a yuan," muttered the barman as he set the drink in front of Deuce.

Deuce flipped a coin to him and took a deep drink. "Good beer." He set the mug on the bar top. "Lookin' to get in touch with someone. A fella named Smolensky. I heard he might check in here now and again."

The barman picked up a cloth and began wiping the bar. He didn't answer.

Meanwhile, Cleo and I sat at a small table near the door. We ordered drinks from the menu interface and they popped up through the service port in the center of the tabletop. I peeled the plastic cover off a shot of 'scotch' and sniffed. It was the right color and clearly packed with alcohol. Any other resemblance to whiskey ended there. But suddenly I didn't care. My body craved a hit of jolt. I downed the shot of ersatz whiskey instead. I ordered another and downed it as well. The third shot blunted the jolt craving, but I looked up to find Cleo staring at me.

"When do we get in touch with Tani?" I avoided her eyes.

"Unless he's changed his ways, he'll be here any minute. The barkeeper likely signaled him the minute we walked in. He's probably monitoring us on one of the security cameras right now. Deuce just upped the ante by asking about Smolensky."

Over at the bar, Deuce sipped his beer. He casually took the pulse rifle off his shoulder and leaned it against the bar near his right leg. He set the beer mug on the bar and swiveled his seat to be able to watch the door and the barkeep at the same time.

I swallowed the ersatz scotch more slowly, welcoming the burn in my throat. Cleo sipped her drink and made a face. "I guess when you're the only game in town..."

She left the sentence unfinished. Two very large men in grey jumpsuits stood in the doorway, looking over the room. Their eyes fell on Deuce and they walked forward, separating by a couple of arm lengths. I eased the Huang out of the holster and snapped the safety off. The nanos woke up, augmenting my hearing and eyesight, extending through my muscles to the finger on the Huang's trigger.

Cleo slipped the needler out of her pocket and laid it in her lap. She was already facing the door, so I concentrated on the guys approaching Deuce.

Deuce watched the two big men impassively. He took a final sip of his beer, set the mug on the bar and motioned to the barkeeper for a refill. The barman set down his rag, turned his back on Deuce and walked to the other end of the bar.

The men in the grey jumpsuits stopped about a meter from Deuce, one on each side of him. Deuce swiveled so that his back was to the bar, the pulse rifle now resting against his left leg.

"You guys want something?" He asked.

"Who are you, spacer?" asked the man to his right.

"Tourist. Just enjoying the local sights."

The man on Deuce's left laughed harshly. He reached into his jumpsuit and pulled out a short barreled pneumatic.

I stood and had the Huang pointed at him before his gun cleared its holster. "I wouldn't do that if I were you," I said. "Lay the gun on the bar, slowly."

They turned and looked at me. The man with the gun moved his hand slowly toward the bar. The other one just smiled. I cocked my head, wondering what he found amusing. Then I heard the voice behind me.

"And you'd do well to follow your own advice. I have a weapon pointed at your head. Raise your arms over your head, holding the pneumatic by the barrel."

The voice seemed familiar and not in a good way. A deep chill settled in the pit of my stomach and a cold sweat broke out on my face. *Where had I heard that voice?*

Deuce nodded, confirming what the man behind me had

said. I raised my hands but maintained my grip on the butt of the Huang.

"By the barrel, I said." The voice was harsher this time.

"Why don't you just calm down, Jake?" said Cleo from behind Tani. "And put down that gun before I have to put a needle in your back."

I dropped my hands and pointed the pneumatic at the man on Deuce's left just as he started to shift it toward Cleo. He stopped and slowly placed it on the bar. He raised his hands when I motioned with my gun.

"Everything alright back there, Cleo?"

"Of course. Jake was just going to sit down and have a drink with us, weren't you Jake?"

"Is that any way to treat a friend, Cleo," asked the man behind me. "I heard there were armed strangers in the bar and was just protecting my investment."

Deuce picked up the pneumatic from the bar and tucked it into his belt. Then he lifted his pulse rifle and nudged the two men in grey toward me. Seeing that he had things under control, I lowered the Huang and turned around to get a look at Jake.

The room spun and there was a roaring in my ears. Burning heat raced along the nanofibers as they strained to pump my own nerves into overdrive. My mind flashed back to the biotank and the choking, drowning sensation as the warm protein laden fluid rose past my nose and mouth and flooded my lungs.

His face had changed. He'd lost weight and may have had some surgery. His eyes were now blue but had the same piercing stare and slight lift at the edges of the eyelids. He could call himself Jake Tani or Jack Frost or Saint Michael. I would know who he was: Major Gamel Samadar of the Third Directorate Black Operations squad. The man who had drugged and beaten me for days on end in the Bear, then tossed me into a biotank.

His eyes widened when he saw my face. With a shout of

animal rage, I launched myself at his throat, forgetting the pneumatic in my fist, wanting only to get my hands on him and tear him to pieces.

Behind me I heard Deuce's pulse rifle sizzle as he dropped Samadar's guards. Cleo stood frozen, her needler still trained on Samadar. My left hand grasped his throat in a grip of iron. The force of my rush drove him to the deck and I landed on top of him, smashing my knee into his groin. I hit him in the face over and over with the barrel of the Huang, feeling the flesh tear and the bones break. He may have tried to struggle, but I took no notice, hitting him again and again until he didn't move anymore. And then he didn't breathe anymore.

I was aware of Cleo punching my head. I ducked it under my left arm to ward off the blows and struck out with my right. I hit her in the chest and knocked her back onto the deck. I raised my right again to hit Samadar but the rage had spent itself. He lay still on the deck, his head a bloody mass of torn skin and broken bone. I wiped blood, not my own, from my eyes and stood up. I turned to Cleo, but she scuttled backwards on hands and feet out of my reach. She got to her knees and brought the needler up in a two-hand grip.

Deuce stood near the bar covering the barkeeper and the few patrons near him with his leveled pulse rifle. He looked at me carefully. "You okay, LT?"

"Yeah," I said, still gasping with the exertion.

"Zack, what the hell?" Cleo's voice shook.

I took a step toward her. She raised the needler, but I didn't care. I took another step, then spun on my left foot and kicked the needler out of her grasp. A blow from the heel of my hand to the center of her chest knocked her back to the deck and I fell on top of her, pinning her arms. My attack was so fast I don't think it even registered with her until she found herself unable to move.

"Let go of me," she shouted. "What is wrong with you?"

"You have two seconds to tell me how you know that man. Make it good, because your life depends on it."

"I told you. I met him in Planetia, before the revolution. He was a liquor distributor. He owned a couple of show bars and imported high-end booze from Earth."

"I don't believe you," I said. "His name isn't Jake Tani. He's Gamel Samadar. He was a major in the Third Directorate, Black Ops section. He spied on political opponents of the Revolution before Metternich took over the government. He was so good at it that Metternich rewarded him with complete run of the Bear. He tortured and killed his way through the prison, cellblock by cellblock, ferreting out 'traitors' and 'counter revolutionaries.' The lucky ones he killed outright. The rest he tossed into the biotanks to die alone and in agony."

"No, I don't believe you," she said. "I knew him. He couldn't have done those things. He had to run from Mars when the Revolution started. He even had to change his appearance to avoid being caught by the secret police."

"Did you actually see him after the Revolution before you reconnected with him here?"

"No, but he—"

"He wasn't running from the secret police. He WAS the secret police. That's what Black Ops does. Check his left wrist. He'll have a tattoo, a black teardrop near the base of his thumb. He might change his face but he'd never remove the black mark. No Black Ops trooper would."

I released her arms, then stood up and backed away, keeping the Huang trained on her. She got up more slowly and walked over to Samadar's motionless form. She stooped and turned over his left hand. By her gasp I knew she had seen the mark. I pointed the pneumatic at the floor as she stood and faced me.

"Truth?" she asked.

I nodded "Major Samadar was in charge of the political section at Bruneault prison. He sent thousands of us into the biotanks. Only one in ten survived and most of them ended up like Rabbit. I'm the only 'tank survivor I know with a functioning nervous system." I didn't mention the nanofibers. I didn't trust her before this, and wasn't about to start now.

"Did you have to kill him?" she asked. "I thought you wanted to find Smolensky."

"I know where Smolensky is," said the barkeeper, suddenly inclined to be helpful after seeing what I'd done to his boss.

"Where is he?" asked Deuce.

"On his way to Mars. He caught the monthly supply shuttle for Tharsis. I heard him telling the boss about it yesterday."

CHAPTER FIFTEEN

"When did that shuttle leave," Deuce asked.

"About four hours ago," replied the barkeeper. "They usually get underway before ten in the morning."

I surveyed the wreckage I'd caused and looked over the small knot of people still clustered around the far end of the bar. It wouldn't be long before the local law heard about this; too many witnesses. I wasn't about to start killing innocent people. Those were Samadar's tactics, not mine. At least, I hoped not. Things had gotten a bit blurry lately.

However justified I might feel in killing my torturer, I doubted I could convince the local sheriff to give me a pass on it. There was only one thing to do.

"Deuce, how long to retrieve the induction coils from the shipyard and install them?"

He rubbed his smooth scalp. "Maybe an hour. Less if Yugo can get 'em out without shutting down the generator."

"Go get them. I'll keep an eye on these folks. Call me when you get to the ship."

"We're runnin'?"

"No choice now. It's that or deal with the law."

"Can't say I like this, LT. Not that I mind killing Samadar. It sounds like he needed it. But I don't know if those coils will get us all the way to Mars."

"We'll make it. Now go. Cleo will stay with me."

I stepped closer to the bar. The barkeeper looked like he wanted to run away. "How do we close the security doors?" I asked him.

He pointed toward the door. "Red switch, next to the coaming."

I looked at Cleo. She nodded and went to the door. A second later a metal shutter rolled down from the overhead and sealed the opening. She skirted Samadar's body and walked over to stand next to me.

"I believe you," she whispered. "Even in the Planetia days, something about him was a little off. He'd disappear for weeks at a time, then pop up unexpectedly. He asked questions you wouldn't expect from a barkeeper." Her face hardened. "But killing him was stupid. We need to be invisible if we're going to avoid the Dragons. You might as well set off a beacon to tell Jones where we are."

"When I walked out of the Bear," I said evenly. "I swore to kill three men. I killed the first on Mars two years ago. He's the second."

She looked away. "Vendetta's are stupid. They're bad business. And getting drunk on a job like this is even more stupid."

"I'm not drunk," I said in that sullen voice that all drunks use.

"You're not sober either. And killing should always be done sober."

"Maybe. I doubt anyone will cry at his funeral." I sighed. "There's bound to be local heat over this, though, and we can't afford that." I keyed my link to the ship. "Sylvia, I need everything you've got on a Martian war criminal named Gamel Samadar. I think there's still a price on his head."

She answered after a brief pause. "He's still wanted by the Federal War Crimes Tribunal. There's a two million yuan reward for him, dead or alive. Do you want me to download the warrants to your link?"

"Hang on a sec." I called to the barkeeper. "You have a comm locus that'll handle text and holo files?"

"Sure. The bulletin board over there." He gave me the locus and I repeated it to Sylvia. A few seconds later Samadar's image in full Third Directorate uniform swam in the holotank along with a rotating DNA profile. The heading above the image read: WANTED FOR CRIMES AGAINST HUMANITY DEAD OR ALIVE

REWARD NY2,000,000

"Everyone over here," I said, waving the pneumatic at the knot of people at the end of the bar. "You, too," I added, speaking to the barkeeper. Once the crowd of a half dozen or so had gathered by the holotank, I pointed to the body on the floor.

"That's what's left of Gamel Samadar. DNA printing will confirm it. There's a two million yuan price on his head and the *Federales* aren't too particular about whether he's alive or dead. Dead saves them the cost of a trial. Two million split six ways comes to more than three hundred thousand each. It's yours on one condition: my crew and I were never here. Any questions?"

They all looked from the image in the holotank to the body and back again. Finally the barkeeper spoke up. "How do we know you're telling the truth?"

"You don't. But the alternative is for my partner and me to kill all of you before we leave." The barkeep was quickly shushed into silence. I waved the small knot of people away and they clustered together near the holotank.

"Are you crazy?" whispered Cleo. "You're turning your back on two million yuan."

"Do you really think the Dragons will let us live long enough to collect? This kind of high profile case brings lots

117

of media attention. The Feds will play it for all they can. We can't be involved in anything like that. At least not until I can make a deal with Jones to get him off our backs."

She drew back, wary. "What kind of deal?"

"The notebook for your life and no reprisals on me or my crew. Or Scalzi for the same price. I've pretty much decided to give him to Jones no matter what."

She smiled. "You'd do that for me?"

"Not for you. I have a ship and crew to protect. Besides, I can't stand that little slime ball. I'd give him to Jones for free."

She cocked her head and looked at me, still smiling and clearly not believing me. I wasn't sure I believed myself. A few minutes ago I'd been ready to kill her, now the thought of Jones getting his hands on her sent a chill through me.

The little crowd around the holotank began to break up. The atmosphere in the bar had changed. No longer hostages or unwilling witnesses, they were now partners in a business enterprise. A few even nodded pleasantly at me when I caught their eye. The beer started to flow again. I holstered the Huang, but kept the security door closed. No sense in inviting more witnesses in. The bar crowd took in the still closed door and nodded sagely to themselves, reaching the same conclusion.

Twenty minutes later, Deuce checked in. "Got the coils, LT. Yugo managed to get part of the degauss done. Maybe it bought us a few more hours of running time. It'll take me about an hour to install and recalibrate 'em."

I turned to the barkeeper who seemed to have become the defacto spokesman for the small group. "Give us twenty minutes, then call the cops. Leave the image up there on the bulletin board. Tell the cops somebody confronted him about it, don't remember who. There was a fight. He lost."

The man nodded coolly, perhaps believing for the first time that he might soon be a very rich man.

Cleo raised the security gate and we stepped out into the

passageway. There was no one around. The gate squealed shut behind us, the barkeeper protecting his investment. I was pretty sure he'd give us at least twenty minutes.

We made our way back to the *Profit*, passing only a few other people in the passageways of Delilah. No one gave us a second look, other than a couple of miners who looked Cleo up and down several times as we passed.

I gave Sylvia the release code and we went aboard. Deuce met us in the cargo bay, wiping coolant fluid from his hands.

"Coils are in and we're ready to go, LT."

"Good job. Give me a couple of minutes to check with Sylvia and we'll get underway."

Cleo and I climbed the ladder to the catwalk. She turned left and went into the salon. I crossed above the hold and swung through the hatch into the cockpit.

"Status report, Sylvia."

"Ship's systems are all nominal. What the hell did you do out there, Zack? There's buzz all over the police net. Some big war criminal's been found right here on Delilah."

"Anything about us?"

"No. Why?"

"Never mind. Tell me about this war criminal."

"It's Samadar. The Black Ops major you asked me about. He was killed in a bar fight down at the Drill Bit. Did you kill him?"

"What are the cops saying?" I asked, avoiding her question.

"There's a barkeeper who's taking credit for it. He says he confronted Samadar and a fight started. All the patrons in the bar got in on it. Three people are dead, Samadar and his two bodyguards."

I smiled. "Get us launch clearance, Sylvia. Take us out as soon as traffic control says we can go."

"You didn't answer my question."

"No, I didn't." I trusted Sylvia with my life every time she piloted the ship. But AI's were property under the law. They didn't have the right to remain silent if a magistrate ordered them to talk.

I left Sylvia to deal with the traffic control AI and made my way aft to the salon. Cleo was still there, slumped in my armchair. I frowned at her but she just took another drag on her cigarette. The needler dangled by the trigger guard from her right forefinger.

"I hope the safety's on that thing." I pointed to the needler.

"Afraid I'll shoot myself?"

"No, me. Put it away."

She pouted, but shifted around in the chair so that she could slide it into a pocket near her hip. "I don't get you, Zack Mbele. You shoot me to protect a man you've barely met only to turn around and help me out of a tight spot with the Red Dragons. Now you're ready to sell out the same man you helped in order to save me from Jones. What's in this for you?"

"Maybe I'm bewitched by your beauty."

She laughed, a short bark of derision. "You're immune. I've been sending you signals since I came aboard. You haven't bitten yet."

"Rabbit and Deuce don't seem to be immune."

Her eyes took on a hard predatory look and she snubbed out the cigarette. "They're not the captain of this ship."

I looked her up and down the way the miners had done. She looked back defiantly. "Don't sell yourself short. Another time, I might be interested. Right now it's all about how much Jones is willing to pay for Scalzi or the notebook or both."

"Bullshit. If all you cared about was money, you'd have collected the reward for Samadar and turned both Marco and me over to Jones to save your own skin." She came to her feet and stood close to me. Her eyes softened as she looked up into mine. "So, Captain, what's in this for you?"

I reached out and took her into my arms. She melted against me, pulling my face down to hers. I kissed her and her lips parted. We held each other for a long minute, then I gently pulled back from her.

"It's still mostly about the money." I let her go and walked out of the salon, a slight smile on my face. *Let her wonder about me for a change.*

CHAPTER SIXTEEN

Sylvia chimed on my link as I reached my cabin. "We're cleared for space, Boss. The docking collar's disengaged and they've out-gassed the bay."

"Take us out, Sylvia. Set a course for Tharsis. Check with Deuce. I want the best speed we can manage without burning out the induction coils."

"What's the rush?"

"I want to beat the supply shuttle that left here earlier today. They have a six-hour head start and I need us to be on the ground before they make orbit around Mars."

"That's going to strain the drive, Boss. We could end up floating home."

"We'll make it. Talk to Deuce. Meanwhile, unlock the door to the spare cabin. I want to have a talk with our other passenger."

I walked down the passageway and kicked open the door to Scalzi's cabin. He jumped to his feet as I entered.

"What the hell is going on, Mbele? We're in space again. I told you Smolensky will be wanting his cut of the money."

"Your silent partner ran out on you, Marco. He left for Tharsis on the supply shuttle four hours before we got here. Why would he do that if he was so anxious to get his money?"

Scalzi's face paled. "Jones. He's going to cut some kind of deal with Jones."

"What does he have to sell? The notebook? Come on, Marco. Tell me what Smolensky's got."

Scalzi refused to look at me. Indecision clouded his face. Finally he said, "The gems. Smolensky's the one who hired me to slice the storage facility. He knew Malloy's stuff was there. I don't know how he tracked it down, but he knew what he was looking for. When I figured out who Malloy was, I re-keyed the lock and made Smolensky cut me in on whatever he found there."

"You told me you sold all the gems from the storage locker. Were there more?" He didn't answer. "Smolensky's already cut you out, Marco. He thinks you're dead or soon will be."

Scalzi slumped down onto the bunk, arms folded, his face a mask of defeat. "Smolensky doesn't need to find more gems. He can grow them. That's what all the chemicals and equipment were for."

"Smolensky found a way to culture glowgems?"

Scalzi shook his head. "Not Smolensky. Malloy. Everyone thinks he was a prospector because he worked out here in the Belt. Most people think that back in those days there wasn't anyone here except miners and freelance prospectors. They forget the science types the government sent out. Malloy was one of them. He figured it out. That's what's in his notebook."

"Smolensky has the notebook?"

"Maybe. I don't know. He understood all the numbers and equations in it. I haven't seen it since we found it."

For some reason my nanos tingled as he was speaking. My vision shifted toward the infrared and my hearing

123

became more acute. Scalzi radiated heat, more than usual. His heartbeat sounded loud in my ears. It increased for a few seconds then returned to normal. He was lying. He was very good at it, and without the nanofibers, I wouldn't have seen the subtle changes. But I'd been trained by my Special Forces mentors to recognize the signs. He knew where the notebook was and didn't want to tell me in spite of Smolensky's double dealing. Interesting. I decided to let it pass. Having him think that he was keeping information from me might be useful.

Instead I said, "We're on our way to Tharsis. If the induction coils hold out, we should get there before the shuttle. We can intercept Smolensky before he can meet with Jones. Maybe even save his life."

"How's that?"

"If he has the notebook and sells it to Jones, he's a dead man. Jones won't need him anymore. If he doesn't, he'll live a little longer; at least until he sets up a culturing facility for the Dragons. After that, he's expendable."

Scalzi looked doubtful. "And you can do better?"

I shrugged. "I'm harder to kill. Jones will know that if he checks me out. Besides, I'm mobile. Harder to catch."

I left him thinking about that and went back to my cabin. Rabbit showed up there a few minutes later. He closed the hatch with a conspiratorial air and spun his chair to face me.

"Sylvia tells me that the White Hand is dead. Is it true? Did you kill him?"

The White Hand was the name we survivors of the Bear gave to Samadar. He'd always worn white linen gloves in the interrogation rooms and on the cellblocks.

"He's dead, Rabbit. Two down, one to go."

"I told you they were here. The Revenants. They'll be coming for us next. You got Clancy on Mars, before the Feds secured the Bear. Nobody even knew it was you. But this is different. Samadar was connected. He's probably part of the inner circle or something. The rest of them will avenge him."

Clancy had been the guard who moved prisoners from the cellblocks to the 'tanks. He'd really enjoyed his job, especially the perk of beating and raping the helpless survivors. He hadn't counted on me.

"Calm yourself. The cops will think the crowd at the Drill Bit did it. I told you before, there is no secret society of Martian diehards hiding out in the Belt."

"But the White Hand was out here. You can't believe that's just coincidence." He lowered his voice to a whisper. "And Marco was here. He must have found them. Why else would a high level slicer be this far out?"

"Because after the war the Feds had no use for him. He was scavenging off the bones of old miners."

"That's what he told you. A good operative will always have a strong cover. The *Federales* put him here to find a way into the organization. To find a way to *him*."

"Listen to me, Rabbit. I killed Clancy because of what he did to us in the cellblock. I killed Samadar for putting us there. I'll find and kill Pedroia for being the one who ran the 'tanks. And that'll be the end of it. Metternich is dead. The Revolution is dead. And when those three are dead, my war is over. If the rest of the high command wants to hide out in the Belt, it's okay with me."

He sat and sulked but didn't speak. He didn't believe me, but he wouldn't argue any more. I touched him on the shoulder. "Don't worry. I can handle the Revenants if they come for us. I got us through the Bear, didn't I?"

He nodded and turned the chair. "He's still out there, Zack. I can feel him." He rolled out of the cabin.

Maybe he was right, but I couldn't see how anyone could have survived the last assault on the Presidential stronghold. Nor did it make sense that the most wanted man in the solar system could slip away from the Fed forces that occupied Mars after the war. Rabbit's paranoia was occasionally useful but hard to live with. And my own sanity depended on the belief that Colonel Metternich was long dead.

Deuce appeared a few seconds after Rabbit rolled out. He stepped in and swung the hatch shut behind him.

"Something on your mind, Deuce?"

"I ain't questioned your judgment before this, LT," he said. "Leastwise, not when you're sober. But killing Samadar was a bad call."

"So Cleo keeps telling me. Something about throwing away two million yuan."

He made a face that told me he didn't give a rat's ass for what Cleo thought. "I don't give a shit about the money. The man needed killing and we'll likely stay clear of the heat."

"So what's your point?"

"You don't kill a man when you're half in the bag if he ain't drawn on you first. A killing like that needs to be cold and sober. You lost it and could have gotten the rest of us killed."

"You weren't in the Bear, Deuce. You didn't see what that bastard did."

He looked away. "No, I wasn't there. And it ain't like you to be holding that against me, LT. You know I'd have taken your place there if I could've."

I sighed. "And you'd be dead now. I didn't mean that the way it sounded."

He didn't say anything to that, just looked at me, waiting.

"Okay," I said. "I lost it. I heard that voice, saw his face and something snapped."

"Get off the jolt, LT. It's eating you up."

"It wasn't the jolt, Deuce. It's the Bear, up here in my head. The jolt, the booze, they help push it down so I can sleep nights instead of bashing my brains out against a bulkhead."

"That's a load of bullshit. You think you need that crap,

okay. But not on the job, and not when I'm watching your back."

I knew he was right. The Colonel had taught us that killing was too serious a business to be done in anger. I might have killed Samadar even if I'd been cold sober, but I would have done it right—quietly, without witnesses. I looked Deuce in the eye and nodded. "Understood."

He held my gaze for a second, looking into me for something that I wasn't sure was there anymore. Then he shrugged and changed the subject. "How much harder do you wanna push the drive? We're runnin' at a steady three G's and looking pretty good for now. But crystallization in the coils is up to seven per cent. If we stress the inertial dampers, the coils could crack."

I took the bait, relieved. "Will we get to Tharsis ahead of the Delilah shuttle?"

"Sylvia says we'll beat 'em to orbit by an hour or so, if they stick to their schedule. They will. It's a low profit run. If anything, they'll be taking it easy."

"Okay, Deuce. We'll hold at three G's for now. Can the dampers take a delayed turnover and five G deceleration at the end?"

He thought for a second. "Don't know. If they fail before they can slow us down, we'll get mighty hungry before help comes."

"They won't fail. And we can always try air braking. It'll cost us plenty in fines, but it's better than starving out here."

His silence told me what he thought of steering the *Profit* into the atmosphere to bleed off speed if our drive failed. I didn't disagree with him. I just didn't see that we'd have other choices at that point. I could slow down now, or shut down the drive and coast to Mars, but Smolensky would be gone by then and with him any chance of saving Cleo.

* * *

It turned out that both Deuce and I were right. The transition from acceleration to deceleration went smoothly with hardly a stutter from the coils or the inertial dampers. We reached the edge of Martian traffic control on course and speed for orbital insertion. Sylvia made one last course correction and was a second away from shutting down the drive and engaging the impulse engines when the coils failed. A shudder ran through the ship, followed by a loud bang from the drive chamber as the primary coil cracked. The secondary followed a second later and we were in free-fall.

CHAPTER SEVENTEEN

"Zack, what the hell?" Cleo's shout came from her cabin.

"No problem. Just a little premature drive shutdown. We'll be landing soon."

Sylvia took us in over the Olympus Highlands, wings extended and engines hot. I rode down in the cockpit with her and thrilled to the sensation of flying low over the rugged landscape. This was better than the smooth elevator ride sensation of a grav field landing.

We touched down at the Tharsis Docks a little before ten in the morning, ship's time. Local time was early afternoon, one of the oddities of space travel. Ships in space operated on Zulu time, the old Greenwich Mean standard. Planets and moons had their own day night cycles and the two rarely matched. Many captains adjusted ship's time to local if their port calls were more than a day or so. I never bothered. I'd grown up underground where the day-night cycle is arbitrary anyway.

A tractor 'bot towed us from the landing field to the environmental dome as Sylvia went through the engine shut-down checklist. I watched from the cockpit until the huge lock cycled and the 'bot parked us at the edge of the transient docks.

Cleo fared better in freefall this time around. Maybe it was the wild ride through the atmosphere. She and Deuce met me near the weapons locker in the cargo hold. Rabbit looked down from the catwalk.

"I don't know why I can't come with you," Rabbit said.

"Because someone has to stay here and keep an eye on Scalzi," I answered. "I need Cleo to talk to Smolensky and Deuce for backup in case the Dragons show up."

"Why Cleo?"

"For the same reason that you can't take your eyes off her. He'll stop and talk with her. That's all Deuce and I will need."

Deuce hefted his pulse rifle and slung it over his shoulder. He handed Cleo a needler and a pair of stun batons that he'd found in a pawnshop in Freetown. She pocketed the needler and smiled as she took the batons.

I pulled out my reliable Huang pneumatic and a pair of spare magazines.

Behind me, I heard a slight crackling sound and turned to see Cleo moving rapidly through a complex *kata* exercise. The batons spun and whirled with blinding speed. She was no stranger to them. She finished with a flourish of crossed batons, then straightened and turned off the electrostatic generators that charged them. She bowed to an imaginary opponent before turning to Deuce.

"Thank you, Deuce."

"No problem, Miss. I enjoyed the show. I never could get the hang of those things."

"Maybe I'll show you sometime."

"Enough," I said as I clipped the Huang's holster to my belt and slid the spare mags into my pocket. "We have work to do and I don't need you two flirting."

Deuce grunted and Cleo smiled at me. Some days I just

get no respect. Deuce tore his eyes off Cleo and went over to the scooter.

The scooter was our three-wheeled all-purpose hauler. There were two seats behind the driver and a two by two meter cargo bed behind them mounted over the rear wheels. It wasn't pretty or fast but it could haul surprisingly heavy loads and was rugged and reliable. Cleo and I climbed into the passenger seats and Deuce started it up. I ordered Sylvia to lock the ship down after we were gone and we rolled down the forward cargo ramp into the sounds and smells of Tharsis Docks.

Unlike Port Tycho with its neat straight rows of berths arrayed around clean, bright service areas, Tharsis Docks was semi-organized chaos. Ships berthed at haphazard angles in any available space. Some hadn't moved in years and had sprouted awnings and attached buildings filled with people and goods. Vendors hawked food and clothes and spare parts from ramshackle storefronts pieced together from old cargo containers. Hookers, thieves, and beggars roamed the winding spaces between ships. The air was thick with the smells of frying food, stale smoke, and humanity. I felt right at home.

Deuce guided the scooter through the winding lanes to the main gate. Beyond lay the city and the commercial passenger terminal. We registered with the AI at the gate control and rode out across the flat plaza leading to the passenger terminals. High overhead, a slight shimmer in the air marked the dome, a clear fabric envelope holding the air in. Mars didn't have much of an atmosphere but it was enough to provide some protection against small meteors and the attenuated solar wind. The electromagnetic radiation shields that kept most of the harmful cosmic rays out caused the shimmer in the air.

I shivered slightly, although it wasn't cold. Too much open space. This was the part of Tharsis that catered to tourists and diplomats. Native Martians lived in safe, sensible tunnels deep under the dome. Neither Deuce nor Cleo seemed concerned, so I swallowed my unease. My nanofibers were tingling nevertheless.

I motioned for Deuce to pull over into a parking area about fifty meters from the main terminal gates. He backed the scooter into a space and set the brake.

"You're on, Cleo," I said.

She hopped to the ground and started walking toward the passenger terminal. The Delilah shuttle had docked a few minutes after we left the *Profit*. With the time needed to pressurize the docking bay, disembark the passengers, and transport them to the terminal building, I figured Smolensky would be just clearing customs. He'd be leaving the security perimeter any minute. The plan was for Cleo to find him and convince him to go with her to a supposed secure transport that would take him to meet Jones. There was some risk that he'd see she didn't have a Dragon palm tattoo, but I was sure he'd be focused on other parts of her anatomy.

I pulled an oil-lens binocular from the scooter's storage locker and focused the visor on Cleo. She walked easily through the crowd, her eyes scanning for her quarry. A few people stopped to look at her briefly, mostly men in business suits, but her business-like air sent no invitations and they quickly moved on. Suddenly she stopped and cocked her head, looking at the main arrival gate. Her posture changed, softening from hard and business-like to open and inviting.

I shifted my gaze to the gate and saw him. He looked pretty much like the hologram Sylvia had found in the Delilah database. About 165 centimeters and stocky, probably close to 100 kilos, broad in the chest and shoulders with a hint of a belly around the middle. He was clean-shaven, his brown hair cropped close to the scalp but not shaved clean. His skin was very light, almost pink. He carried himself erect and scanned the crowd with sharp eyes. He'd been a soldier once; it showed in his bearing and posture. But he'd been living a softer, more indulgent, life for some time now and the hard edges of his past were almost gone.

Cleo stepped close and spoke to him. I could see the slight tilt of her head and her dazzling smile. His suspicious look faded almost immediately as his eye swept over her. After a brief exchange, he nodded and followed Cleo toward us, his gaze fixed on her trim bottom and swaying hips. He didn't quite lick his lips.

"Get ready, Deuce." I stowed the binoculars in their case and settled into the scooter's seat. "Almost showtime."

Deuce released the break and eased the scooter out of the parking place. He drove slowly down the lane that led to the main plaza, approaching it at an oblique angle. Cleo and Smolensky were ahead of us, approaching the area where limos and transports waited to pick up their passengers.

Just as we came up to about ten meters away from them, Smolensky stopped and said something to Cleo. She turned back and smiled at him, indicating a limo at the end of the short line. Deuce increased his speed. Smolensky hesitated, took a step forward and then stopped as three men climbed out of the limo. Cleo turned back to look at them, surprised. One of them reached into his breast pocket. Cleo dropped into a fighting stance and drew her stun batons. Smolensky reached into the small bag he'd carried and drew a short needler.

"Step on it, Deuce," I said and drew the Huang. My nanos shot out and the world seemed to slow down as my awareness sped up under their influence.

The man from the limo pulled a pneumatic from his breast pocket. I dropped him with a shot through his forehead before he could bring it to bear on Cleo. One of his mates rushed at Smolensky. He fired a needler, but the shot went wide. Cleo spun on one heel and slammed a kick into the man's thigh causing him to stagger and almost fall. The stun batons whirled and struck him on the neck and right shoulder. He crumpled and went down, unconscious. The third man spoke urgently into a wrist comm as he ducked behind the limo. A pulse from Deuce's rifle sparkled and cracked along the fender, just missing.

Smolensky aimed his own needler at Cleo, but she was faster. One baton swept up from low ready and crackled as it touched his wrist. His hand jerked and he dropped the weapon. The other baton swung in from his left and found his neck right at the base of the skull. He crumpled to the ground.

Deuce jumped down from the scooter and hoisted Smolensky onto his shoulder. Cleo sheathed the batons and drew her needler. I ran over to the man Cleo had stunned and reached for his needler. As I pulled it from his grasp I noticed the Dragon tattoo on his palm. No surprise there. Time to get moving.

Deuce dumped Smolensky into the bed of the scooter and wrapped his hands and feet with cargo strapping. We climbed aboard just as a black ground car spun into the plaza. Deuce fed power to the scooter and it jumped forward. I ducked involuntarily as a pulse rifle bolt sizzled overhead.

I turned and returned fire with the pneumatic. Slugs ricocheted off of the fender of the car and kicked up small showers of chips as they slammed into the concrete of the plaza. A man holding a pulse rifle leaned out of the passenger side and fired. Deuce slewed the scooter to the right and the bolt missed. Cleo took aim with her needler, but lowered it when she realized needles would be futile.

We careened across the open plaza, zigzagging as pneumatic slugs and pulse bolts bracketed us. I crouched on the seat facing backwards as I fired the Huang. I emptied one clip, doing little more that punching a few holes in the hood and windscreen of the car. Deuce threw the scooter into a sharp left turn, nearly pitching me from my perch. Cleo caught my belt and pulled me back. I reloaded the pneumatic and aimed again. My vision narrowed and my time sense seemed to slow everything down. The arm holding the pulse rifle out the side of the car stood out in sharp relief against the black surface of the door. I fired twice. The arm jerked and the rifle fell. It hit the ground and the rear wheel rolled over it with a shower of blue sparks. The car swerved to the left. I fired twice more, aiming at the blurred shadow in the driver's seat.

I was either lucky or a better shot than I thought. The car swerved violently back and forth until the front wheels bit into the pavement and it rolled to its side.

Deuce gunned the scooter and we left the wreckage behind. I scanned the plaza but saw no other pursuit. Deuce took us down several winding pathways and around the rear fence of the commercial port before heading back to the Docks. We rolled up to the rear gate, clear across the Docks from our starting point, a few minutes later. The AI passed us and we drove slowly through the crowds toward home.

CHAPTER EIGHTEEN

By the time Deuce drove the scooter up the ramp and into the *Profit*'s hold, Smolensky had begun to stir. I cut him loose while Deuce parked the scooter and Cleo collected and stowed Deuce's pulse rifle and her own stun batons. I noticed that she kept the needler and made a mental note to take it from her later. No harm in letting her feel like part of the crew, for now.

Smolensky moaned and opened his eyes. I grabbed him by the collar and hauled him to a sitting position. His eyes cleared and he looked around in alarm. He saw Cleo and his face reddened.

I shook him slightly. "Don't look at her. Look at me." I held up my left hand, palm out. "Look at my hand. No tattoo. We're not Dragons, and you're a lucky man." He shook his head, still confused from the stun baton. "If you'd met with Jones, you'd only live long enough to show him how to culture the gems. After that, he'd have killed you. Maybe quick and easy instead of hanging you by your heels and slicing off pieces, but you'd be dead just the same."

I caught the startled look in his eye before his expression closed down into a blank mask. "Oh, yes. We know about the glowgems. Marco Scalzi was very helpful with that after we saved his ass from the Dragons back on Highpoint."

He started to speak, coughed and cleared his throat and then said, "Who are you?"

My vision blurred for a second and my legs felt weak. I'd heard that voice before. The nanofibers burned in my arms and legs as heat coursed along my spine and seemed to explode behind my eyes. I heard the voice again in my head, this time as a memory, coming from behind and above me as I was lowered into the biotank.

He coughed again and I came back to myself. I stared into his eyes until he looked away. He struggled weakly in my grip. I let him go and stepped back, my head still spinning.

"Where am I?" he asked.

"Everything Jake, LT?" Deuce stepped up beside me and put a hand on my shoulder.

"Golden, Deuce." I looked at the man with the familiar voice. I'd never seen his face, but the voice echoed in my memory through long years of nightmares. Pedroia. Jaime Velasco Pedroia. Metternich's witch doctor, head of the Human Subjects Division in the Bear.

Maybe Rabbit wasn't just paranoid, after all. First Samadar, now Pedroia, both on Delilah at the same time and clearly working together. I forced myself to be calm, to look at him. He was rapidly recovering from the effects of the stun baton. If he recognized me, he was hiding it well.

"As to where you are, you're aboard the free trading vessel *Profit*. My name is Zack Mbele. This is my ship and you're now my guest."

His head snapped up when he heard my name. He knew who I was all right. As one of only three survivors of the biotanks with a stable nanofiber bond, I was well known to him and to his boss. His eyes narrowed as he tried to catch any hint of recognition in my face. I managed to keep my expression neutral. I didn't want him to know I knew his true name just yet. He probably felt safe, since he never actually entered the 'tank rooms, only directed things from the control booth. None of us prisoners ever saw him in person.

"Guest, eh? What if I want to leave?"

"Then I'll have to have Deuce here make sure you don't." Deuce grinned savagely and cracked his knuckles. A bit melodramatic, maybe, but it got the point across.

Pedroia looked Deuce over and nodded. "All right. What do you want with me?"

"Art," I said pleasantly, using his alias. "We're all friends here. Marco was worried about you. Imagine his surprise when he got back to Delilah with your share of the money and learned you'd shipped out for Tharsis."

"I heard Scalzi was dead. Killed by a bounty hunter working for Colin Jones."

"Not dead, yet. He's one deck up in our spare cabin."

"Glad to hear it."

I smiled at him. "Sure you are. That's why you're here trying to cut a deal with Jones. Tell me, did you plan to sell him the notebook? Or did you think you could make a deal to grow gems for him? Are you naive or just stupid?"

He flushed and pushed himself upright from the scooter's cargo bed. "Do you have something to say or are you just going to insult me?"

"If you think Jones would let you live once he got control of the process to make glowgems, then you're either naive or stupid."

He leaned back against the scooter, folding his arms. "And you're going to give me a better alternative?"

"I'm going to keep you alive." *At least for now.*

He looked smug. "You don't have a clue what you're talking about."

"Don't be so sure. What did Jones tell you? That he'd

split the profits with you? Or maybe that he'd set you up for life with a big payoff. Why do you think you can trust him? He's got no reason to keep you alive if he gets his hands on the notebook."

Pedroia didn't answer. He still believed he could keep the upper hand with Jones. *Interesting.*

I turned to Deuce. "Get Mr. Smolensky settled in the salon. I'll be up in a few minutes." I lowered my voice so only Deuce could hear. "And make sure to keep Rabbit away from him." Deuce nodded. He didn't ask why.

Deuce and Padroia climbed the ladder to the upper deck and turned left down the passageway to the salon. Cleo leaned against the weapons locker, watching them.

"He's an arrogant son of bitch," she said after they were out of sight.

"You don't know the half of it."

"What?"

"Never mind." I shook my head. "What's your take on him?"

"He thinks he's got something on Jones that he can use to keep himself alive. He's either onto something very big, or he's incredibly stupid. Maybe both."

"I agree. You think the notebook would be big enough?"

She shook her head. "Once Jones has it, he can get his own people to grow the gems. He won't need Smolensky. Even if he has the process in his head, it won't keep him alive for long. Once Jones' people learn the process, Smolensky's even more of a liability."

I liked the way she thought. I still didn't trust her, but she was right about the situation and she'd performed beautifully during the fight in the plaza. Her motives were still uncertain. Saving her own skin, of course, but she didn't need to risk her neck to ensure that. She could have told me to pound sand when I asked her to help lure Smolensky into our hands. Maybe it was just for the love of the game. Or maybe she thought she could make a play for a share of the money, not that we'd seen much of that yet.

I winked at her. "Time to shake things up." She looked puzzled but didn't ask questions as she followed me up to the salon.

Deuce stood near the hatch, arms folded, face impassive. Pedroia sat at the table, trying to look relaxed. I stepped aside and let Cleo enter first. As expected, Pedroia followed her with his eyes. While he was distracted, I motioned Deuce out. "See what you can do about replacing those coils. We need to be ready to move."

I took Deuce's place, leaning near the hatch before Pedroia noticed the switch. He glanced back at me, stopped, and looked again.

Cleo settled into my armchair and drew her needler. She went from soft to hard in an instant, holding the needler on Pedroia with a steady hand. We hadn't talked about it or rehearsed it, but it was perfectly played.

He tried to look calm, but my nano augmented senses picked up the surge in his heart rate, the sudden sweat on his brow and the increased heat from his face.

"Let's talk some more, Jaime," I said quietly, barely above a whisper.

The effect was electrifying. His eyes widened and he went rigid in the chair. Cleo sat up in the armchair, puzzled but seeing immediately that I'd struck a nerve.

"What did you call me?" Pedroia's voice was hoarse.

"You are Jaime Velasco Pedroia. Art Smolensky is a fiction."

"You're insane."

"And you're a liar," Cleo said, gesturing with the needler. "You recognized Zack as soon as he said his name. I saw it in your face."

I think I fell in love with her at that moment. She saw a change in the situation, played her part exactly right and, through it all, believed in me enough to take a stand on my side.

BRUCE DAVIS

I raised my voice, drawing his attention back to me. "You were Metternich's witch-doctor, the man behind the biotanks. How many thousands did you kill, Jaime? Ten? Twenty? I'm your worst nightmare: a prisoner with attitude and a gun. Give me a reason not to kill you, right now."

I drew the Huang with nano-augmented speed and pressed it to his forehead. I heard Cleo's gasp of surprise. The move was so fast that she hadn't followed it until I was in her line of fire. She shifted the needler away toward the right and leapt out of the chair to cover Pedroia from another angle.

"No, wait," he cried. "It wasn't me. I just operated the 'tank room. I didn't direct the experiments."

"No good, Jaime. Your voice was the last thing we heard as they lowered us into that 'tank. Sometimes, I think the prisoners who died were the lucky ones. They don't have to live with the dreams of drowning and panic. They don't have to hear your voice droning on and on as they choke on their own spit. They don't have to live with these damned things growing inside their own bodies."

"I can give you the glowgem formula," he said desperately. "It's all in my head. I can make you rich."

"What about Malloy's notebook? Where is it?"

"I don't know." He was sobbing now. "I haven't seen it since Scalzi left Delilah. Ask him where it is. When I heard he'd been killed, I thought the Dragons would come after me next. I got word to Jones that I knew everything that was in the notebook. That I wanted to make a deal."

I lowered the pneumatic. "That's better, Jaime. But why did you think Jones would deal. If he has the notebook, he'll have no use for you."

"I kept the last page of Malloy's notes. Without it, the technique won't work. I memorized it, then destroyed it. Without me, the notebook's worthless."

You stupid SOB, I thought. *Of all people, you should know that anyone can be broken. You might as well have asked*

Jones to get it out of you.

"What you're going to do is write it down for me. That's my price to keep you alive."

"How do I know you won't just kill me once I tell you."

"I might. But since I don't really give a shit one way or another about the gems, I'll make sure Jones keeps you alive as part of any deal I cut with him. Either that, or I'll send you back to Delilah. That's a guarantee."

"All right. I'll do it."

"Good boy. Wait just a minute. There's someone else you need to meet. He'll be the one to take down what you say. He's the most likely to understand it. Then I'll put you in with your old friend Marco. You two will have a lot to talk about."

I hesitated for a second. I needed Rabbit for this. I didn't know if he'd recognize Pedroia's voice or, if he did, what it would do to him. He was barely keeping a grip on reality as it was. I decided I didn't have a choice. I'd deal with the fallout if Rabbit had a breakdown after meeting Pedroia, but I needed the recording as insurance before I tried to strike a bargain with Jones.

CHAPTER NINETEEN

"Rabbit," I called over the intraship link. "Come up to the salon. I have a job for you." I turned to speak to Pedroia. "Rabbit's also a 'tank survivor. If I were you, I'd go on being Art Smolensky around him and Deuce. They might not be as understanding as I am." I looked at Cleo and she nodded. Pedroia's real identity would remain between us, at least for now.

Rabbit rolled in a few seconds later. "Hi Zack. Is this Smolensky?" He looked at Pedroia. "I'm Eddie Conejo, but most folks call me Rabbit. That's my slicer handle—Eddie the Rabbit. Marco Scalzi's with us, too. He and I spent a lot of time data sparring during the war. He's one of the best. But you probably knew that, right? Isn't that why you teamed up with him?"

"Rabbit," I interrupted. "Art has information about the glowgems. He's going to give it to you. I want a full record—text, audio, video, in a secure file. This is important. Cleo's life and maybe mine may depend on keeping that information secure until I'm ready to use it. Understand?"

He nodded vigorously. "Sure, Zack. I can do all that. I'll build a security net around it with data traps and then..." He went on for several seconds. I didn't catch most of it. It didn't matter. If Rabbit said it would be safe, I knew I could count on it.

"Good," I said as he wound down. "You and Art get started. I'm going to see what I can do to help Deuce."

I turned to leave, motioning Cleo to follow me. I caught a glimpse of her expression as she watched Rabbit set up his virtual keyboard and activate the holomatrix in the tabletop. She looked tender and indulgent, like a protective older sibling. It surprised me. There was more to Cleopatra Lee than first impressions indicated. The thought scared me a little.

Cleo followed me out. "Thanks for backing me up," I said.

"You didn't give me much to work with in there. Is he really a war criminal?"

"Jaime Pedroia's voice was the last thing most prisoners who went into the 'tanks heard before they died. For two years he sent thousands of us into a very isolated and private hell. I said before that I'd sworn to kill three men before I died. He's the last."

She drew back from me. "You're going to kill him?"

"Not right away." I looked away, unable to meet her eyes. "I still need him. Whether he lives or dies after we settle with Jones...I haven't decided that yet."

"Killing him wouldn't be smart. If Samadar was worth two million, what would Pedroia bring?"

"Last I checked, a little more than two and a half."

She grasped my chin with both hands and turned my face to hers. Her eyes bored into mine. "Vendetta's are stupid, especially where large paydays are involved. Be smart, Zack. Turn him over to the *Federales*."

Sylvia chimed on my link before I could answer. "There's a call for you, Zack. It's Colin Jones."

"I'll take it in the cockpit, Sylvia." I pulled Cleo's hands away from my face, holding them in my own. "Go back to the cabin. Jones is calling. I'll let you know how this goes down."

She nodded and turned away. "Think about the money, Zack," she said.

I walked quickly to the cockpit. I wasn't afraid of Jones, but I didn't want to keep him waiting. You may not fear a poisonous snake, but you still don't poke it with a stick. I swung through the hatch and settled into the command chair before activating my link.

"This is Zack Mbele," I said to the image that formed in the holotank. "What can I do for you?"

Jones wasn't what I expected. He was a small man, thin and wiry. He wore his light brown hair long, not stylishly shaved in the current fashion. It was drawn back in a short ponytail at the nape of his neck. His skin was pale, his face set off by high cheekbones and a thin, delicate nose. He looked more like a clerk or a shopkeeper than a crime boss. But his eyes corrected that impression. Pale green and hard as emeralds, they regarded me with the intensity of a hawk sizing up its next prey.

"So you're Zachariah Mbele." He smiled. "A right pain in the ass, you are."

"I'm told it's one of my more endearing qualities."

He laughed in genuine amusement. "You've got sand, I'll say that for you, Cobber. You know who I am?"

"Colin Jones. Drug runner, slave trader, extortionist, murderer. Have I missed anything?"

"No, that about covers it," he said calmly. Clearly a man who was comfortable with his reputation. "A more sensitive guy might get testy being called names like that. Me, I don't give a rat's ass as long as I get respect. No wonder Patel wants your bollocks on a plate."

"Then he'll have to get a lot tougher. Or hire more muscle."

"Careful, Cobber. He's a bit stuck on himself, I'll admit. But he's still a dangerous man to cross."

"So am I. Does this conversation have a point, Colin? Or are we going to trade bad-ass insults all day?"

"Right. It's business, then. Smolensky. You have him, I want him."

"No problem there. As long as the price is right."

His laugh was harsher this time. "How about I let you live if you turn him over now. Is that good enough?"

"How about I tell you to eat shit and die. I have Smolensky and Scalzi. One of them knows where the notebook is, the other knows the final step in the culture process. One's no good without the other."

He frowned. "Don't push me, Cobber. I admire a bit of pluck, but don't try to shake me down."

"No shakedown, Colin. Fair price. You want a monopoly on the gems; I've got the guys who can give it to you."

"You think you're pretty smart?" His smile was thin and cold, no amusement in it. "You and that bitch Lee cooked up a scheme to snag Scalzi. Now you know about the gems and you figure to get in on the action. Not gonna happen that way. You turn Scalzi and the bitch over to me, turn Smolensky loose and, if I'm feeling generous, I'll let you live."

It was my turn to laugh. "If I was worried about being killed, I wouldn't have tweaked Patel's nose. You won't kill me, Colin. I know the gems are cultured. If word of that gets out, they won't be worth squat."

"All the more reason to kill you now."

"Too late," I bluffed. "There's a cop back on Highpoint. Friend of mine. I gave him a video file of Scalzi talking his head off. If anything happens to me or my ship, it goes to the news media."

He crossed his arms and pursed his lips. "I'm not sure I buy what you're selling, but you're right. It isn't worth taking a chance. How much?"

"I figure the information will net you at least two and a half million." His eyes widened at the figure. Interesting.

"But I'm not greedy. Let's say ten percent—two hundred fifty thousand."

"I like your nerve, Mbele. All right. Two fifty for Scalzi, Lee and Smolensky."

"Not Lee. She stays with me."

He laughed, low and wicked. "Sure. Good luck with that. She conned Patel into sending her after Scalzi; she's conning you, too."

"That'll be my problem, Colin. When do we make the exchange."

"This time tomorrow. Spaceport plaza, the same place you gave my boys the slip. You and your man; Patel and two of my boys."

"Three to two, Colin? You think your guys will be safe?"

"Like I said, Cobber. Don't push me." He reached out and broke the connection.

I sat there for a second, considering. Jones had reacted differently than I'd expected. The bluster and threats were standard for this sort of thing. But he'd recognized the significance of the two million yuan figure—the reward for Pedroia; and he'd agreed too quickly to the offer of two hundred fifty thousand. Did he know who Pedroia was? It seemed likely. No skin off my nose if Jones planned to give Pedroia to the Feds, but why would he do that? He'd been apolitical during the time I was underground here in Tharsis. Not particularly supportive of the Revolution, but no friend to the Feds either. I doubted he'd try to buy favor with the current governor by turning over Pedroia.

I heaved myself out of the command chair and returned to the salon. Rabbit was just rolling out. He gave me a thumbs-up and went aft to our shared cabin. Pedroia sat in the chair, head down and looking defeated. His head jerked up as I walked in.

"What now, Mbele?"

"Now you go aft and I lock you in the spare cabin with your buddy Marco. Tomorrow I turn you both over to

GLOWGEMS

Jones. He's still willing to trade, but you two are a package deal. Scalzi knows where the notebook is, you know the culture technique. I convinced Jones that each of you was worthless without the other. The two of you better get your story straight before tomorrow, or one of you is going to die."

"That wasn't the deal," he yelled, jumping to his feet. I crossed the room and had him by the throat before he could say any more.

"The deal is what I say it is. I swore to kill you the day I walked out of the Bear. I'm breaking that oath right now. I don't give a shit what Jones does with you after tomorrow."

"You're a fool," he said, his voice croaking. "Those gems could make us all rich. Scalzi's expendable. I already know everything in that notebook. All I need is financing. Forget Jones. We can be a team."

I eased my grip on his throat. He settled back on his heels, a shrewd look crossing his face. I erased it with a left jab to his jaw. It hurt my hand but it felt good to see him drop to the floor.

"Luckily for you, I am a fool. Otherwise you'd be dead by now. Try selling it to Jones." I grabbed him by the wrist, hauling him to his feet and twisting his arm into a hammerlock. Then I marched him down the passageway to the spare cabin.

Scalzi looked up in surprise as we entered. I shoved Pedroia into the cabin and closed the hatch.

CHAPTER TWENTY

Cleo reclined on the bunk. Her hair was wet and she wore nothing but a towel. She looked up from the palm reader she was viewing as I entered.

"I see you made yourself to home," I said, looking her over.

She stretched, a movement of natural grace and animal enticement. "Fighting bad guys is hot work. I couldn't stand my own stink. You wouldn't have a laundry sanitizer on the boat, would you. I only have the one change of clothes."

"There's a receptacle in the head," I pointed to the small alcove at the back of the cabin. Damp spots on the deck showed that she'd already found the room itself. "Behind the sink, the chute pulls out of the bulkhead. Basic clean and dry only, I'm afraid. Special handling or pressing aren't included."

"No problem. My travel clothes are always wash and wear." She propped her head on one hand, elbow resting on the pillow. "Did you want something in particular, or did you just come to tuck me in?"

"I cut a deal with Jones. Scalzi and Smolensky for two hundred fifty thousand in cash." She opened her mouth to speak but I held up my hand. "And he lets you live."

"We could get two million for Pedroia if he's who you say he is."

"If we survived to collect. There's something deeper than the gems going on here. Jones knows something about Pedroia, maybe the whole story. I think he plans to turn Pedroia over to the Feds, and he won't take kindly to us beating him to it."

"That doesn't sound like the Colin Jones I know," she said with a frown.

"No, it doesn't. Which is why I'm going to take this deal and walk away. Too much heat for a small time operator like me. You can come with us back to Tycho City or take your chances here on Mars."

She stood and faced me. "I thought the answer would be obvious by now."

I hoped it was, but it had to be her choice. If she stayed it would be because she truly wanted to. "Whatever you decide. You earned a share of the money, so you'll be okay financially for a while."

She stepped close. I could feel her breath on my face. The towel fell away. Her perfect breasts pressed against my chest, the nipples hard through the thin fabric of my shirt. Her arms came up around my neck. I bent my head and kissed her, wrapping my arms around her and pulling her close. One of us found the lights and the room darkened. She led me to the bunk and we fell into it, entwined as a single body.

* * *

I awoke later, after we were both spent and had fallen asleep in each other's arms. She lay next to me breathing softly and evenly. I got up, found my clothes, and made my way to the cockpit. Rabbit would be asleep in my cabin. I didn't want to wake him or deal with his questions. I needed to think this through.

For all our passion, I still didn't understand her motives or trust her intentions. And I didn't care. That was the thing that surprised and disturbed me. She was a liar and a grifter and that was fine with me as long as she chose to stay.

I fell asleep again in the command chair and dreamed of green fields under the double moons of Mars.

* * *

It was still dark when I awoke. Ship's time glowed on the chronometer next to the nav panel. Just before three in the morning, Zulu time. That would make it almost dawn, Martian time. We had at least eight hours before we'd need to leave to meet Jones.

"Status report, Sylvia." No answer. "Sylvia, what's going on?" Nothing. I leaned forward and checked the status board. Life support, hull integrity, reactor temperature; all were nominal. But the security system was offline. "Sylvia, security protocol, Tharsis seventeen. Sylvia, respond."

I jumped out of the chair and ran along the catwalk. The intraship link was down. The outside datalink as well. We had air and gravity but every other ship's system was either off line or functioning at failsafe level.

"Rabbit!" I shouted. I slammed open the hatch to my quarters. "Rabbit, get up. Sylvia's offline. We're wide open."

"Huh? Zack? What?" He lifted himself on his elbows. "Sylvia can't go offline. Her failsafe protocols won't allow it. She should reboot in a few seconds."

"I'm telling you, she's offline. All the security systems are off, too. It's been more than five minutes, at least. I don't know how long before that. Get up, damn it."

"Okay, okay. I'm awake. Give me a second to get into my

chair."

I fumed and fidgeted while he swung his legs off the bunk and levered himself into the chair. I pushed his chair over to the small desk across from the bunk. He opened his virtual keyboard and a data display. He grunted, made a few keystrokes, then whistled softly.

"Sylvia's off line," he said.

"Yeah, I know that, Rabbit. Now bring her back."

"Sure, give me a few seconds. It was neatly done. Someone inserted a looping time query into her reboot protocol with a null value in her clock readout. She's stuck."

"So unstick her."

He worked for a few more seconds at the keyboard, then checked a line of code in the display. "Go up to the cockpit. Trip the main bus breaker, count to ten, then reset it. Sylvia should come back online after that."

"And if she doesn't?" I didn't much like the idea of shutting down all power aboard the ship, even for a few seconds.

"She will, Zack. I know what I'm doing."

I walked back to the cockpit. With the electrical power cut, the reactor would be okay and the gravity grid was fed directly from the reactor. But the life support, air scrubbers, lights, heat, all ran off the main bus. We'd be stuck on Mars if the power didn't come back on.

I reached the cockpit and unlatched the tool chest from the bulkhead. I pulled out the power driver and unscrewed the panel under the nav station. Power conduits snaked in from below and fed a panel of breakers. At the top was a large double handled switch with a red tag. I grasped it with both hands and pulled.

The air handlers sighed and spun down and the cockpit went dark. I counted to ten, held my breath, and pushed the breaker back into place. The lights came on immediately and a faint whine echoed through the ducts as the air handlers spun up.

The cockpit rang with a shrill whistling feedback howl.

The sound dampened after a second, followed by a garbled voice counting down from ten. With each number, the sound became clearer and by five, it was recognizable as Sylvia.

I screwed the panel back into place as she continued to count down. We finished at the same time.

"Status report, Sylvia."

"All ship's systems are nominal. Ships time is…wait, that can't be right. It should be just after midnight, but local time is after six in the morning. We've gained three hours and twenty eight minutes."

"No mistake, Sylvia. You've been off line for that long."

"How could I be off line that long?" There was a note of fear in her voice that surprised me. "I should have rebooted within a few seconds."

"Somebody sabotaged your reboot protocol. And I'm pretty sure I know who."

The lights above the cargo hold were bright as I strode across the catwalk. Deuce came out of the passageway under the ladder and looked up at me.

"Everything Jake, LT?"

"Golden, Deuce. Just a computer glitch. Rabbit fixed it."

He nodded and went back to his quarters. He'd gotten two coils from the shipyard earlier in the day and had replaced the primary coil already. A few more hours work and he'd have the auxiliary in place and calibrated; then we'd be mobile again.

I continued aft to the spare cabin. Scalzi was the only one aboard with the skill and the motive to mess with Sylvia's security protocols. Rabbit could have done it, but had no reason to. It hadn't done him much good. As soon as Sylvia went off line, the outer locks had sealed shut. He might have had the run of the ship, but he couldn't leave.

I spun the dogs on the spare cabin hatch and called to Sylvia. "Release the lock on the spare cabin, please Sylvia."

"Done, Boss."

I pushed the hatch open with my foot, standing back from the coaming in case Scalzi and Pedroia had cooked up a surprise for me. As soon as the hatch swung open, I knew they hadn't.

"Oh, shit," I whispered.

Pedroia lay face down on the deck, three needles protruding from his back. All had black fins—cyanide. Scalzi lay sprawled across the bunk, his face purple, eyes open and bloodshot. A power cord from the data display was wrapped around his neck.

"Sylvia, monitor and record the spare cabin, secure file, my voiceprint."

"Recording. Are they both dead, Boss?"

"Yeah. Get Deuce up here. Is Cleo still in her cabin?"

"Ms. Lee is in the charter cabin. She appears to be asleep."

"Lock down her hatch. Tell Rabbit to stay put in my quarters." I didn't want either one of them in here. Cleo because I figured she had been behind this. Rabbit because I couldn't handle his incessant chatter right now.

I entered and knelt next to Pedroia. I checked his pulse, a useless gesture considering the black needles in his back, but I had to be sure. His neck was cold and rigid. He'd been dead for a while. Scalzi was more obviously dead, unless he'd developed a talent for breath holding. I pulled out one of the needles, careful to avoid the point. I sniffed. Cyanide all right. The needle itself was a Smith and Wesson 5.5 mm. Cleo used an S&W 5.5mm, and she hadn't stowed it in the weapons locker after the fight in the plaza.

I moved over to Scalzi. The cord around his neck had been pulled tight enough to cut into the flesh. I glanced back at Pedroia. He'd been strong enough to do this. I doubted that Cleo, for all her ability, would have taken Pedroia out with the needler, then strangled Marco with the power cord. She'd more likely have shot him as well. It would have been quicker and cleaner.

I checked for needles but found none. So what had

happened here? I could believe Pedroia had killed Scalzi. Either in a fight over how they planned to deal with Jones, or as a cold-blooded calculation. If the notebook was irrelevant to him, then so was Scalzi. Less baggage to deal with.

But if Scalzi was dead, then who had sliced Sylvia's reboot protocol, and who had killed Pedroia? I stood between the dead men, pondering this. Deuce arrived and took in the scene at a glance.

"You didn't do this," he said. "What's going on, LT?"

"I don't know. We're screwed and that's for certain. These two were our ticket to money and freedom. Without them, we've got nothing to sell to Jones.

"When can we be ready for space?"

"Couple of hours. Coils are in, just need calibration. And we need some rock for the CO2 scrubbers. It wouldn't hurt to top up the water storage, too."

"Do what you can, but I want us underway in two hours."

"Will do, LT. What about these two? I don't think the cops'll let us go if we report this."

I thought a minute. "Scalzi we'll dump in space. No one's likely to miss him."

Deuce stood impassively, looking down at Pedroia. "And this one?"

"He's not who we thought he was. His real name's Jaime Pedroia. He's wanted by the Feds and has a two and a half million yuan price on his head. They didn't specify alive or dead."

"Ain't he one of the guys you wanted to kill?" Deuce asked, his face carefully blank.

"I didn't do this, Deuce. The deal was Scalzi and Pedroia to Jones for a quarter million cash and Cleo's life, as long as she stayed with us. I think Jones knows who he is."

Finally Deuce's face changed. He frowned and looked away. "You figure on including her in this crew?"

"Only as far as Tycho. After that, we'll see."

"Your call, LT. Not up to me."

"Maybe not. But I wouldn't bring her in without talking to you first." I looked down at Pedroia. "We'll wrap this one up in some cargo tape and leave him for Jones. Maybe the bounty will satisfy him."

"Would it be enough for you?" he asked.

I smiled and shook my head. "No, probably not. Go get the coils calibrated. I'll clean up here."

Deuce nodded and left the cabin. I went back to Scalzi and unwound the power cord from his neck. It had been wrapped twice around and pulled tight. It had taken some strength to cut into the skin that way. I tossed the cord aside and lifted his torso back up onto the bed. The lapel of his jacket was torn. I looked closer. There had been a small pocket sewn into the inner fold of the lapel, now torn open.

I went back to Pedroia and rolled him onto his back, scattering the needles. There was nothing in his pockets or lying under him. Then I noticed his left hand, closed tightly around something. I pried it open and whistled softly. Clutched in his palm were two glowgems, about a centimeter each, and a small data stick.

CHAPTER TWENTY-ONE

I left both bodies laid out in the cabin and returned to my own quarters. Rabbit was still there, now fully awake and dressed.

"What's going on, Zack?"

"Marco and Smolensky are both dead. Smolensky had this in his hand." I held up the data stick. "Can you access it?"

Rabbit blinked a couple of times and cocked his head. "Dead?"

"That's what I said," I answered impatiently.

I should have noticed something was wrong then and there. Rabbit never used one word when ten would do. But I was distracted by my suspicions about Cleo and my fear that they might be true. "Can you access the stick or not?"

"Sure. Let me take a look."

I gave him the stick and he plugged it into a dataport next to the desk. He opened his virtual keyboard and data display. After a second he said, "It's not a data stick. It's a key."

"A key?"

"Yeah. You know, it unlocks a door or a safe or some kind of secure container."

"I know what a key does. What I mean is, can you tell what it opens?"

He rubbed his chin. "Maybe. They often have a code that verifies the lock's location. I might be able slice it without screwing up the unlocking code."

"Do it. It was important enough that Scalzi had it hidden in a secret pocket."

Rabbit made a few keystrokes and said, "Well that was easy. The key's labeled so that it can be returned to the owner if lost. It's for a safe deposit box at the Highpoint Security and Trust Bank."

That made sense. Scalzi had been hedging all the time, holding something back. I'd have bet my last yuan he had the notebook hidden somewhere. Now I knew where. Getting it might prove difficult, even with the key. But Highpoint banks were known for asking few questions of their customers. Unless Scalzi had secured the box with a separate pass code, we might be able to bluff our way out of this mess yet.

I took the key from Rabbit and locked it and the gems in my locker. It was low-tech security, but no one was leaving the ship so the key wouldn't get far. I trusted Deuce and Rabbit; Cleo's freedom would depend on how she answered a few questions.

"See if you can reconstruct what happened to Sylvia," I said to Rabbit. "I want to know how Scalzi did it."

"Okay, Zack. But if he did what I think he did, there won't be many traces."

I left him to his work. I had questions for Cleo.

I knocked at the charter cabin door, had Sylvia unlock it, then swung the hatch open. Cleo stood in the middle of the cabin, hands on hips, fire in her eyes.

"You son of a bitch. You leave me in the middle of the

night after what we shared and then have the nerve to lock me in? What the hell are you playing at?"

"Shut up. Scalzi and Pedroia are dead." Her arms dropped to her sides as her face registered genuine surprise. Either that or she was still playing a part. I couldn't tell any longer.

After a second, her face hardened again. "What does that have to do with me?"

"Oh that's rich," I laughed. "That really is. Our only bargaining chip with Jones is gone and you ask what it has to do with you. You're a real piece of work, lady. Did you think our little fling last night would buy you a place on this ship?" It had, at least until Pedroia had turned up with her needles in his back.

I expected the anger. I didn't expect the attack. Those amazing eyes flashed again, filling with rage and hatred. She spun on her heel, launching a roundhouse kick at my head. I ducked, just barely avoiding the blow. The nanofibers activated and I fended off the *chu-don* punch that followed the kick. She rained blow after blow on me. Even with my nano-augmented speed, I staggered back, just blocking her attacks. She spun, thrust, and moved in ways that I'd never seen a person move before. I backed almost to the bulkhead before I saw an opening. I thrust out, speed and strength augmented by the nanofibers, and smashed a fist into her breastbone. She flew backward across the room. I launched myself from the wall landing on top of her. Another blow to the side of her head stunned her. I hooked a leg behind her knees and pinned them together, then grabbed both wrists and pinned them to the floor.

She writhed and bucked; she spat and cursed at me. But I held fast and she eventually stopped struggling. She lay still and glared at me, meeting my eye defiantly.

"Scalzi and Pedroia are dead," I repeated. "Scalzi was strangled with a power cord. Not your style, so I figure Pedroia did it. Maybe they fought. Maybe Pedroia figured to limit competition. I don't know. He can't tell us because he's dead, too. He had three 5.5mm Smith and Wesson needles in his back; black loads. Where's your needler, Cleo?"

"In the weapons locker." She spat in my face and struggled again. She'd have gotten loose if my strength hadn't been augmented. Damn, but she was strong.

"No, it isn't. I saw you put the stun batons in there, but you kept the needler."

She looked away. "I put it in there later." Her voice was sullen.

"Try again. There wasn't time. You weren't out of sight long enough. Sylvia can verify it."

"I don't know where it is," she shouted. "I woke up and you were gone and the door was locked. And the needler was missing."

"Convenient."

"It's true. I was here with you. How could I have killed them?"

"I got up and left, remember. You could have done the job while I was in the cockpit."

She laughed. "So you prefer your virtual woman to the real thing?" I frowned and she knew the barb had hit home. "Think, you idiot. Silly me, I planned to wake up and find you next to me. How could I know you'd leave and give me the perfect opportunity to sneak through a strange ship, open a locked door and shoot the one man who might keep me from being Patel's target of the week?"

My head hurt. The nanos were retracting and I could feel the deep ache in my muscles. What was worse, she made sense. Everything would have to fall in place exactly right for her to get to Pedroia. And she had no good motive for wanting him dead. She didn't do it.

I pushed off the floor and stood, giving her plenty of room. I didn't need another kick in the head. She sat up and got slowly to her feet.

"So, smart guy, if I didn't do it, who did."

160

I didn't answer her question. I knew the answer; there couldn't be another. "Deuce, get up here. Bring plenty of cargo tape."

"Who killed them?" demanded Cleo.

"I did."

I turned and left the cabin, ignoring the stunned look on her face.

Deuce met me at the spare cabin. Together we wrapped cargo tape around Pedroia's torso to keep his arms in close to his chest and bound his legs together. It wasn't like he would be trying to get away, but for what I had in mind, he needed to look like a prisoner. Deuce hoisted Pedroia onto his shoulder. I lifted Scalzi. Deuce was right; he was a heavy boy.

Down on the cargo deck, Scalzi went into the port-side lock. We'd flush him into space once we cleared orbit. We attached Pedroia to the loading winch using more cargo tape. We'd drop him near one of Jones' legitimate businesses on our way out. We'd have to make up some sort of malfunction to explain our erratic departure path to traffic control. If Jones knew who Pedroia really was, and I was betting that he did, the two million in bounty money might buy us some time. But Deuce was right. I didn't think Jones would let it go at that.

"Sylvia, get us out of here. Give me a low pass over the industrial park on the south side of the spaceport."

"Yes, Boss. What'll I tell traffic control?"

"Tell them we had a grav boot failure. Old ship; happens all the time."

"If you say so." Sylvia's voice sounded doubtful.

We were cleared for departure in less than fifteen minutes. The tractor 'bots towed us out to the launch area. Sylvia took us up smoothly then sheared off and flew an erratic path over the south edge of the environment dome. There was an industrial area there with chemical and recycling businesses that were too toxic or dangerous to allow inside the enclosure. Sylvia slowed to a hover over a nondescript salvage yard and lowered the cargo ramp. Deuce depressurized the forward lock, swung the winch out and lowered away, dropping Pedroia into the yard. Sylvia pulled up and rejoined the outbound traffic pattern. The whole maneuver had taken only forty seconds.

Deuce closed the outer lock and secured the cargo winch and then walked over to the port-side airlock. As soon as we cleared orbit and were safely in freefall space, he'd flush the lock. I went aft and climbed the ladder to the second deck. I wasn't looking forward to the next conversation.

"Sylvia, is Rabbit still in my cabin?"

"Yes, Zack. Should I call him?"

"No. I want to speak to him there. Make sure we're not disturbed."

"You want me to lock down the charter cabin again?" She sounded positively eager to do it.

"No, just let Cleo know I need some time alone. I think she'll understand."

I walked slowly down the passageway to my cabin. Rabbit was there, sitting in his powerchair. He looked up as I entered and his face fell when he saw the look in my eyes.

"When did you find out about Pedroia?" I asked, sitting down on the bunk facing him.

"As soon as he opened his mouth. It was like I was back in the 'tank. I almost let it slip right there, but I didn't. You wanted information from him and that was more important. But it was hard, Zack, really hard. After you left he got nasty with me. He said he was only going along because you were a pirate and threatened to kill him. He bragged that he'd make Jones cut your throat and toss you in a recycling pit before he'd tell him how to make the gems. I managed to stay all meek and just set up the recorder. He wasn't going to say anything even then but I said I'd call you back into the salon if he didn't. He was still scared of you, so he talked. I made the video and print files just like you asked."

"And then?" I asked as gently as possible.

Rabbit looked away. Tears gathered in his eyes and he wiped them away with his sleeve before continuing. "He said I was a worthless cripple and he didn't understand why you kept me around. He said he'd heard all about me from Scalzi. He said I may have been a hot-shot slicer once, but now I was nothing but a paranoid nutcase and that I should have done the universe a favor and died in the Bear. I know you wanted to kill him yourself, Zack. But I couldn't let it go."

"Did you take Sylvia offline?"

He nodded. "I knew she'd have the cabin under surveillance. The only way to stop her from recording everything was to shut her down for a while. After I thought about it, I figured I could make it look like Marco had done it."

"How did you get the needler?"

He blushed. "I went by the charter cabin. I was going to see if I could get Cleo to keep you busy while I shut Sylvia down. She was in the shower and didn't hear me open the hatch. Her needler was on the bunk, next to her clothes. I just rolled in and took it. I was just passing the salon again when you came by."

"What about Scalzi? Did you plan to kill him, too?"

Rabbit's face turned grim in a way I'd never seen before. "If I had to. Pedroia was going to die. If Scalzi got in the way, I'd have killed him, too."

"But Pedroia had already done the job?"

Rabbit nodded again. "I opened the hatch very slowly. Pedroia had his back to me. Marco was dead. I could tell just by looking. It was like when we were in the Bear. You learn to tell dead from just sleeping real quick in the Bear. I shot Pedroia before he could turn around. He was dead, too, before he hit the floor."

"Where's the needler?" I asked.

He reached into a compartment next to the chair's right armrest and drew out the weapon. He held it out between his thumb and forefinger. "Here. Tell Cleo I'm sorry for making it look like she did it."

I took the weapon and checked the safety, clicked it on. "Cleo will get over it. Besides, she's mad at me, not you."

"Are you mad at me, Zack?" he asked timidly.

I shook my head. "No. If anything, I owe you an apology. I shouldn't have sent you into that room without telling you who Smolensky really was."

"That was okay," he said, surprised at my apology. "I knew you must have some plan for him. The information was more important than my revenge. I should have trusted you to take care of him instead of trying to do it myself."

I couldn't tell him that the plan was to let Pedroia walk in exchange for Cleo. Why was she suddenly more important to me than my promise to myself and to all of Pedroia's other victims? Rabbit still trusted me to stand by my word.

I got up from the bunk and slid the needler into the waistband of my trousers. "Don't worry about it, Rabbit. What's done is done."

I still couldn't meet his eye.

CHAPTER TWENTY-TWO

"What about the rest of the Revenants?" Rabbit asked, as I was about to leave the cabin.

I started to tell him to quit obsessing about his imaginary villains but stopped myself. A cold chill settled in my gut. How likely was it that both Pedroia and Samadar would turn up on Delilah? I'd been searching for them for nearly three years without a hint of success. To find them on a backwater rock like Delilah was too convenient to be a coincidence.

"Nothing we can do right now," I said.

"They'll hear about this. They'll know we did it. We need to beef up our security. How soon before we get to Tycho? I've got a lot of reprogramming to do."

I wanted to ridicule his paranoia, but I couldn't. I still found it hard to buy a secret society of revolutionary fanatics hiding in the Belt, but I didn't believe in coincidence. Pedroia and Samadar had found each other somehow, and that might mean there were more Martian fugitives out there. Maybe connected with the Dragons. Jones had operations in the Belt; a bunch of 'roids he controlled outright, if the stories were to be believed. And he ran most of his smuggling operations from Tharsis, a perfect way to get people out of Mars without the Feds knowing about it.

Where Rabbit saw a threat to be feared, I was beginning to see opportunity. I'd drawn the line at bounty hunting, figuring most folks on the run weren't too much different than Deuce and me. But I might make an exception when it came to the people who had stuck Rabbit and me in the Bear. That could be considered a public service.

I realized one other thing. If Jones had helped fugitives get out of Mars after the war, he must have some use for them. He wouldn't appreciate me poaching in his territory. I needed to settle with him over this glowgems deal before tweaking his nose again.

"We're not going to Tycho," I said to Rabbit. "We're going back to Highpoint. Scalzi hid the notebook in that safety deposit box. We need it to buy off Jones. We can't worry about him coming after us if we're going to hunt Revenants."

I left him in the cabin. I had apologies to offer to Cleo and a course to set with Sylvia. I spoke to Sylvia first and had her put us on a roundabout course for Highpoint, just in case the Dragons were already looking for us. I figured we still had a few hours before Jones put the word out to kill us but didn't want to get overconfident.

I knocked on the hatch coaming before I entered the charter cabin. Cleo was sitting in the only chair, waiting for me.

"Did you talk to Rabbit?" she asked.

"How did you know it was Rabbit?"

"It's the only thing that made sense. I know I didn't kill them and you could have done it sooner and cleaner if that's what you wanted. My impression of Deuce is that if he kills someone, he'll do it face to face. That only leaves Rabbit."

I settled on the bunk with a sigh. She had us all pegged

and catalogued. It was a little frightening, all the more so because it was correct. "Pedroia killed Scalzi. For something he was carrying, apparently." I told her about the small gems and the key. "Rabbit lifted your needler while you were in the shower, took Sylvia off line once everyone was bedded down for the night, then shot Pedroia."

"Was it bad for him?" she asked. "In prison, I mean."

"It was bad for all of us. But Rabbit was a slicer, not a soldier. He didn't know how to survive. He'd have died in there if we hadn't been cellmates. Even then, we both came close to dying more than once. Rabbit needed me, and that gave me a reason to survive."

"And you both swore to kill the people who hurt you."

"Not Rabbit," I said. "He came out of the Bear broken, obsessed with conspiracy theories, but not dangerous. At least I didn't think so. I underestimated him and how much he was counting on me to bring him some kind of justice."

"And now we're all screwed. I feel sorry for Rabbit. But vendettas are still stupid."

"This is down to me. I didn't trust Rabbit with Pedroia's identity. I should have explained the plan to him. Jones would have obliged us by killing him eventually."

"So now what?" she asked as she leaned forward in the chair.

I felt her full attention was on me, like I was the only person in the world. How did she do that? "We head back to Highpoint."

"What?"

"The electronic key I found in Pedroia's hand is for a safe deposit box in a bank on Highpoint. Scalzi had it hidden in a secret pocket sewn into his lapel. I'm betting the notebook is hidden there. We'll need it to buy off Jones."

"That's a long-odds bet."

"You have a better idea?" She didn't reply. "Neither do I. If we don't find a way to get Jones off our backs, we might as well head for the Belt and join Rabbit's Revenants."

She laughed. "You ridicule Fingal's Cave and then tell me about Revenants?"

I laughed with her, but it was an uneasy laugh. Rabbit's tall tales seemed a lot harder to dismiss. "I think Rabbit would like to talk to you. He feels badly about stealing your needler."

"And he wants me to forgive him. Rabbit isn't the problem, Zack."

I knew she was right. But I wasn't about to grovel any more than I already had. She'd played me from the first minute I saw her in the food court. She was playing me now. I'd been a willing participant maybe, but this was my ship and my crew. She was the problem, not me.

"Do you want to talk to him, or not?"

She cocked her head in that way she had. "Sure, I'll talk with him."

"I'll tell him," I said, aware that I'd lost control of the conversation once again. I left her there and went to find Rabbit.

He was where I'd left him, sitting in the middle of my cabin looking miserable. He looked up as I came in. "Is Cleo going to kill me?"

"No Rabbit. But she wants to talk to you. She doesn't seem upset with you. It's me she's pissed at."

"Why you? I stole her needler."

"And I accused her of killing Pedroia without thinking it through. She wants me to believe in her, no matter what."

"Do you? She's really beautiful, Zack. Nobody could blame you for wanting her."

I walked over and touched him on the shoulder. "I accused her because I trust you with my life. She hasn't earned that trust yet."

"But she could, right?"

"Maybe. Why is that important to you?"

He shrugged. "You need her. You need something to keep you believing in the good part of life. Even in the Bear, I always believed there would be something better. I never lost hope. You never had any. The only thing you've lived for since we left the 'tanks has been revenge. Maybe she can change that."

I didn't answer. He rolled past me and turned down the passageway to the charter cabin.

* * *

I don't know what he and Cleo talked about. He was in there a long time.

I spent the time in the cockpit, sitting in the command chair, staring out into the black. Sylvia had the good sense to keep quiet and leave me to my thoughts. Pedroia was dead. So were Samadar and Clancy. I'd sworn to kill all three of them and now the job was done. So why the hell did I feel so empty?

What did you expect, idiot? A chorus of halleluiahs? You got what you wanted. Now get on with business.

Business. What business? I was nearly broke once again. I'd made a powerful enemy and my only bargaining chip was a mythical notebook that might turn out to be worthless. Worse, I'd been willing to betray a friend's trust for money. I could tell myself it was part of a plan to save us all, but I knew better. That's why the revenge felt so hollow. I'd seen a way to make more money than I'd ever dreamed of and had sold out.

CHAPTER TWENTY-THREE

We made good time to Highpoint, despite the roundabout route Sylvia plotted for us. I spent the nights with Cleo in the charter cabin. She seemed quieter since our fight, more observer than manipulator.

Rabbit had persuaded me to hold onto Scalzi's body. It was now packed in the galley freezer. I didn't like it, but Rabbit said he had his reasons.

I went up to the cockpit as we entered the Highpoint zone of control.

"Highpoint Control," said Sylvia as we approached. "This is VC-334 *Profit*, entering Highpoint zone of control. Request approach and landing clearance."

"*Profit*, this is Highpoint Control. You are cleared to the first marker; hold there and await final approach vector. And welcome back to Highpoint, Ma'am."

"Why thank you," cooed Sylvia. "You remembered us."

"Yes, Ma'am. How is your husband?"

"He's an old grouch. I'm much younger than he is, you know."

The controller didn't answer.

"I think you scared him, Sylvia," I said.

"Then he shouldn't try to flirt with married women."

I pointed out that she was neither married nor a woman, but she just made a rude noise with her vocal synthesizer.

We were held at the first marker for about ten minutes before we got a final approach vector and landing clearance. There wasn't much traffic; the wait seemed longer than needed. As soon as we were docked and the bay pressurized, the reason for the delay became clear. Instead of the usual customs official, Inspector Kensai stepped into the bay. I was suddenly very aware of the body in my galley freezer.

"Sylvia, keep the cargo ramp locked. I'm going out through the starboard sally port to talk with Kensai."

"What if he has a warrant?"

"Then we're in for a long stay." I ducked out of the cockpit and ran across the catwalk. Kensai called Sylvia as I slid down the ladder. I could hear her over my link.

"Captain Mbele will be right out to speak to you Inspector Kensai."

I didn't hear his reply as I cycled the starboard lock and lowered the stairs from the sally port. Kensai stood a few paces away, arms at his sides, left hand resting half in his pocket. He looked at ease, maybe even slightly amused.

"I didn't expect to see you back in my jurisdiction so soon, Mbele. I thought we had an understanding."

"Just doing a little banking business, Inspector Kensai. And I thought we'd only agreed that I wouldn't pick on any more Dragons here on Highpoint."

"Yes, that's true. Your banking tips have proven very profitable, by the way. My squad plans to cash in on them very soon. I hope your business won't interfere with theirs."

I smiled. "No. I doubt you'll even know we're here."

His light tone hardened slightly. "I'm counting on it. May I come aboard?"

"Is this a customs inspection? Or a police matter?"

"Is there a difference?"

I shrugged. "Customs inspections are limited to my holds and personal baggage. Police searches can be more extensive, if there's a warrant. Do you have a warrant, Inspector Kensai?"

"No. No warrant," he said with a chuckle. "This one's on me. You're a very interesting guy, Mbele. And interesting isn't a good thing to a cop. Watch your step while you're here. And give my regards to Ms. Lee." He turned and walked away.

I climbed through the sally port to find Cleo in the cargo hold, waiting for me.

"How did he know I was here?" she asked.

"He didn't hear it from me. He's a smart guy; doesn't take much of a detective to realize that you disappeared at the same time we left."

"Coming back here was a bad idea. How do we know he won't tell the Dragons we're here?"

"Not Kensai," I said, confident that it was true. "That's why he was here, not the usual customs inspector."

"You're sure you can trust him?"

I nodded. "He'll keep quiet about us, at least to the Dragons, and to the other cops. He may be the only honest policeman on Highpoint. He'll leave us alone as long as we don't do something illegal."

"That won't take long if we try to access Marco's safe deposit box," she said, a wry smile crossing her face.

"So we won't let Kensai find out about it."

We climbed back up to the salon and I called Deuce and Rabbit to join us there. Cleo started toward my chair but stopped, and then turned aside to sit in one of the metal ones around the table. I settled into the armchair.

Deuce stepped through the hatch, glanced at Cleo, but remained standing, leaning against the bulkhead. Rabbit followed and rolled over to the table next to Cleo. She smiled at him. Deuce grunted softly.

"Rabbit," I said. "Have you learned anything more about the key?"

"Not much. It's a pretty standard key. I did some digging on Highpoint bank procedures. In addition to the key, we'll need some sort of secure ID. If Scalzi used a password, we may be out of luck. Figuring out a random password is nearly impossible and we have no real clues to what he might choose. On the other hand, a lot of banks are requiring a DNA profile as the secure ID. It can't be forgotten, can't be discovered or deduced, and is hard to fake."

"And impossible for us to use, unless we want to haul a frozen body into the bank lobby," Cleo said.

"Not necessarily. That's why I told Zack we had to bring Marco along with us. The DNA sensors sample skin cells, usually from a hand or fingertip. We only need part of Marco to pass the screen."

"So much better," she said. "Carrying around a frozen hand. Don't you think the bank will notice that?"

"Maybe not. The key will get us access to the vault. The DNA confirmation is on the box itself and releases the lock after the key is inserted. Usually the vault officer leaves the customer alone to retrieve his box. It's part of their privacy policy. They offer complete secrecy as to what the customer places in the box. Good for business and it gives the bank cover for anything illegal. If they don't know what's in the boxes, they can't be responsible for informing the Feds if there are illegal goods in them."

"What about basic identification?" I asked. "Won't they ask for some ID besides just the key?"

Rabbit grinned. "Probably. But I can handle that. I've sliced their security system before. I can insert your image into Scalzi's profile with the bank. I can't do anything about the DNA screen since that's encoded in the lock itself. But I'll get you into the vault, no problem."

"How long to slice the system?"

"A few minutes. Long before you can get there."

"Okay, do it. Deuce and Cleo, I want you both with me. I don't know if Jones knows we're here yet, but I'm willing to bet the Dragons will be watching the bank if they know Scalzi did business there. They may even have somebody on the inside. We need to be ready for trouble."

Deuce just nodded. Cleo looked thoughtful but not worried.

"Something on your mind, Cleo?" I asked.

"Just thinking about Marco. He was always looking over his shoulder, even before the Dragons got involved with this business. It was like he was worried about someone else following him. That was part of why he wanted me for protection."

"You think there's someone else interested in Malloy's notebook?"

"Maybe. It's only a feeling, nothing solid. Like you said, we should be ready for trouble."

"Go down to the cargo deck with Deuce. Draw whatever weapons you think you need from the locker. I'll be down in a few minutes."

She nodded and touched me on the hand as she stepped through the hatch. I went aft to the galley and opened the freezer. We'd bent Scalzi over double to fit him in. Even then it was tight. I worked his hand loose from the plastic wrap that covered him. I debated taking the whole hand but couldn't see an easy way to remove it. A large wire cutter was enough to remove his forefinger. I wrapped it in a scrap of plastic and put it in my pocket.

Deuce and Cleo waited down on the cargo deck. There was an awkward silence between them. Cleo had her needler holstered at her waist and the stun batons tucked into a cloth bag that hung from her left shoulder. Deuce carried his pulse rifle slung over his shoulder, concealed by a long gray overcoat. I took my Huang pneumatic and the short bladed sheath knife that I'd carried the last time we were on Highpoint. I tucked a pair of extra magazines for the Huang into my back pocket.

"Lock down, Sylvia," I called as we exited through the sally port. "Release code: Tharsis seventeen."

"Someday you'll have to tell me why that phrase is important to you," Cleo said.

"No, I won't." The Revolution might be long dead, but there were some things that I wouldn't talk about, ever.

Deuce smiled faintly at the exchange. I don't think Cleo saw him.

We left the cargo bay and walked to the main tube station. Rabbit downloaded a map to my link and I checked the information kiosk at the station. We boarded a tube for the main level, just spinward of the balcony where I'd gotten the open space shakes a while ago.

The directors of the Highpoint Security and Trust Bank had gone to great lengths to create an impression of solidity and permanency in the facade of their institution. Faux marble columns flanked the wide bronze plated doors. The metal detectors and security scanners were carefully concealed behind decorative cornices above the doorframe. I left the Huang and the knife with Deuce. He and Cleo sat at an open-air cafe just across the main thoroughfare from the bank.

The bank interior was cool and dark, a solid looking space of black marble and cherry wood. The security guards were conspicuous in the corners and the overhead cameras and weapons turrets were just as inconspicuous behind the dark ceiling tiles. Hanging chandeliers of cut crystal cast cones of light on the deposit terminals and desks scattered across the floor.

I walked across the open space with a slow measured pace, my footsteps echoing in the air.

The desk marked 'Vault Officer' was near the back wall. A small, neatly dressed man with a thin black moustache and fashionable shaved scalp sat behind it, typing briskly on an old-fashioned keyboard in front of a flat screen monitor. He looked up as I approached.

"May I help you?" he asked in a carefully neutral tone.

I held up the key between my thumb and forefinger. He took it from me and plugged it into a port on his gleaming desktop. He glanced at the monitor in front of him, looked at my face and nodded.

"Welcome back, Mr. Scalzi." He handed the key back to me. "Do you wish to access your box?"

I nodded, placing the key back in my pocket next to the plastic wrapped finger. I kept my hand casually in the pocket and worked the plastic off of the now thawed fingertip.

The small man stood and motioned for me to follow. He led me through an archway behind his desk and into a very well-lit concrete and steel anteroom. He pressed his palm to a reader and a steel door slid open revealing a long vault. The walls on either side were lined floor to ceiling with lock boxes. He stepped aside and held out his hand with a slight bow, inviting me to enter.

"Place your key in the input port on the console and your finger in the DNA reader next to it. When you are finished, press the button on the top of the console and I will open the vault again."

I nodded my thanks and stepped into the vault. The steel door slid shut behind me. I looked around. If there were security cameras in here they were well concealed. I clicked my link but got a no-service tone. I stepped up to the console in the center of the room. It stood about chest high. There was an input port on the left, a small DNA reader on the right and a red button on the top. To the left of the console were a small table and a real wooden chair with leather padding on the arms and seat.

I plugged the key into the input port. A blinking red light appeared in the DNA sensor. I removed the finger from my pocket and pressed it to the sensor. After a long second the light turned green. There was a whirring sound overhead as a robotic arm descended from the ceiling and traveled along a track down the center of the vault.

The whining whir of the servo in the otherwise deep silence of the vault took me back to the biotank where the only sound you ever heard was the high pitched hum of the injectors as they pumped the nanos into your spine. I broke into a sweat and the vault suddenly felt uncomfortably cold.

The arm stopped, bent, and removed a box from the left wall. It turned and ran back up the track to the table where it deposited the box next to the chair. I flinched away from it, but it didn't reach for me, just pulled back up into its recess in the ceiling.

I took a deep breath and swallowed the bile in the back of my throat. I stepped around to the table and sat down.

The box had a hinged top and a simple latch in the front. I opened the latch and lifted the top. The notebook was smaller than I expected, only about ten by twelve centimeters and less than three thick. The synthetic leather cover was spotted and frayed at the edges. I reached in, lifted it out of the box, and opened the cover. Scrawled in a cramped hand at the top of the first page was the name: F. Malloy.

CHAPTER TWENTY-FOUR

I slid the notebook into my jacket pocket, and closed and latched the box. I went to the console and retrieved the key. The arm reached down, took the box and returned it to its place in the vault. I pushed the button on the top of the console and turned to face the door just as the vault manager opened it.

"I trust everything was satisfactory, sir?" he asked.

"Yes, thank you." I spoke to him for the first time. I started to brush past him but stopped as he pressed a wicked looking needler into my ribs.

"I'll take the notebook," he said quietly.

I looked him in the eye. His gaze was hard, the look of a trained killer, not a banker. I raised my hands to shoulder level. I moved my chin downward indicating my right lapel. "It's in my jacket pocket."

He stepped back, the needler leveled at my chest. "Reach in slowly and pull it out."

I could feel the nanofibers extending into my muscles. I tensed my left arm as I reached for the pocket. He followed the movement with his eyes, giving me an opening. I lifted up on the toes of my left foot and lashed out at his groin with my right as I swept my left hand down and knocked the needler aside. He doubled over in pain and I hit him behind the ear with the heel of my right hand. He dropped to the floor.

I picked up the needler and checked the mag. He was packing sleepers, so I shot him in the left thigh to make sure he stayed down. Kneeling next to him, I checked his pockets. No ID, no other weapons. I checked his palm, expecting a Dragon tattoo.

A chill ran through me. Instead of a Dragon, a black teardrop was tattooed at the base of his thumb—Black Ops squad.

I pulled him all the way into the vault and slipped through the door just as it slid shut. I dropped the needler on the floor and walked out through the archway into the bank's main lobby. The security guards hadn't moved. The doors to the street opened smoothly as I approached. I walked through and turned right onto the crowded thoroughfare. No cries or challenges from behind me. I breathed a little easier.

Deuce and Cleo walked up beside me. I nodded in reply to Cleo's questioning look. She handed me the Huang, which I clipped to my belt, and the knife, which went into the top of my boot. Deuce held his rifle slung over his shoulder and scanned the street ahead.

"Any trouble?" asked Cleo.

"A bit. One of the bank clerks tried to take the notebook away from me with a needler. He knew what I'd come for. I left him to sleep it off in the vault."

"Dragon?"

"No, former Black Ops. Teardrop tattoo and all."

Deuce looked sharply at me. "Ain't supposed to be any of those guys left."

"So I've heard. But I've run into two of them in the last

few days. First Samadar and now this guy. I don't know if he's free-lancing, working for Jones or for someone else. But he knew what was in that lockbox and pretty soon his employer will know we have it."

"We should get back to the ship," Deuce said. "But I'm thinking the tubes are a bad idea."

"Right." I activated my link. "Rabbit, we need an alternate route home. We're about fifty meters from the tube station. What are our options?"

"Give me a second, Zack." A pause. "Okay, turn spinward at the next junction. There's a lift that'll take you down. Head for deck sixteen. It's mostly warehousing and light manufacturing. You can walk the whole deck, or hop a cargo pod at any of a half dozen stations."

"Thanks. Everything okay there?"

Sylvia replied. "I've had two requests from Customs to file a cargo declaration. I told them we weren't offloading, only refueling, but they're getting testy about it. What should I do?"

"Tell them to breathe vacuum. Then call Kensai and have him contact me on my link."

"Will do, Boss. That Customs AI is an arrogant bitch. I'm going to enjoy telling her off."

"Rabbit," I said. "Stay in touch. Track me by my link."

"Okay, Zack."

We turned at the junction and saw the lift station off to our right. Deuce touched my arm and pointed behind us. Three men in dark jackets moved purposefully through the crowd, coming our way. Cleo drew her needler, but I grabbed her wrist and shook my head. There were too many people about. A firefight here would attract a lot of attention. We couldn't afford any official investigation until the notebook was safe. And I didn't want to explain the dismembered finger in my pocket or the dead man in my freezer.

We reached the lift with several seconds lead on our

unknown pursuers. A few working people joined us and Deuce punched the button for deck sixteen. Other decks were selected, but all were below ours.

The lift stopped and we stepped out into a wide space with a low overhead, maybe three meters high. Lighting panels spaced every ten meters or so made the whole area look dim and filled with shadows. Wide aisles on either side were lined with storage rooms and small manufacturing centers. None of them seemed to be occupied at present. I consulted the map Rabbit had downloaded to my link and pointed off to the left.

"The cargo terminal is that way. We can probably hitch a ride on a container bound for the terminal, or we can walk."

"What about the men from the plaza?" Cleo asked. "They saw us get into the lift. It shouldn't be too hard to figure out where we went."

"I'm counting on it. Deuce, take a position over there by that recycling bin. I'll cover the other side from around that corner. Cleo, you take the middle. Get behind the corner of the next aisle and stay low. Shoot from kneeling or prone position. Deuce will aim high. I'll take the center of mass."

"I know what to do," she said coolly.

We separated and took our places. After a few minutes I began to wonder if I'd misjudged our friends in the dark jackets. Deuce looked calm, hardly moving as he stood behind the battered metal bin and sighted along his rifle. I couldn't see Cleo. I shifted my weight, easing pressure on my right shoulder.

The lift doors opened; no one came out immediately, then a hand holding a pneumatic appeared on the side closest to me. I tightened my grip on the Huang. They exited carefully, quickly, first to the right, then the left, then the center, each covering the other with raised weapons. I sighted along my pneumatic and fired. Deuce and Cleo opened up immediately. Only one of the three got a shot off, and it went wide in Deuce's general direction.

I rushed forward, kicking a loose pneumatic out of the way. I knelt next to the man I'd shot, covering the other two with the Huang. I could hear Cleo approaching rapidly from behind me. Deuce stayed in place covering us both with his pulse rifle. The man I'd shot was dead, a ragged hole in his right temple. Three black needles protruded from the man in the middle, stitching a neat line from right thigh to left ribcage. Cleo only glanced at him before kneeling next to the man closest to Deuce. She looked back at me and shook her head.

I waved to Deuce and he lowered his rifle. Cleo searched the man closest to her while I did the same with the one in front of me. A pair of extra magazines for the pneumatic and a cheap tourist map of the arcology were all I found. That and the teardrop tattoo on his left hand.

I looked up to find Deuce standing over me. I rolled the man's palm over so Deuce could see the tattoo. "Shit," was his only comment. I stood up and pointed left in the general direction of the cargo terminal. Deuce nodded and took off at a brisk walk, pulse rifle held low at the ready.

"Time to go," I said to Cleo as she searched the third dead man.

She looked up and saw Deuce walking rapidly away. "What's the rush," she asked coming smoothly to her feet.

"These guys are Black Ops. Third Directorate death squads. They're supposed to all be dead or locked up in the Antarctica maximum security prison."

"They don't look like much of a threat right now."

"There's usually six men in a squad. We only got three, maybe four if the bank clerk was with them." I now regretted not killing him. "They won't walk into a trap like this again. We need to move right now."

Cleo didn't say anything, just fell in beside me as we walked quickly after Deuce. She kept her needler drawn and ready. I motioned her to move ahead and fell a couple of paces behind as a rear guard.

We made good time through the warehouse district. We saw occasional 'bots and workers but they went about their business. They seemed oblivious to us. After a kilometer or so of zigzag travel we entered an area made up of light manufacturing businesses. There were more people around, moving between the large enclosed spaces where the real work was done. A few noticed Deuce's pulse rifle and looked alarmed, but no one challenged us. Deuce took off the overcoat he'd been wearing and wrapped the rifle in it, which cut down on the worried glances from passersby.

I checked the map on my link. We were about eight hundred meters, straight-line travel, from the cargo terminal and still sixteen decks down. If the guys we'd killed at the lift had back-up, they knew where we were by now and would be covering the lift station near the terminal. It was time to do something unexpected.

"Rabbit," I called over the link. "I need a lift near our present position."

"To your left, about fifty meters, there's a cargo lift. It'll take you to the main level; it doesn't stop anywhere else."

I whistled to attract Deuce's attention. He turned and I waved him back to me. Cleo stood by.

"We're going to throw them a curve. If those Black Ops guys had back-up, they'll be expecting us to come up in the lift closest to the terminal. We're going left. There's a cargo lift that'll take us to the main level."

"So much for staying inconspicuous." Cleo said.

"That went away the minute we shot those guys back there. The local law may not be aware, but someone is. We need to change the game."

"No argument," she said. "Just pointing out that things could get messy in a crowded public place."

I nodded. "No good choices. Let's hope we get lucky. Deuce, take point."

He set off at a brisk walk. Cleo and I followed close behind. The cargo lift was open, waiting for the next load when we arrived. I called Rabbit again and he overrode the control AI. We boarded the lift and Rabbit took us up to the main level. Deuce surveyed the area and waved us out.

The lift opened into a cargo yard separated from the main thoroughfare by high decorative fences. Boxes and cargo containers of various sizes were laid out in neat rows as delivery 'bots entered and left the yard carrying goods to the stores and businesses in the area.

We followed the line of fully laden 'bots to the exit and stepped out onto the pedestrian walkway. The passenger terminal loomed at the end of the street with its sweeping steel and glass facade. The cargo terminal was more modest, set off to the right with a wide businesslike gate at the end of a short driveway.

We walked toward the terminal, slower than the moving crowd, but not slow enough to attract attention. There was an arcade near the terminal filled with stalls catering to the last minute needs of travelers. Deuce ducked into the entrance and Cleo followed. I leaned casually against a post and watched the cargo terminal. From inside the arcade, Deuce and Cleo did the same.

The crowd ebbed and flowed through the gates of the spaceport, crossing the wide plaza fronting the tube and lift stations. They say patience is a virtue, although not one that I practice much. I forced myself to stand easy and watch the plaza. Somewhere out there, men were waiting to kill us. I remembered my training. Lessons learned long ago during more idealistic times resurfaced. I slowed my breathing and waited.

The nanofibers tingled and I knew that something had changed, just beneath my conscious awareness. I scanned the crowd, jumping from face to face. They blurred and ran together, as if the nanos were eliminating any that didn't fit, until one stood out sharp and clear.

He stood across the plaza, near the drive leading to the cargo terminal. He was partially hidden by a tall support pillar, watching the crowd as people entered and left the spaceport. Ashok Patel.

I turned slightly so my face was hidden, then walked casually into the arcade. I flipped through a display of toiletries, paying little attention to the images as they flashed in the holotank. Deuce was close enough to hear me whisper.

"Patel is standing next to the cargo terminal entrance. You and Cleo wait here. Give me five minutes, then walk out together. Make sure he sees you."

I turned and left the arcade as Deuce spoke to Cleo. I walked quickly away from the spaceport until I was out of Patel's line of sight, then crossed to the opposite walkway. I was walking against the flow of foot traffic and got a few annoyed looks from people in the crowd, but no one spoke to me. Within two minutes, I was across the plaza from the arcade, working my way toward Patel.

He was too good to stand where I could come up on his blind side. I worked as close as I could, using the flow of the crowd for cover. Right on time, Deuce and Cleo walked out of the arcade and crossed the plaza toward the passenger terminal.

Patel's head came up and followed them until they had passed him. He straightened and took a step forward, his eyes focused on Cleo. I moved fast, augmented by the nanofibers. In half a second I was behind him, my left hand gripping his arm and my knife pressed into his back. The tip penetrated his jacket and touched the skin just above his kidney.

"Hi, Ashok. I didn't expect to see you here today." He stiffened. "No, don't turn around. This knife will find your heart before you can take a breath."

He stopped walking. "What are you going to do, Mbele? Kill me right here in the plaza? That'd be a stupid move. Even dumber than backing out on the deal with Jones."

"I may not be very bright, but I'll still be alive. You won't be. I have what Jones wants. But you already know that."

"Know what?"

I nudged his back with the knife, making him gasp. A small spot of blood soaked through his jacket. "Now you're being stupid. You know I have the notebook. You sent your hired assassins to take it from me."

"Assassins? What the hell are you talking about? Jones wants your head and sent me to get it. I have my own people."

"Good luck with that. Didn't Jones appreciate the present I sent him? It was worth two million and change."

He laughed at that. "You don't know what you're into, Mbele. Jones isn't going to let you get away with cheating him. He had other plans for Pedroia."

"Did Jones hire the Black Ops freelancers? Or was that your idea?"

"Black Ops? You're losing it. You've been hanging around that twitch, Conejo, too long." I pushed with the knife again. He stifled a cry. "Go ahead. Kill me if you've got it in you. I told you, I have my own people. I don't need freelancers."

"Maybe not. But there are three dead commandos down on deck sixteen and they all have teardrop tattoos on their hands."

"Your problem, not mine. Who else have you pissed off?"

I thought about that, but couldn't come up with any answers I could believe in. If the commandos weren't his, then someone else knew about the notebook.

"Come on," I said. "We're going for a walk." I opened my link. "Deuce, everything Jake?

"Golden, LT. We're just inside the terminal. What's the plan?"

"Patel and I are heading for the cargo terminal. You and Cleo join us there. Watch out for Dragons. I doubt he's alone."

"On our way."

I pushed Patel ahead of me and we made our way across

a short parking apron toward the cargo terminal. I slowed as Cleo and Deuce approached. Cleo stepped up next to me as Deuce double-timed ahead to take up point. He stopped at the big automatic doors that marked the entrance to the terminal lobby and turned to cover us. They hit us just before we reached the doors.

CHAPTER TWENTY-FIVE

As soon as I saw Deuce raise the pulse rifle to his shoulder, I swept Patel's feet and shoved him to the deck, holding him down with my forearm across the back of his neck. The knife went into the sheath in my boot and I drew my pneumatic.

I leaned down so Patel could hear me. "Stay down, you son of a bitch. I'll deal with you after I finish with your boys."

I pressed the pneumatic to his right calf and pulled the trigger. The slug tore through the meaty part of his lower leg. It would hurt like hell but wasn't life threatening. He shouted with pain and alarm and clutched his leg. He wouldn't get far, even if he tried to run. A slug clanged off the deck next to me and I flinched even as the nanos extended into my nerves and muscles.

Cleo dropped to a crouch. Deuce's pulse rifle sizzled and a man in dark coveralls fell to the deck. Pneumatic slugs bracketed Cleo's position. She returned fire with her needler and dropped another Dragon. There were two more that I could see, both half-concealed behind support columns on opposite sides of the apron.

"Deuce," I shouted. "Crossfire cover." I dove to my right without waiting for a reply. Deuce's pulse bolts sparked and sizzled along the column closest to me, pinning down the gunman behind it. I rolled across my shoulder and came up firing. The second gunman stepped out to draw a bead on me. He was a heartbeat too slow and I put a slug through his chest.

Deuce sidestepped to his left drawing fire from the remaining gunman. Cleo's needler snapped and the last Dragon fell, twitching slightly as the poison found his heart. I swiveled and covered Patel with my pneumatic. He lay very still.

I walked over and nudged him with a toe. "Get on your feet. Your boys screwed up." He didn't move. That was when I noticed the black finned needle stuck in his neck. I spun to face Cleo.

"Cleo, what the hell did you do?"

"He was going to make a break for it," she said holstering the needler. "The firefight distracted you. I could see him getting ready to run."

"He had a hole in his leg. How far was he going to get?" I said. "We needed him alive."

Her voice hardened. "You're not the only one with scores to settle."

I stared at her. "You're the one who said vendettas were stupid. Or was there something else going on here?"

She held my gaze, not backing down. "No one lays hands on me without my permission. No one." There was a desperate fury in her eyes that I'd seen before—on Clancy's rape victims in the Bear.

I leaned close and spoke softly to her. "What did Patel do to you?"

"We'd better get out of here, LT." Deuce broke in before she could answer. He pointed to a trio of official looking cars pulling into the short parking apron leading to the cargo area.

I nodded, retrieving Cleo's needle from Patel's neck and handing it to her. We moved as fast as we could without appearing to run through the cargo offices and staging areas in the open part of the terminal. Our bay was several frames spinward on the cargo deck, about five hundred meters from where we stood. Once we were out of sight of the main terminal, we broke into a run.

The bay was open but there were three men in customs uniforms standing around the ship. I stopped as I entered the bay. Deuce and Cleo almost ran into me. The customs men hadn't seen us. Two were busy adjusting the height of a laser torch propped on a heavy jack stand while the third attached a pair of wrist-thick power cables to its base. We ducked behind a blast shield next to a pile of boxes and a bundle of old tarps.

"Rabbit, Sylvia, what's going on." I hissed over the link.

Rabbit answered. "Sylvia did as you said, Zack. She really gave it to that customs AI. Called her names I didn't know were in her vocabulary program. But I think the AI got mad. She sent these guys down and they're threatening to cut us out if we don't let them in. Sylvia explained that her programming won't let her open up without the proper release code, but I don't think they believe her. Where have you been all this time?"

"Never mind. Sylvia, did you get in touch with Kensai?"

"Yes, Boss. But he just said to stall as long as I could and that the situation would change very soon. He said if they really started cutting into my hull that I should just open up and let them in. What should I do, Zack?"

"Sit tight. We'll work on it from this side."

I turned as Deuce tapped me on the shoulder. He pointed to the bundle of tarps. Cleo knelt next to it and raised one corner of the heavy nanocloth. Under it was a body. She pulled the cloth back to reveal two more. All three wore customs uniforms and all three had pneumo wounds in their foreheads.

I motioned Deuce to take a position where he could cover the space between the ship and us. There wasn't room for all three of us to fire around the shield. I knelt below Deuce and looked out. The man handling the power cables was out of sight on the far side of the bay. Both cables were connected to the torch. The other two stood next to the torch's control panel. Deuce had a clear shot at one of them but the other one was partially concealed by the jack stand. No chance to get all three from here.

I waved Cleo up next to me. I handed her my pneumatic. "Stay low and cover me. Give me your needler."

"What are you doing," she asked.

"These guys aren't customs. Either they're Dragons or they're the rest of that commando team. We can't get a clean shot at them from here, and if I'm right, we're going to have the cops all over this bay in a few minutes. We have to get the notebook aboard the ship before that."

She handed me the needler and I tucked it into the back of my waistband. She grabbed my face between her hands and kissed me firmly then let me go and raised the pneumatic.

I took a deep breath and closed my eyes for a second, concentrating. The nanos stirred and then activated. I could feel my muscles twitch slightly as the nanofibers entered them. My hearing became sharper and when I opened my eyes the ghostly glow of infrared wreathed the lighting panels and Cleo's body. The nanos had never responded to my command before, but I was glad they'd done it now.

I stood and walked casually into the open bay. The men at the laser torch didn't look up until I was within two meters of them. "Can I help you, gentlemen?" I asked.

The man at the control panel turned to face me; the other one moved to keep the jack stand between us.

"Official customs business," said the first man. My hyper

acute ears could hear the third one working around the far side of the bay to get behind me. "Are you the captain of this vessel?"

"At your service," I said breezily.

"Give your AI the release code. We have orders to search your ship."

"Of course. As soon as I see a warrant. We're not offloading, just refueling."

"It's right here," he said, reaching into his rear pocket. I leapt aside as he whipped out a short barreled pneumatic. He was fast. The round clipped the sleeve of my jacket. I was fast, too. I pumped two needles into him just before the bolt from Deuce's pulse rifle made a mess of his head.

My jump cleared the edge of the jack stand and I brought the needler around and put two into the second man's chest before I hit the ground. Pneumatic rounds from my left spalled off of the metal deck as I rolled across my shoulder to my feet.

A second pneumatic coughed twice as Cleo fired on the third man.

Deuce ran out from behind the blast shield, covering the far side of the bay, but Cleo's aim had been true.

I lowered the needler and checked the man I'd shot. He was dead, needles in his neck and left arm. I turned up his palm and saw the black teardrop.

"Over here, LT." Deuce stood over the man Cleo had shot. I rushed to his side.

The man was still alive, but in bad shape with two wounds in his chest. His eyes were glazed and he gasped for breath, small bubbles of red froth pushing out from the wounds as his chest heaved.

I knelt next to him and grabbed him by the chin forcing him to look at me. "Who are you? Who are you working for?"

His eyes focused on mine for a brief second. A trace of a smile crossed his face before it was wiped away by the pain.

He struggled to speak and I bent closer.

"*Non sibi sed Mars*," he whispered, then chuckled. It brought on a spasm of coughing and the red foam bubbled from his lips. He gasped once and died.

Cleo had crossed the deck and stood behind me. "What did he say?"

"Not self, but Mars." I translated the Latin. "It's the Special Forces motto. We found the rest of the Black Ops team."

"What the hell is going on, LT?" Deuce asked. "These guys ain't supposed to exist anymore."

"I don't know, Deuce. Yesterday, I'd have sworn the Revolution was dead and the Revenants were just a fairy tale. Now I'm not so sure. But what do they want with the notebook? Unless they're tied to the Dragons."

A loud pounding on the bay's main hatch interrupted us. I jumped to my feet and ran for the ship, Deuce and Cleo close behind. "Release code Sylvia," I shouted. "Tharsis seventeen."

The starboard sally port hissed open and I turned to cover the door as Cleo and Deuce climbed aboard. I caught a glimpse of gray police uniforms rushing through the hatch as I climbed the ladder and slammed the port closed.

CHAPTER TWENTY-SIX

"Sylvia," I said as I crossed the hold to the ladder. "We're going to be hailed in a minute. Stall them. Insist on speaking to Kensai."

I climbed the ladder two steps at a time to the second deck. Rabbit was on the catwalk. I pulled the notebook from my jacket and tossed it to him. "Make a copy of this, full scan."

"Okay, Zack," he said. "But what's going on outside. We saw you take out the Customs guys. That's going to land us in a lot of trouble, with the law I mean. They may be crooked, but you can't just shoot them."

"They weren't Customs agents. And we're already in trouble with the law. Now get that notebook copied as fast as you can and add the file you made of Pedroia explaining the culture process to the end of it."

He nodded and rolled away to my cabin. I turned to look down onto the hold where Deuce and Cleo stood.

"Deuce, how much of that Selenite do you have left?"

"About a kilo," he said, his voice full of reservation. "What have you got in mind, LT?"

"Rig a charge to the reactor housing and a dead man switch for me. If things go sideways, I'll blow her up here in the hold before I let these bastards take her."

He folded his arms and gave me a hard look. "You know I'm with you, LT; whatever happens. But Conejo and Cleo, they ain't shipmates, not like us. They've got a right to jump ship if they want."

"No fear, Deuce. When the time comes I'll want you to take them off. I'll be the only one aboard."

He shook his head. "Can't let you do that. I left you once and you ended up in the Bear for two years. I ain't gonna do it again."

His stubborn expression told me there was no point in arguing with him. There wasn't time for that anyway. I needed the threat to be real, even if I had little desire to follow through with it. What surprised me was the fierce conviction inside me that, if pushed hard enough, I would indeed follow through.

Cleo saw it. Her face paled, but she held my eye. "You are the craziest man I've ever met," she said. "What do you think blowing yourself up will accomplish?"

"Nothing that you'd understand. And I don't plan to do it. Not unless the Highpoint cops leave me with no other choice."

"There's always another choice!" she insisted. "Dying for honor is as stupid as vendetta."

Sylvia interrupted before I could answer. "You were right, Boss. The Highpoint cops are hailing us. I told them we wanted Kensai. He's on his way."

I nodded to Deuce. "Get started. Let me know when you have the charges rigged. Then we'll see what Inspector Kensai has to say."

We didn't have to wait long. By the time I crossed the catwalk to the cockpit and eased into the command chair, Kensai was standing in the bay near the door. Through the forward viewport, I could see a handful of Highpoint cops in gray combat uniforms taking up firing positions around the bay. Two of them flanked Kensai, pulse rifles at low ready. Kensai looked up at the cockpit and tapped his ear.

"Okay, Sylvia," I said. "Put me through to him."

"Mbele? I thought I told you to keep your fight with the Dragons out of my jurisdiction."

"I didn't start the fight, Kensai. They jumped us outside the freight terminal."

"Did the Customs officers attack you too?" He pointed at the bodies on the deck in front of him. "Open up your locks, now! We're coming aboard."

"Sure." I struggled to keep my voice calm. "As soon as I see a warrant."

"I don't need a damn warrant," he replied evenly. "I've got probable cause spread all over this deck. Now open up before I cut you out of there."

"Hang on, Kensai. Give me a minute here. Those guys on the deck aren't Customs and you know it. The real Customs officers are under a tarp near the door. If your guys are worth a damn, they must have found them by now."

"We found them. Doesn't change anything. I told you to keep the Dragons off my beat. Instead, you fight running gun battles all the way back here to your ship."

Deuce swung through the hatch behind me and handed me a remote detonator switch. "All set, LT," he whispered so Kensai couldn't hear. "Push the button down to arm it, release to set off the charges."

I nodded. "Get back to the main deck and keep Rabbit and Cleo down there. Be ready to put them out through the port side lock if I give the word." I looked him in the eye. "I want you to go with them, Deuce. Look out for them."

"Can't do that, LT. We've been over this. I stay with you."

"Call it an order if you want, but I need you to get off with them." I held up a hand, silencing his protest. "Somebody has to look out for Rabbit. Cleo can take care of herself, but

Rabbit can't. Get him home to Tycho."

Deuce's face contorted in a spasm emotion. "LT," he pleaded.

"Just do it," I said softly. "Now get below."

"Mbele. What's going on in there?" Kensai's tone was harsh, his patience wearing thin.

"Just a little personal business, Inspector Kensai," I replied. "Check the bodies on the deck. They aren't Dragons. No palm tattoos."

He motioned to one of the riflemen standing next to him. The man rushed forward to the nearest corpse and turned its left hand over. He shook his head and returned to Kansai's side. They exchanged a few words before the rifleman nodded and left the bay.

"Sylvia," I said, keeping the channel open so Kensai could hear. "Download the last thirty minutes of recording from your external cameras to Inspector Kensai's link."

"Yes, Boss."

Kensai pulled a datapad from his breast pocket and opened the file. He spent a long couple of minutes reviewing it at high speed. When he was finished, he put the pad away and stood silent for a second.

"Sergeant," he said to one of the snipers in the bay. "Pull your men back, outside the docking bay."

The gunmen kept their weapons pointed at the ship as they backed out through the hatch to the passageway.

Kensai motioned for the remaining cop to stay put and stepped forward a couple of paces to the nearest body. He bent and studied the teardrop tattoo.

"Who are these guys, Mbele?" he asked. "I just got a report of three more bodies down on deck sixteen with the same marks on their hands."

"Martian Black Ops squad. The teardrop mark is their calling card. They were supposed to have been disbanded after Reunification. Most of them ended up in Antarctica with the other war criminals."

"So what are they doing here, and on my watch?" He stood and looked up at the cockpit, his hands on his hips.

I looked down at the deadman switch in my hand. Time to put up or shut up. "I'm coming out," I said. "We need to talk."

"Keep your hands where I can see them and open your locks for my men," he said.

"We talk first. Then we'll see if you still want to arrest someone."

I climbed out of the chair and went aft to the ladder. Deuce, Rabbit and Cleo stood below near the port side lock. None of them looked up as I climbed down to the main deck and approached the lock. I reached out and touched Rabbit on the shoulder.

"Whatever happens," I said. "Go with Deuce. Do what he says. He'll get you home to Tycho."

Cleo wouldn't look at me. I cycled the lock and stepped in. Deuce secured the inner hatch and I popped the outer one. The ladder extended automatically and I climbed down to the deck.

Kensai didn't move, but the man with the pulse rifle who had been standing next to him started forward. I held up my hands, making sure they both could see the detonator switch in my left. I depressed the button on the top, activating the detonator.

"Stop right there," I said. "This is a remote detonator keyed to a half kilo of Selenite attached to my reactor housing. If I release this button, it'll take out this bay and a good chunk of the station's outer hull."

The rifleman stopped and looked back at Kensai.

"You're bluffing," Kensai said.

"Maybe. Are you ready to find out?"

He paused a second, then waved his man back. "What do you want?"

"Ten minutes alone with you. If you still want to arrest someone after that, I'll give it up, provided you let my crew go."

"I don't bargain with terrorists," he said. "I won't let you hold this whole station hostage." He waved a finger at the man next to him who raised his pulse rifle again.

I held up the detonator. "It's a deadman switch, Kensai. You really don't want to shoot me."

"Damn it, Mbele, stop screwing around."

"Send your man out and talk to me," I said calmly. "Where am I going to go? You don't dare shoot me. You might as well hear what I have to say."

He folded his arms and looked hard at me before jerking his head toward the hatch. The pulse rifleman backed out and the hatch closed and sealed.

"At least now you can't decompress the whole spaceport." Kensai slid his hands into his coat pockets and walked toward me. "Your turn, Mbele. Tell me why I shouldn't shoot you, now that you and I are the only ones at risk here."

I noticed he didn't mention my crew but decided not to bring that up. "Why are you here in force, Inspector Kensai?" I asked instead. "I assume we aren't your primary target."

"No, you're not. At least not yet. In a way, I owe you. Your dossier on Zink's finances opened the door for us. We're rolling up the whole rotten network today. The Minister of Customs and Immigration himself is under arrest." He looked down at the bodies on the deck. "You didn't kill the real Customs agents. What went down here?"

"You saw it on the holofile." I pointed to the nearest corpse. "These goons were trying to break into my ship."

"I saw the first one draw on you. Then I saw you move faster than any human being should move and kill two of them before you hit the ground. Who the hell are you?"

"Just a poor ship driver trying to make a living."

He laughed at that, a harsh barking sound. "Don't hand me that bullshit. You run around picking fights with the likes of Colin Jones and you slice into financial databases that my people have been trying to crack for months. You knew who these guys were. I'm thinking you used to be one of them."

I held out my left hand, palm up. "No black mark. Don't confuse me with one of these animals. I was Martian Special Forces—same boss, different service. Black Ops commandos were Metternich's own personal hit men; Martian Way fanatics to a man. They make the Dragons look like a bunch of schoolyard bullies."

"Why are a bunch of die-hard fanatics here on Highpoint? And why are they after you?" he asked.

"I don't know. The Dragons I understand. I have something Jones wants and I tweaked his nose over it back in Tharsis. Ashok Patel was one of his enforcers. He and a few of his boys jumped us at the entrance to the terminal. You probably ran across them on your way here."

Kensai nodded. "There were enough witnesses to that firefight to give us a clear picture of what happened."

"When we got here, the Customs agents were already dead and the Black Ops goons were setting up the laser torch. You saw the rest for yourself."

"Why is Jones after you?"

"I have Cleopatra Lee. Jones paid her to get Marco Scalzi for the Dragons, but I messed up her play at the food court and Scalzi got away. Jones doesn't give second chances."

He shook his head as he gave me a doubtful look. "Jones wouldn't risk a firefight in a public passageway just to get back at a bounty hunter. And why did he want Scalzi in the first place? Our dossier pegs him as a small time gem dealer."

" He was a slicer for the Feds back during the Reunification War."

"And I was an infantry squad leader. So what? Why would Jones care about his war service?"

"He's not. Scalzi used his slicing skills to break into dormant bank accounts. He found something that's worth a lot to Jones."

"What would that be?" Kensai's tone was impatient.

I didn't answer right away, considering how hard to push Kensai. "Before I tell you that, I need some immunity."

"You're in no position to bargain, Mbele. At least a dozen people are dead because of you. My bosses aren't going to let that slide."

"Come on, Kensai," I said. "You said there were witnesses to the firefight with the Dragons. And you saw how things went down here. Even if you arrest us, it'll be ruled self defense. We'll get misdemeanor weapons charges, pay a fine and that'll be all. Not worth your time or the magistrate's."

"That's not my call," he answered. "What happens at trial is up to the magistrate

"Maybe. But you decide who gets arrested in the first place. And do you want to try to explain where you got the financial dossier on Zink? What will the magistrate do if he finds out where you got your information?"

He looked like he'd just eaten something nasty. "This better be good."

"Then I have my immunity?" I asked. "No arrest, no prosecution based on what I tell you here?"

"You won't be arrested based on anything you tell me now. Hold anything back and there's no deal. Understood?"

I nodded and keyed my link. "Sylvia, get the file Rabbit made from Malloy's notebook and Smolensky's interview. When I give the word, download it to Inspector Kensai's link."

I waited for a second, then went on. "Scalzi found a storage compartment on Delilah that used to belong to Fingal Malloy."

"Fingal's Cave? Give me a break, Mbele."

I held up a hand. "Just listen, it'll make sense. Scalzi had help. A guy named Art Smolensky who backed him with cash and contacts. They opened the storage facility and found a cache of glowgems, a bunch of old equipment and a notebook. Smolensky fronted some cash for Scalzi to peddle the gems around the system. He sold to dealers in Tycho City, Tharsis and here on Highpoint. Made a lot of money, most of which went for equipment and raw materials that were shipped back to Delilah."

"We know about the gems," said Kensai. "No one knew where they came from, but there's no question they were new to the market. Not one of them was tagged."

"That's not the half of it," I said. "What do you know about Fingal Malloy?"

"He was a scientist of some kind, went a little crazy out in the Belt and dropped out of sight for a few years. He showed up on Delilah with a backpack full of glowgems the day before he died. Set off the gem rush and started the legend of Fingal's Cave."

I was impressed and told him so. "Most people only know the story that he was some kind of burned-out prospector."

He smiled. "I used to be a Cave buff. When I was a kid, I dreamed about finding it. I learned everything I could about Malloy. Enough to figure out that there was no Cave, just a sick old guy who made a lucky find."

"Did you know he was a biochemist? Specialized in xenobiology." Kensai shook his head, a spark of interest lighting up his eye. I continued, "Malloy didn't find those gems. He grew them. He figured out a way to culture glowgems. The details of the process were in the notebook that Scalzi found."

"And that's what Jones wants," Kensai said. "No wonder he hired a bounty hunter to track Scalzi down." He looked hard at me. "Where is Scalzi? I know you got him out of here along with Ms. Lee. That must have been an interesting trip."

"Yeah, about that." I looked down at the deadman switch in my hand. Kensai caught the gesture and frowned. "That's another reason I need that immunity deal."

"Better let me have it all," he said.

"Scalzi's dead. He's in my galley freezer." I held up my hands as Kensai exhaled sharply and took half a step forward. "I didn't kill him. He had a falling out with his partner. They fought and Smolensky killed him."

"If you didn't kill him, then why is he in your freezer? And where the Hell is this Smolensky person? Damn it, Mbele. I'm tired of playing games with you. Spill the whole story or you can forget any kind of deal with me."

"Okay, okay. Don't get your knickers in a twist. Scalzi wanted to go to Delilah to pay Smolensky off. Smolensky wasn't there. He'd run off to Tharsis to cut his own deal with Jones. We ran him down on Tharsis before he could talk to the Dragons and brought him back to the ship." I didn't mention the bar on Delilah, or the firefight at the Tharsis spaceport. "I threw Smolensky and Scalzi together, hoping to shake them up and find out where Malloy's notebook was hidden. One of them had it, but neither one was talking."

Kensai's look was doubtful. "You put the two of them together and let one of them kill the other? I thought you were smarter than that."

My face burned with embarrassment. "I had them under surveillance. Besides, they were partners as far as I knew. But there was a glitch in our AI. The surveillance got interrupted. Smolensky killed Scalzi, but not before he took a slow poison needle himself. We bundled Smolensky up in cargo tape and dropped him off at one of Jones' legitimate businesses."

"Why would Jones want a dead body?"

"Because Smolensky's real name was Jaime Pedroia. Even dead he was worth over two million yuan."

Kensai's eyes widened in recognition when I said Pedroia's name. "What was a Martian war criminal doing on Delilah? And why didn't you turn him in yourself, if you knew who he was?"

I shrugged. "Why not Delilah? It's not like he was going

to rent a penthouse here on Highpoint." I didn't go into why I hadn't killed him on sight. "I traded him to Jones after he killed Scalzi. I didn't have the notebook yet and thought I'd get the Dragons off my back in return for a two million yuan payoff. Check your cop updates. I'm sure you have them. It'll show Pedroia is dead or captured."

"If you gave them Pedroia, then why did the Dragons make a run at you outside the terminal?" Kensai asked, still not buying this version of events.

"I don't know. Why don't you ask him? Maybe he still wants the notebook."

"Which I take it you now have?"

I nodded. "That's why I needed Scalzi, or at least his DNA. The book was in a safe deposit box at the Highpoint Trust Bank. You might want to get a few of your boys over there, by the way. I left another of these Black Ops commandos in the vault, sleeping off a needle. They knew I was after the notebook."

"Now, you tell me?" Kensai pulled out a datalink and spoke rapidly into it. He waited a second for a reply and then put the link back in his pocket. "So we're back to these jokers. Are they working for Jones?"

"No, I don't think so. Patel didn't seem to know anything about them. Why would Jones send in his own people if he hired freelancers?"

"But they knew you were after the notebook," Kensai pointed out.

"I think they knew where it was all along. They just couldn't get at it without Scalzi's DNA. Either that or a few kilos of Selenite. I don't know if they knew anything about me, or if they targeted us after we got our hands on the book."

Kensai folded his arms. "That doesn't help me, Mbele. I've got to explain all this to my bosses and what you've given me so far doesn't amount to much more than a bedtime story. I've half a mind to haul you in front of a magistrate right now."

I shrugged and held up the detonator. "We can end this right now if that's the way you want to play it."

He didn't flinch, just stood there looking at me, his arms folded, calling my bluff. "Or?" he asked.

"You let us go and I give you all I have on Malloy, Scalzi and Pedroia, including the process for culturing glowgems. You can do whatever you like with it; but it'll confirm my story. Or, you can try to arrest us and take a chance that I won't blow a hole in this bay, or that a magistrate won't throw out your entire Customs bust because the evidence was tainted. Your choice."

He didn't answer right away. He stood his ground, staring down at the body of the nearest commando. When he spoke, I wasn't sure if he was talking to me or to himself. "You spend a whole career trying to do the right thing. It shouldn't be hard, but it always is." He looked up at me. "All right. You have thirty minutes to get your ship out of my jurisdiction. And if you so much as pass through Highpoint space again, I'll have you blown away. Are we clear on this?"

"Absolutely. Sylvia, download the notebook file to Inspector Kensai."

He nodded to confirm that he'd received the download.

"That information could make you a very rich man, Akira," I said. "But I won't be surprised if it shows up on the public net in the next few days. Then every dreamer with a few spare cubic meters of space will be culturing glowgems for fun and profit."

He smiled wryly. "I'd like to see Jones' face when he finds out."

"I'll have a front row seat for that," I said. "Good bye, Inspector Kensai."

"Get out of here before I change my mind." He turned and stalked toward the exit hatch.

I watched until he left the bay, then disarmed the

detonator. I shook my hand to get the stiffness out of it. I'd been gripping the dead man switch for almost an hour. "Get us a launch clearance, Sylvia. We're getting out of here."

CHAPTER TWENTY-SEVEN

I met Deuce on the cargo deck and handed him the detonator. "It's disarmed," I said. "Get that Selenite off of the reactor housing. We're leaving. And Deuce, be very careful."

He grinned. "You know it, LT."

Rabbit and Cleo were next to the ladder at the rear of the hold. I sent Rabbit up to the cockpit to monitor the arcology security net. Kensai could keep a rein on his own men, but I didn't want to be surprised by a bunch of Customs agents on the make for some sort of redemption. They'd already tried to shake us down once.

"Sylvia, are we cleared yet?"

"Not yet, Boss. Things seem pretty chaotic up in traffic control."

"Call me as soon as we're cleared but launch without waiting for me. I want us out of here before Kensai changes his mind."

Cleo remained standing by the ladder. "You can drop me at your first port. I'll have my things packed and ready.

There's not much anyway." She turned to climb the ladder but stopped when I grabbed her shoulder. "Don't do that. I figured I've paid my way already between Delilah and here. It's been interesting."

I let go of her shoulder, but she didn't move. "I thought you might sign on permanently," I said. "Or at least consider a full share as a crewmate."

She shook her head, not meeting my eye. "No, that wouldn't be a good idea. I'm a solo act, not a team player."

I touched her shoulder again and felt her start to lean toward me, then catch herself and pull away.

"I wouldn't ask for much," I said. "I need you nearby, that's all. It's been a long time since I had anything to live for except revenge. And as you said, vendettas are stupid. Not much of a reason to keep living."

She turned to face me. "I can't, Zack. I need more than a bed and an occasional tumble. I've had that all my life. I need to build something lasting, some sort of security."

"But that's what I'm offering. A life aboard this ship. Being a part of something."

"No, that's not what you really want. You think you need me, but you know nothing about me. You only know that what you've had up until now isn't enough anymore. That's good. But you live like there's no one else in the universe." Her eyes finally met mine. They were filled with tears, but her voice shook with anger, not sadness. "Did you think about Deuce or Rabbit when you brought me on board? Did you think twice, or even once, before you rubbed Patel's nose in it the day we first met? You're reckless, even when you're sober; worse when you drink. The only rest you seem to get is when you're dead drunk or on the jolt. Don't tell me that's a good way to build a future."

I stepped back from her but said nothing.

She shook the tears from her eyes. "I'd like to believe it would work. I really would. But I can't." She climbed the ladder to the second deck and disappeared down the passageway toward her cabin. Still, I said nothing.

I started up the ladder, not really following her, just headed for the upper deck.

Sylvia called as I reached the catwalk. "We're cleared for launch, Boss. They're outgassing the bay."

Kensai may have collected the bodies of the real Customs agents. I doubted he cared about the Black Ops guys. Less to explain if they were vented to space before they attracted official attention.

"Take us out as soon as they open the outer doors. I'll be in my cabin." I caught a glimpse of Rabbit in the salon as I passed, absorbed in his virtual keyboard and the holotank. Just as well. I'd have kicked him out anyway. The spare cabin was empty now that Scalzi was in the freezer. We'd have to do something about that, too, but I wasn't ready to think about it right now.

Rabbit had already moved his stuff out of the cabin. I slumped on the bed, then held on to the grab bar along the bulkhead next to it as the gravity field in the docking bay cut off. I barely noticed the slight sensation of movement as Sylvia took us out under impulse power.

I floated a few inches above the bunk, brooding about Cleo's words. Sure I took chances. You had to if you wanted to make a living as a small freighter. But reckless? She took jobs as a bounty hunter and had the nerve to call me reckless? I knew what I was doing. I was going...nowhere.

"Gravity in thirty seconds," Sylvia announced over the intercom.

I barely noticed as I dropped to the bunk. I sat up, recognizing the truth behind what she had said. For all my maneuvering to make a big score off Jones for the notebook, I'd blown it. If I was lucky, I could cut a deal that would keep us all alive. But I wouldn't see a single yuan of profit. It had taken most of Scalzi's money to replace the induction coils I'd burned out on the run to Delilah. And I'd lost the bounties on Pedroia and Samadar because of my own stupidity. Stupid to kill Samadar in front of witnesses and doubly stupid to leave Rabbit out of the loop on Pedroia.

I crossed the cabin and opened the cabinet above the desk. The bottle of single malt stood there, dark and inviting. I could taste the smoky flavors rolling across my tongue, feel the pleasant burn in my throat and the warmth in my gut. I picked up the bottle, pulled the cork, and inhaled the sharp alcoholic vapors. My hand shook slightly and my mouth went dry with anticipation.

I started to raise the bottle to my lips but stopped. Her words looped over and over in my head—*reckless even when you're sober, worse when you're drunk*. I lowered the bottle and stood staring at it for a long time. Then I put it back in the cabinet and closed the door.

"Boss?" Sylvia called tentatively. "We're clear of the Highpoint zone of control. What's my course?"

"Tharsis. Standard acceleration profile."

"Okay," she said doubtfully. "If you say so."

"Don't give me grief, Sylvia. I'm tired of sneaking around. We're taking this to Jones on his home turf. Tell everyone to meet me in the salon in ten minutes."

I walked slowly to the salon. Rabbit was already there. I nodded to him, but just sat in my chair without speaking. Deuce arrived, looking curious, but caught my mood and crossed to the table. He swung out a metal chair and sat down. Cleo wouldn't meet my eye as she walked in. She sat next to Rabbit and greeted him warmly, which only made him blush and stammer something unintelligible.

"I have a couple of announcements to make and I want us all on the same page," I said once everyone was quiet. "First, we're bound for Tharsis. Jones wants us dead. I figure running and hiding won't put him off the trail for long, so I'm going to take the fight to him. We have the notebook; he wants it. He doesn't know I gave the file to Kensai, and I don't plan on telling him. If I can cut a deal to keep us alive, great. If not, I won't hide until he sends another hit squad after us. He'll take me in a stand-up fight or not or all.

"Which brings me to my second point; Cleo has already asked to get off at our next stop." I looked at her. "You may want to reconsider that, seeing as how it's Tharsis, but if you like, I can put down at Utopia Planetia for a few minutes on our way in. You can catch a shuttle to Tycho from there. Rabbit, you may want to consider doing the same. We're liable to be in a running fight with the Dragons once we hit Tharsis Docks."

"I won't run out on you, Zack," Rabbit said. "I might be able to help."

Cleo didn't answer. I sat waiting, but she looked away.

"What about the Black Ops guys, LT?" asked Deuce. "You figure they're working for the Dragons?"

"I don't think so," I said. Patel had denied it and I had a feeling there's another party interested in the notebook. "We'll worry about them after we deal with Jones."

"So what's the plan, Zack?" Rabbit asked.

"We land at Tharsis Docks like we own the place, then give Jones a call. Offer him the notebook for the right price. No fear, no compromise, no sneaking around. We give him a straight up deal or a straight up fight." Cleo snorted loudly at that. I scowled at her. "You have a better idea?"

"Any idea is better than that. It's suicide."

"You've already opted out of this. What do you care?"

"Let's just say I have a low tolerance for stupidity. Besides, I like Rabbit. I wouldn't want him to get hurt."

I folded my arms. "So how would you handle it?"

"Put Jones in danger. We make him trade his own personal safety for ours. The notebook is just a sweetener. It lets him save some face."

"We?"

She made a face. "All right, I'm in. Okay?"

"You're sure?" I said. "Jones wants to kill you. You can still walk away, let us take the heat; maybe take him out."

She smiled. "He wants to fuck me first. Then he'll kill me. And that's how we'll take him." My face must have betrayed me because she said, "Oh, come on Zack. You think I can't tell. I met him in person. He was with Patel in that warehouse when they sent me after Scalzi. It was in his eyes. He'll try to convince me that he'll let me live if I give in willingly. But if I don't, he'll have his boys strap me down and do it anyway. It's all the same to him."

"So you give yourself up to the Dragons. How does that help us?"

"That depends on Rabbit," she said.

"Me?" his voice squeaked.

She nodded. "Can you come up with a tracker that will let Deuce and Zack follow me but won't be detectable by Jones and his people?"

Rabbit thought for a second. "I may have something that will work. I can rig a carrier wave to your link that'll send out a signal even if they turn the link off. I'll need to access the..."

"Enough, Rabbit," Cleo and I said together.

She continued. "I'm sorry. I wouldn't understand it, anyway. It's just important that it work."

"Oh, it'll work."

"So, we can track you. What then?" I asked.

"I leave the ship as soon as we reach Tharsis. I take the notebook, minus the last page, the part Smolensky, or Pedroia or whatever you call him, destroyed. I offer it to Jones in return for my life. He'll bite. I know he will."

"Maybe. And maybe he'll just kill you, or give you to his boys for a bit of fun."

She shook her head. "Not Jones. He'll want me for himself. And if he kills me, he'll do the job himself. That's part of the thrill for him. He'll make sure whatever happens to me will be personal and private."

"Even if we can track you, he'll be covered by some serious muscle. How are we supposed to get in and force him to deal?"

"I don't know," she admitted. "You and Deuce are good enough to take his guards. Once you're in, he'll keep his guys under control."

"That's not a plan, Cleo," I said. "For this to work, Jones has to believe we'd *kamikaze* ourselves to cut a deal with him. What if he calls our bluff?"

"So what? You were ready to blow up this ship rather than lose it back on Highpoint. Jones means to kill us if we don't get to him first. What have you got to lose?"

Part of me had to admit she was right. I was the one who had invited a stand up fight with the Dragons. But assaulting them on their home turf with Cleo as a hostage didn't sound like a fight we could win. We didn't have the firepower.

"Walking into a meat grinder isn't going to get you out or save the ship," I said.

"But it doesn't have to be that bad," she said. "If I go in alone, with the notebook and with proof that Scalzi is dead, I can try to claim my fee. I'll say that you took me against my will or that I decided you were too crazy to be trusted. He'll buy it. He'll let his guard down and you and Deuce will be able to take him."

"If he doesn't just kill you on sight and take the notebook."

"He won't," she said.

I shook my head. "I don't like it. I don't have a better idea, but this isn't a plan. It's wishful thinking." I checked the time through my link. "We'll be in Martian space in a few hours. There's still time to divert to Planetia, if you want to get off. If not, we'll sit tight at Tharsis Docks and see if Jones comes at us. If he doesn't, then we'll look at other ideas to get at him."

CHAPTER TWENTY-EIGHT

I didn't ask again if Cleo wanted to get off. She stayed in the cabin as we touched down at Tharsis and the tractor 'bots towed us to a berth not far from where we'd been placed the last time. Sylvia confirmed our registration with the Port Authority and paid the docking fee. Then she sent a message to Jones through one of his front businesses telling him where we were and that I wanted to deal. I sat in the command chair and watched the Docks below us.

I'd have been happier with a clearer field of fire to the starboard side, but didn't see a better berth nearby. Asking to move would just attract more attention. I set Sylvia's security screens for ten meters on all sides of the ship. We were in a low traffic area and there were few casual passersby, so I hoped the alarms wouldn't be so frequent that they made us complacent.

I left Sylvia to monitor things and returned to my cabin. She'd put the call through to me if Jones responded. Cleo and Rabbit sat in the salon talking. I glanced in and she smiled at me but didn't stop listening to Rabbit ramble on about link interfaces and carrier waves. I should have realized something was up right then.

Jones didn't answer my message. A bad sign. He didn't even call to make threats, but then, he wouldn't. Guys like Jones only made threats when they wanted something from you before they killed you. To him, we were already dead. It was just a question of how long it would take his boys to do the job.

After two hours, I headed back to the command chair to look over the Docks again. Rabbit and Cleo weren't in the salon. Rabbit was in his cabin, consumed as usual with his gadgetry. Cleo's hatch was closed. I passed it by and headed for the cockpit.

"Situation, Sylvia," I said as I swung through the hatch into the cockpit.

"Quiet, Boss. No response from Jones, no sign of any unusual activity since Ms. Lee left."

"What? Cleo left the ship? Why didn't you tell me?"

"I had no orders to tell you." Sylvia's voice was frosty. "You said to watch for an attack, not watch for people leaving the ship. I assumed Ms. Lee was free to come and go as she pleased."

"Don't give me that crap, Sylvia," I yelled. "You knew the plan. Did she and Rabbit cook this scheme up and get you to go along? Or were you just happy to be rid of her?"

"It wasn't my idea to keep it secret, Zack," she cried. "Edward put an inhibitory command in my surveillance routine. I couldn't say anything about Cleo leaving until you asked for a sitrep."

"Of all the idiotic...RABBIT!" I shouted as I swung through the hatch and stalked across the catwalk. "Rabbit! What the hell do you think you're playing at?"

"Sylvia told you, didn't she?" He peeked out through the hatch of the spare cabin. "It was Cleo's idea. She made me do it."

"She made you do it," I mocked. "How, Rabbit? At

gunpoint? You two looked pretty cozy, last I saw you."

He blushed. "She looked at me, Zack. You know how she does that thing with her eyes. I've seen her do it to you."

I bit back an angry retort. The fact that he was right only made it worse. "Are you at least able to track her?"

"Oh, sure. That was the whole point, wasn't it? The tracking signal uses the locator embedded in her datalink. Even if she turns it off, I can still find her."

"How did she plan to contact Jones?"

"She didn't tell me. I think she had a prearranged comm locus from when she was working for him, tracking Scalzi, you know? She took the original notebook but left the last part, the part you had me record from Pedroia. She said she was also taking proof that Scalzi was dead but she wouldn't tell me what. I was supposed to tell you after she had a two-hour start, but you started yelling before I got a chance to." He paused, searching my face. "You'll be able to get her back, won't you, Zack? She said you were the best she'd ever seen. And Deuce is almost as good. You'll get her back."

"Maybe," I sighed. "Or maybe I'll just lift the ship and head for Tycho. Jones can have her." I saw the stricken look on his face. "Oh, relax, Rabbit. I'll go after her. It was a stupid thing to do, but now she's forced my hand. You may want to get off the ship and find a place to hole up for a while. If Deuce and I fail, we'll be dead and the Dragons may decide to come after you just for sport."

"Let them try," he said. "Sylvia and I can cook up some surprises for them."

I smiled. Maybe they could at that. "How do we track Cleo?"

"I can feed the coordinates to your link. They'll show up on your heads-up map as a red blip. You can follow it straight to her."

"Okay, set it up so I can suppress it if I need to. If she stops, find the address and see if you can access a floor plan for whatever building she's in."

"Will do, Zack. I'll get to work on slicing the Tharsis police and municipal services network. I should be able to access surveillance cameras, building permits, plans, utility hookups, and the like. It may help us find her."

I nodded and he rolled back into his cabin. I went forward and slid down the ladder to the main deck. I found Deuce in his workshop.

"What's up, LT?" he asked as I stepped through the hatch.

"We've got a situation. How far are you willing to go for Cleo Lee?"

"She's in trouble?"

"By now, Jones has her. She set herself up as bait to draw him out. Rabbit rigged her link so we can track her. She thinks we can take him and force him to deal for the notebook."

He exhaled slowly. "You offer her a share?"

I nodded. "I asked her about it just after we left Highpoint. She turned me down."

Deuce shrugged. "Don't see what we owe her, then. You sure she's not just trying to play you? Sell you out to Jones for her own skin."

"I don't know," I admitted. "She worked the tracker out with Rabbit and left the ship without telling me. It's not like she went out of her way to get me on board with this. If she wanted to sell me out, she'd have to be able to guarantee Jones I'd take the bait."

Deuce gave me a wry smile. "But still, you're going after her."

"Yeah, I guess I am."

"I'll get my pulse rifle," he said.

I held up a hand. "Are you sure, Deuce? Like you said, you don't owe her anything."

"She's a shipmate, or will be if you get her back. I guess that's good enough for me."

"Okay. Better take a pneumatic as backup. Maybe a blade or two as well. This could get ugly."

When we got to the weapons locker, Rabbit was waiting above us on the catwalk. "Catch," he said, and tossed a handheld datapad down to me. "That's the tracker. Sync it to your link and keep it with you. It'll send a signal to your heads-up display with an arrow pointing toward Cleo. The readout on the datapad will give you a range."

"Got it," I said. "If we're not back in two hours, get out of here and find a safe place to hole up, understood?"

He nodded but didn't say anything—unusual for Rabbit.

Deuce tapped me on the shoulder and handed me my needler, a pair of throwing knives and a black, long-barreled Huang pneumatic in a belt clip. He had his pulse rifle in his right hand and a 7mm Smith and Wesson pneumatic in a shoulder holster. I still had the short-bladed sheath knife in my boot. I slid the needler into my jacket pocket, clipped the pneumatic to my belt, and strapped the sheaths for the throwing knives to my wrists. We pulled out a half-dozen spare mags for the pneumatics and I pocketed a couple for the needler, black for cyanide. I wasn't playing games anymore.

We descended the ladder from the starboard sally port and set out toward the main terminal. There were no direct routes across Tharsis Docks. Ships, hangers, shanties, and vendor stalls crowded every available space. Paths through the jumble wove this way and that, all radiating from the spaceport gates. The Docks never slept. Any hour of the day or night, people crowded the narrow paths. The smells of frying food, lubricants and human waste mingled with the sharp scents of spices and stale sweat. Music blared from open-air bars and tents marked with the red inverted triangle symbol of registered brothels. No one asked how many of the tents actually bothered to register.

The crowd seemed to sense that we were dangerous. People edged away or lowered their eyes as we passed.

Deuce kept the pulse rifle at low ready, partially covered by a loose jacket draped over his arm. I wore my short garrison jacket. It didn't cover the pneumatic in the belt clip, but the sleeves were wide enough to allow a smooth drop from the wrist sheaths.

Closer to the gate, the structures built up around the grounded ships were taller and more substantial. Some of the ships in these old berths hadn't moved in a generation. The path we followed threaded between a pair of Leviathan class cargo haulers that had been cut in half years before and their decks converted to cheap rooming houses. I stopped and looked down the hundred-meter long steel and plascrete canyon. If the Dragons were looking to ambush us, this would be the place.

Deuce stood at my elbow. "I'm thinking this is a good spot for a bushwhacking."

"Most likely," I said. "We could backtrack and come at the gate from the East path. But there's the crossroads just past the salvage yard. It's just as tight and they probably have it covered, too."

He checked the power level on his pulse rifle and clicked the safety off. "If they've gone to the trouble of planning a party, I'd hate to disappoint 'em."

I moved the needler from my jacket pocket to my waistband, drew the pneumatic and jacked a round into the chamber. I nodded to Deuce. We separated, moving to opposite sides of the narrow passage before starting in. Deuce led the way. I stayed a couple of paces behind so I could keep him in sight and cover his advance.

We moved slowly, scanning ahead and behind as well as overhead. Balconies and overhanging catwalks sprouted from the curved sides of the hulks providing hiding places and firing positions that looked down on the path. We reached the halfway point before they hit us. Four of them stepped out of a hatch ahead of Deuce and blocked the path.

The nanofibers shot out into my muscles and time seemed to slow. Deuce dropped to one knee and brought the pulse rifle to his shoulder. A pneumatic round slammed into the metal wall next to my head. I brought the Huang up, aiming overhead. There were two of them on a balcony above me and two more across the way on a wide catwalk. The catwalk was a better shot and I took it, firing twice.

I hit the first gunman in the chest, two slugs, center of mass. I shifted aim before he slumped to the deck and fired twice more. One slug rang off the railing of the catwalk. The second hit the other gunman in the neck. He dropped his pneumatic with a wet, strangled cry. He coughed, sending a small geyser of blood cascading over the rail to splatter on the deck before he pitched forward and tumbled after it. I dove across the path, rolling on my shoulder to come up facing the balcony.

Deuce fired at the four Dragons blocking our path, oblivious to the pneumatic rounds that bracketed him. He dropped two before the others scrambled for cover in open doorways on either side of the path. I pumped more rounds into the balcony. Plascrete fragments rained down, but the shooters ducked back under cover. I heard the sound of running footsteps behind me but didn't dare turn and lose the shot above me. Deuce kept up a steady fire, pinning down the two remaining Dragons at our front.

The running footsteps closed on me. I slid one of the throwing knives into my left palm, keeping the right, with the Huang, pointed at the balcony. My nano-augmented ears pinpointed the running feet and I thrust my left hand outward casting the knife in a sharp underhanded throw. A coarse grunt followed by a gurgling sigh rewarded my toss.

The shooter above me thrust his pneumatic over the side of the balcony and fired blindly downward. I put a round into his forearm and he dropped the gun. His partner made the mistake of popping his head up and caught a pneumo slug between the eyes for it.

I turned, trusting Deuce to cover my back. My knife had taken one of the Dragons in the gut, just below the breastbone. If he wasn't dead, he was doing a good imitation. A pneumo round plucked at my sleeve. I returned fire forcing the two remaining gunmen at that end of the passage to dive for cover.

"Which way, LT," Deuce shouted.

Combat doctrine said to take the fight to the ambushers. "You lead," I said. "I've got your back."

He fired twice more, forcing the Dragons at his end of the path to keep their heads down, then charged. I emptied the Huang's clip at the two goons behind us, drew the needler and followed Deuce. He cut right as he reached the doorway where one of the gunmen crouched. I cut left and put a needle in the man's chest as he tracked Deuce with the muzzle of his pneumatic. Deuce's pulse rifle crackled and a bolt of coherent microwaves sang past my ear as he dropped the second man.

We dashed into the open plaza that fronted the gate to the spaceport. The last two Dragons didn't follow us. Deuce slowed his pace and looked back while I looked ahead toward the gate.

The Tharsis Port Authority didn't care what happened on the Docks as long as it didn't spill over onto the tourist sections of the spaceport. The casinos and entertainment companies that ran the city were careful to preserve the veneer of safety that kept their marks happy and spending money. I wasn't surprised that the gate guards paid no attention to the fight in the nearby street. But when they studiously ignored the knot of hard-looking men in black jumpsuits walking toward me from the gate, I knew we weren't out of trouble.

"Deuce, front and center," I said as I slapped a fresh clip into the Huang. I held the needler in my left hand and the Huang in my right like some kind of old-time cowboy. Deuce spun around and dropped to a crouch next to me, snapping the pulse rifle to his shoulder.

The men in black approached slowly but casually, as if we presented no threat. The one in the lead raised his arms, hands open, and palms out toward us. After a few more steps, he brought them together and began clapping in slow applause. The other men fanned out behind him until they covered our front from right to left, too many and too far apart to be taken out by the two of us.

"Well done, Zack," said the clapping man. "I haven't seen that crossfire gambit since before the Revolution."

I recognized the voice. "Sanchez? I thought you were dead."

"I thought the same about you until my team on Highpoint turned up dead. As soon as I heard, I said to myself 'Zack Mbele.' Nobody else is that good."

"Don't bullshit me, Roberto. Your guys had the bank staked out. They knew exactly who they were dealing with."

"Not so, Zack. They thought it was Scalzi. The guy we planted in the bank said you had the right DNA signature. *Verdad.* They were looking for Scalzi."

I lowered the needler but kept the Huang trained on Sanchez. He looked heavier than I remembered, but the eyes and that thin moustache were the same. "Since when are you Black Ops? You ran guns and money to the revolutionary cells in Planetia last I remember."

He lowered his hands and shrugged. "Since the Colonel made me see the light. The old order's gonna fall, Zack. The revolution was just a bit premature, that's all."

I laughed at that. "Roberto Sanchez a Martian Way fanatic? That's really funny. Did the Colonel find out about the money you were skimming? Is that when you discovered your devotion to the cause?"

He smiled. "There are many paths to righteousness, *Amigo.*" He pulled back the cuff of his shirt, stepped close to me and showed me the black teardrop on his wrist. "The Colonel was a great man. He used to speak fondly of you."

"Right. He always threw his favorites into Hell. I should be grateful he loved me so much."

Sanchez leaned closer and lowered his voice, ignoring the gun I press into his neck. "Come on, Zack," he whispered. "I know you came out of the Bear with more than you took in. I know about Clancy and Pedroia and somehow, I doubt a bunch of *pendejos* on a backwater asteroid got the drop on Samadar."

CHAPTER TWENTY-NINE

I lowered the pneumatic and stared at him. "What the hell is going on, Roberto?" I asked. "First Samadar, then Pedroia, now you? Tell me Rabbit hasn't been right all along."

"Is he still paranoid? Still seeing Revenants in the closet?" Sanchez laughed. "Maybe he's right, *Amigo.*" He became serious. "Now do you and Deuce want to stand down, or do my boys have to shoot you."

I nodded to Deuce and he lowered the pulse rifle. I holstered the Huang and was mildly surprised when Sanchez made no move to take it from me.

"Stand down, boys," he said to the gunmen. "Zack and Deuce are old friends."

They lifted the business ends of their weapons and pointed them away from our general direction. They didn't exactly lower them, though.

"What's the matter, Roberto?" I asked. "Don't you trust me?"

"Trust is a relative term, Zack. I trust you're not going

to do anything stupid until we have a chance to talk. After that, *quien sabe?*"

I shrugged. "So talk."

"Not here. We have a spot nearby, inside the gate. We'll go there, have a drink or two, and talk about old times. Get reacquainted."

"I haven't got time for small talk, Roberto."

He smiled. "Make time. Jones won't kill Cleo Lee until he knows you're out of the way. I don't think any of the boys he sent after you will be reporting in. My guys are taking care of the ones you missed."

I managed to keep my face neutral. "How do you know about Cleo?"

He smiled. "Let's have that drink, Zack." He raised his hand and signaled to his men. They eased back and put away their guns. Deuce stood and slung his pulse rifle. Sanchez nodded to him. "*Como'sta*, Deuce?"

"Not bad, Lieutenant. You?"

"Still alive, Deuce. Still alive. And it's Major now."

"That so?" Deuce grunted.

Sanchez held his eye for a second, then turned and started toward the gate. I followed, swallowing my questions for the time being. He knew too much about us and our business and that scared the hell out of me.

The black-clad gunmen fell in behind us and we passed through the gate into the spaceport terminal area. The guards nodded to Sanchez and didn't give us a second look. Must be nice to be so well connected.

We walked the length of the passenger terminal, and then turned left along a row of nondescript storage facilities. At the third, Sanchez stopped and motioned toward one of his guys. The man ran ahead and thumbed a print lock next to the oversized door. It rolled up with a screech of metal on metal and we stepped into the darkened interior of an empty warehouse.

The door rolled down behind us, and someone turned on

the overhead lights. Sanchez touched my arm and pointed toward a partitioned room at the rear. Deuce and I followed him as his men began stripping off gear and stowing weapons in lockers along the wall. Scattered across the warehouse floor were several banks of holomatrices, a few tables surrounded by high-backed chairs, two universal exercise machines, and batches of free weights. Along the wall to my left, across from the lockers, was a practice range with firing stations for pneumatic pistols, needlers, and pulse rifles. A metal stairway led to the top of the partitioned room where a row of bunks was visible. These guys were pros, well funded, and well trained. Suddenly, Rabbit's paranoia seemed a lot less crazy.

Sanchez opened the door to the partitioned area and waved Deuce and me in. A large conference table with a built-in holomatrix dominated the center of the room. A bunk, a metal desk, and an oversized locker lined one wall. Racks for weapons lined the others. He pointed toward chairs at the conference table and strode to the desk. He pulled a bottle of McAllen Single Malt and three glasses out of a drawer and joined us.

He poured a couple of centimeters of amber liquid into the glasses and passed one to me, another to Deuce. "To Mars," he said, lifting his glass.

Deuce tossed his drink back in a single gulp. My hand twitched toward the glass in front of me, then I jerked it back. I could taste the alcohol, feel it roll across my tongue. I desperately wanted that drink. Which was why I wouldn't take it.

Sanchez smiled. "What's the matter, Zack? Not your brand?"

"Answers first, Roberto," I said, looking him in the eye so I wouldn't be able to look at the glass. "Who the hell are you guys and how do you know about Cleo Lee?"

"I have sources inside the Dragons," he answered. "Colin Jones is really pissed at you, by the way."

"I'm heartbroken. You didn't answer the first part of the question."

He shrugged. "You know who we are. We're all that's left of the First Covert Operations Battalion, Martian Third Directorate. Metternich's Finest. *Semper Vigilantis.*"

"Metternich's dead. He took the Directorate with him."

"Not all of us. After the war, some of us got out and made it to the Belt. There were certain rally points out there where we managed to find each other." He sipped his drink. "With the Colonel and most of the High Command dead or taken, we were on our own. So we went free-lance. The Dragons have a lot of influence here on Mars, even with the *Federales*, but they needed muscle to run their operations in the Belt. It was a win-win."

"What about Samadar and Pedroia?" I asked. "Were they in charge of the operation?"

Sanchez laughed. "Get real, Zack. Samadar was a martinet with a talent for torture and lining his own pockets. And Pedroia was a twisted psycho with a medical degree. They were liabilities. You did me a favor by killing them."

"Then why didn't you do the job yourself?"

"They had their uses. They were the last direct links to Metternich. Links that were important for the true believers." He smiled. "You were right about me, *Amigo*. I'm no Martian Way fanatic. I go where the money and power lead."

I nodded. "And that leads to Jones."

"It did. Until Pedroia and Scalzi found Malloy's notebook."

"I was wondering about that," I said. "If your team was working for Jones, why didn't Patel know about them? And why didn't Jones know the notebook was in Scalzi's safe deposit box?"

"Because I never told him and Pedroia never knew. As to Patel, after he fired on your ship, Jones ordered us to eliminate him. Jones has other plans for his job. Lee beat us to it, but I'm not complaining." He sipped his scotch and went on.

"Pedroia found out about Malloy's storage locker on Delilah. The stupid bastard thought he could keep it to himself. He didn't tell us and brought Scalzi in to slice it open. But Scalzi was no fool. He cut himself in for a share as soon as he saw what they'd found. He didn't trust Pedroia and went to Samadar for some muscle. That's how Cleo Lee got involved."

"Did Scalzi know who he was dealing with?" I asked.

"Of course. He'd sliced the military database in his former life and knew exactly who they were. He told Samadar what he had and where he intended to hide the notebook in return for a guarantee of protection. Samadar didn't pass that little bit of information on to us until Scalzi had already made it to Highpoint and hidden the notebook. Our only option by then was to place one of my guys in the vault and wait for Scalzi to return. We hadn't counted on you and Deuce, or on Lee being such a pain in the ass."

"So you planned to double-cross Jones all along."

He shrugged, sipping more scotch. "That's a harsh word, Zack. I prefer to think of it as a renegotiation of our agreement. Jones got wind of the gems as soon as Scalzi started to sell them. By the time the Dragons made a run at Lee and Scalzi, Pedroia had already contacted him to try to cut his own deal. With Pedroia dead, the only record of Malloy's process is that notebook. Whoever has it controls the gem market. I mean to have it myself. I'm tired of being Jones' hired hand. Once we control the gems, we'll have all the funds we need to resurrect the Revolution."

"So, we're back to that again, are we?"

"For now." Sanchez winked at me. "The boys outside think that's what I'm about. I shouldn't have any trouble skimming off enough to live out my days in comfort Earthside. I hear it's easy enough to buy citizenship in the old U.S. of A. Especially after I tell the Feds about a nest of real live Revenants here on Mars. I'll be long gone by the time they come to roll up this outfit."

This was the Roberto Sanchez I'd known: devious, cunning, and self-serving. Despite the implications of a network of former Black Ops troops bent on resurrecting the Revolution, here was something I understood. Metternich had seduced the people of Mars with his Martian Way rhetoric, only to leave them battered and broken, sacrificed to his twisted ego. Now Sanchez was repeating the pattern, milking the dreams of his own men for money. I looked down at my untouched drink and knew I no longer needed it. I wouldn't drink with Sanchez to save my own life.

"What do you want with Deuce and me?" I asked.

"Don't be coy, *Amigo*. You're tracking Cleopatra Lee. I don't know how, but you have a way of finding her. You and Deuce wouldn't be out here, armed to the teeth, if you didn't."

"Why should you care about that? Jones will get the notebook, but you're still on his payroll. Why not bide your time and take over the operation once he has the gem cultures up and running?"

He tossed back the dregs of his drink before answering. "Because I don't have the muscle. What you saw outside is all that's left. They're good. But Jones has good men, too, and more of them. Even if I could knock him off, the rest of the Dragons would never follow an outsider." His eyes gleamed with determination. "This is my chance. Take the notebook, use the equipment and supplies Pedroia stockpiled on Delilah and go into business for myself. There are plenty of believers out in the Belt who will flock to a resurgent Revolution. Once we get to Delilah, the Dragons won't be able to stop us."

"What about Cleo?" I asked.

"That's up to you, *Amigo*. The two of you alone don't stand a chance." Deuce shifted in his chair at that and Sanchez raised a hand to calm him. "No offense, Deuce. Just fact. You won't get within a hundred meters of Jones. You just don't have the firepower."

"Whereas you and your men..." I said.

He nodded. "We can't track Lee and Jones. It's a good bet he's got her in one of his safe houses. You can find her and my men can provide the tactical support for the three of us to get to Jones. I get the notebook and you and Lee can do as you please. You could even come with us. You're still known among the faithful. There's a place for you if you want it."

"No, thanks," I said. "I've been screwed once by the Martian Way. I don't need to repeat the lesson."

"Suit yourself. But a cut of the money could set you both up for life. The Way is dead. If those fanatics out there are too stupid to realize it, they deserve what they get."

I looked at Deuce. He shrugged. "Your call, LT. I ain't saying we need his help, but some more guns would make the job a lot easier."

"And after?" I asked.

Deuce spat into his empty glass and stared at Sanchez. "I don't think we should drink with this snake no more."

"I guess that's it then," I said to Sanchez. "You get the notebook and we go our separate ways."

"You always were a fucking *sangron*," Sanchez said. "I don't think I can trust a man who doesn't look out for his own interests."

"I'm not sanctimonious. I've just had a belly full of Metternich's Martian Way bullshit. If it's a choice between staying poor or listening to that crap again, I'll pass on the money."

"*Bien*," Sanchez said with a curt nod. "We're agreed. How are you tracking Lee?"

I looked at Deuce again and he nodded. "Rabbit came up with a way to follow her through her link, even if it's jammed or turned off. We can track her with this." I held up the datapad.

"How does it work?" Sanchez asked.

I laughed. "Hell if I know. Some of Rabbit's slicer magic. It uploads a signal to my link and gives me a directional arrow on my heads up." I blinked twice to activate the display, then pointed toward the back wall. "Cleo's that way."

Sanchez clenched his jaw twice, activating his comlink. "Saddle up, team. We've got a mission."

By the time the three of us crossed the open warehouse floor to the outer door, a half dozen of Sanchez's men were waiting for us. They all held Nakajima pulse rifles. Deuce sighed audibly and I suppressed a smile. He'd wanted a Nakajima for years but the price tag was out of our league. I didn't see Jones paying freelancers enough to afford fancy rifles or a setup like this warehouse. I wondered who else was backing Sanchez.

We crossed the spaceport concourse, Sanchez's men spreading out ahead and behind us, their weapons concealed beneath long black coats. The directional arrow in my heads up display blinked, and then angled downward.

"She's in the tunnels," I said, masking some of my own relief. The casino district loomed high above the spaceport terminal. Searching there would mean a lot of time in the open and attract more attention. Jones might know Deuce and I were coming, but we didn't want to advertise our new partnership until the last minute. Armed men in the mean tunnels where the working class of Tharsis lived wouldn't raise many eyebrows.

Sanchez stayed on my elbow, not quite close enough to touch me, but the message was clear. He didn't trust me any more than I trusted him. This alliance would last only as long as I was useful. I glanced back at Deuce. Two of Sanchez's men walked with elaborate casualness a half pace behind him. We were outnumbered and outgunned and had no choice but to see this thing through.

And why the hell was I here in the first place? I wondered. *Because I had the hots for some woman?* I sighed inwardly. No, it was more than that, and I'd known it from the first moment I saw her. For the past two years, I'd acted alive but had been mostly dead. I'd kidded myself that the jolt and the booze helped me cope with the nightmare that was the Bear, but I knew all along that they were just a way to maintain a state of walking death. Seeing Cleo, touching her and feeling her breath on my face made me want to live. Rabbit was right; vengeance is a lousy reason to go on living.

I took a right just past the terminal and followed the gentle slope of a broad tunnel entrance down one level. The short tunnel opened onto a wide underground plaza. On the far side, was the tube station with capsules ready to whisk passengers into central Tharsis or take them up to Planetia, 1500 kilometers away. To our left were the Beta dropshafts. Upper Beta was the preferred address for skilled workers and the middle class. Lower Beta, on the other hand, was a tangle of cheap hotels where rooms rented by the hour, pawnshops, run-down bars, and dead-end flophouses. Just the sort of neighborhood Jones would pick for a safe house.

Sure enough, the arrow pointed toward the dropshafts, angling downward to vertical as we approached. We commandeered a platform to ourselves and rode slowly down the shaft until the arrow went horizontal at level 18, right in the middle of Lower Beta.

We stepped out of the shaft into a central plaza. Sanchez's men spread out without waiting for orders, covering our entrance and the three wide tunnels that fed into the plaza from the rest of the level.

It had been a long time since I'd last visited Tharsis and couldn't remember if I'd ever been on this level of Lower Beta. I probably had at some time or another, but unlike Alpha Three with its shiny new nightspots or Upper Gamma with its old Martian colonial ambience, Beta Eighteen was depressingly similar to most other down and out areas of Tharsis. *Just like home.*

The overhead lighting panels were spotted with dust and less identifiable substances that cast vague shadows across the open plaza. The floor had once been tiled with a white and red fractal pattern. The tiles were chipped and worn, the red faded to a pinkish orange and the white now a yellowed ivory. Layers of black grime replaced the grout and filled the gaps where tiles were missing. A large flickering hologram ran along one wall advertising 'Chang's Yuan Saver Emporium.' A green arrow pointed to a dilapidated storefront, long vacant. The plaza was empty of people, but the faint strains of music from a bar near the far tunnel entrance showed that the level wasn't deserted.

Sanchez looked at me and I checked my display. I pointed to the far tunnel and we set off across the plaza. I eased the Huang out of its holster and Deuce swung his pulse rifle to low ready. Sanchez flashed hand signals to two of his men and they moved quickly ahead of us into the tunnel.

As we passed the bar at the far end of the plaza, a sudden flash of movement caught my eye. I spun, raising my weapon. Deuce and Sanchez did the same, a half second behind me. The man who had staggered out of the bar stopped short, eyes wide as he raised his hands. One of Sanchez's men rushed up and said a few words in his ear and the drunk took off running across the plaza. I smiled at the situation. We were a real bad-ass bunch, all right. Ambushed by a drunkard. I hoped the Dragons were less stealthy.

The broad tunnel ahead of us branched into three smaller passageways, right, left and center. Typical Martian habitat construction. Apartments and business spaces would line each passageway. At the end there would be an open space in front of a shopping mall or a light-manufacturing center. I'd grown up here, in tunnels just like this one. In my head, I could see the cluttered passageway, the brightly painted doors, the dim lighting panels overhead. The air would be rich with the smells of tightly packed humanity, a mix of spices, sweat, sewage, and cooking oil.

Sanchez glanced at me and I indicated the left tunnel. His team moved forward in two staggered parallel lines, swiftly clearing the passageway ahead of us. With the sixth sense common to all Martian tunnel dwellers, the people around us recognized trouble as we approached and cleared the area. We moved fast.

Two hundred meters in, the lead element of the team suddenly halted and we all took a knee, covering the tunnel ahead.

A few seconds later, one of the point men made his way back to Sanchez. "There's an open plaza fifty meters ahead, Major. On the far side there's a block of apartments. We can see three guards near the tunnel, two more flanking the main entrance to the block. There are oversight windows facing the plaza. Most are closed, but at least three are open and well positioned to provide covering fire for the guards."

"Has your team been spotted?" Sanchez asked.

The man shook his head. "Not yet, but it's certain they've got eyes all along this tunnel. They know we're here."

"Can we take the plaza?" I asked.

Sanchez's man looked at his boss who nodded slightly. "Maybe," the man said. "It'll be ugly until we take out the high cover from those windows."

"No choice," Sanchez said.

"Maybe, maybe not," I said. I keyed my link. "Sylvia?"

"Yes, Boss," her voice was flat but clear. Jones was well guarded but he didn't have any scramblers or dampening fields up.

"Download my position and the info files in my link buffer, then have Rabbit check out the apartment block at..." I glanced at the address readout over one of the doors across from me. "...Green Six Plaza, Level Eighteen, Lower Beta."

Sanchez started to speak, but I held up my hand as

Rabbit came on the link.

"What do you need to know, Zack," Rabbit asked.

"I need a way into the apartment block that fronts onto Green Six Plaza."

"Well, the main entrance is directly across the plaza from the tunnel where you are now."

"Rabbit..."

"I know," he said. "You need another option. There's an access tunnel behind the drop shaft station. It leads to a utility space that circles the entire level. From there you can get to the main air and power feeds behind the apartment block. The inspection panel will be sealed from the inside, but it's only metal plate a few millimeters thick."

I looked at Deuce. He shrugged. "A little Selenite, no problem. It'll be noisy though."

"Jones will have someone on the other side," I said. "I would."

"Need a diversion," said Deuce.

"My guys will handle that," Sanchez said. He looked at his man. "I need two men, make it Lynch and Kanawa, with me. Tell Kanawa to bring his demo stuff. When I give the word, make a show of attacking the guards in the plaza. Engage the high cover in the building, but don't waste men on a full assault. Just keep them busy for a few minutes. I'll signal once we're in." The man nodded and hurried away.

"Rabbit," I said, "What have you got on the apartment block?"

"There are two units each on the two lower levels and a large single apartment on the top deck, five units total. All of them are owned by an outfit called Cardiff Properties. They're owned by..."

"Rabbit, stop," I interrupted. "I just need a floor plan and some idea of where Jones is holding Cleo."

"Oh," he said. "Right. One second—okay, there's a central hallway, two stairwells, front and back, no lift or dropshaft. This must be a really old place, Zack. There is a room for the power and utility feeds below the rear stairs. The access panel is in there. Only the rear stairs lead to the upper apartment. That's where Cleo's signal seems to be."

"Any utility voids or service shafts?" I asked.

"No. Power feeds, air and water are all integrated onto the bearing walls."

I turned to Sanchez. "Only one way up. The Dragons are sure to have a guard in the hall and one on the stairs. Your diversion better be a good one."

Sanchez's two men joined us, and we set off, back down the tunnel and across the main plaza. Behind the dropshaft station, we found the access and entered the utility void. A few minutes of quick walking brought us to the panel Rabbit had described.

Deuce examined it for a few seconds, then held out his hand to Kanawa, Sanchez's demolition guy. "Selenite," he said.

The man reached into a belt pouch and handed Deuce a sealed foil packet about six centimeters square and ten or twelve millimeters thick. Deuce peeled open the foil and a sharp, ammonia tinged odor wafted out. He stripped the foil away from the gray clay-like explosive and began kneading it in his hands. He rolled the Selenite into a ball, then broke it into thirds. Each chunk he then rolled out into a long cord. He pressed two of the cords against opposite sides of the access panel, near the seals. The third, he split in two and stretched the shorter pieces top and bottom across the gap between long ones.

"Igniter," he said, again holding out a palm. Kanawa handed him a small silver disc. Deuce pressed it into the corner of the explosive. "Ready when you are," he said to Sanchez.

Roberto activated his link. "This is Sanchez. Start your attack now." He listened for a second, and then turned to Deuce. "Thirty seconds to get into position, then give them a minute to draw the guards to the front."

Deuce nodded and counted off the time. At ninety seconds he said quietly, "Fire in the hole." He slapped the igniter with the butt of his pulse rifle and averted his face.

Selenite can be detonated in two modes. Send an electrical charge through it and it explodes. A half-kilo of the stuff would collapse the void we were in and a good bit of the apartment block as well. Messy and far more destructive than we needed for this job. Even tiny charges set against the access panel would blow outward along the path of least resistance and do little more than dent the metal.

What we needed was Selenite's second mode of destruction. It's hard to ignite, but once you get it burning it flares hotter than a small sun. It burns out quickly but anything it touches is vaporized. The igniter Deuce planted in the Selenite ropes contained a small magnesium flare, plenty hot to light off the explosive.

White light and thin, acrid vapor filled the air around us. A second later, a two square meter section of the access panel clanged to the deck at Deuce's feet. Deuce already had his pulse rifle up and moved into the opening. Sanchez's guys flanked him.

I drew my pneumatic and motioned Sanchez ahead of me. He hesitated a half second, not wanting me at his back any more than I wanted him at mine. His men were already through the opening, though, and he didn't make an issue of it. He stepped through the gap and I followed. Up ahead, I heard the crackle of Deuce's pulse rifle.

The sounds of a firefight rattled through the front of the hall. Sanchez's men held their weapons ready, facing the sounds, and covering the foot of the stairs. A Dragon with a scorched pulse wound in the middle of his chest lay at their feet. Deuce was halfway up the stairwell, pulse rifle covering the next landing.

Sanchez flashed a quick hand signal to one of his men, the one called Lynch, who nodded and took a knee next to the stairwell, his rifle covering the hallway. I started up the stairs toward Deuce, one eye on Sanchez and his other guy.

Deuce's rifle cracked again. "Clear," he said as he rushed up the stairs to the second level. I followed and found another dead Dragon. Deuce waited just below the landing leading to the top level. He held up a fist as I approached and I stopped. He held up two fingers and pointed up toward the top level, then placed his open hand in front of the two fingers.

I nodded and relayed to Sanchez, "Two guards at the top, behind a barricade. They know we're here."

"How do you want to play it?" he asked. "We need to make a move fast before my guys back off. They can't take this place with a frontal assault and in a few minutes it'll be clear they aren't trying to."

"Any flash-bangs in that belt of yours?" I asked Kanawa as he crouched next to Sanchez.

"Two," he said. "But no launcher. Silas has it for the HE grenades out front. I'll have to set the fuses by hand and toss them over the barricade."

"Do it," said Sanchez. "Deuce and I will cover you. Zack, you hold this flight until Deuce gives you the all clear. I know you won't trust me at your back."

Kanawa nodded and opened the flap on his belt pouch. He drew out a pair of five by two centimeter cylinders. He adjusted a small dial on the top of each one before nodding to Sanchez again. The two of them moved up next to Deuce and spoke to him in hushed tones.

Deuce stood and lifted his pulse rifle to his shoulder. He tapped Kanawa on the shoulder, then stepped around the corner of the stairwell and laid down several bolts from the rifle as covering fire. Kanawa stepped out onto the landing and threw the grenades in an underhand toss. He and Deuce ducked back below the landing, averting their heads away from the grenades.

Even though I had my head turned, the double *thump* and brilliant flash of the detonations made me wince. I waited a half second for the thin smoke to clear, then charged up the stairs after Deuce and Sanchez. Deuce's pulse rifle crackled and hummed over the dull reports of pneumatics and the *snap-ping* sound of a rapid-fire needler. I fired over Sanchez's head at a dark figure behind a low wall at the top of the stairs. A swarm of needles stitched its way up the wall and across the overhead above me. Sanchez dodged to one side. Kanawa wasn't so lucky. He tumbled past me down the stairs, a pair of needles in his neck.

Deuce reached the top of the stairs and vaulted over the barricade. He swept his pulse rifle from side to side before shouting, "Clear!"

I reached Deuce's side a second later. Sanchez had stopped to check Kanawa. He came up to us after a few more seconds and responded to my questioning look with a small shake of his head. He handed the pouch from Kanawa's belt to Deuce. Deuce frowned and slung the pouch from his own belt.

We stood on a landing at the top of the stairwell about two meters wide and half as deep. The barricade, a simple construction of plasteel wall panels, ran across the top step and the outer edge of the landing. An airtight hatch with a central wheel and thick metal dogs at the back of the landing was the only way out of the stairwell. I tried the wheel and was surprised when it moved easily. I'd have expected Jones to lock the inner dogs as an added security measure.

"Don't look like he was expecting company from this side," Deuce said, echoing my own thoughts.

"Or he's got other nasty surprises waiting inside."

"Only one way to find out." Deuce spun the wheel and released the dogs from the hatch coaming.

It swung inward like any good Martian would expect, until it stood half open. I started to push it wider, but Deuce grabbed my arm and pointed toward the deck. A tripwire led from the lower edge of the hatch to a hook in the base of the coaming and then out of sight behind the left hand side of the opening. I peeked around that side and could see a small clump of Selenite stuck to the wall, studded with black tipped needles. A crude but effective booby trap. Deuce pulled a multitool from his belt and cut the wire. With the tip of his pulse rifle he swung the hatch fully open.

We waited a second, but nothing happened. Deuce stepped cautiously through the hatch, pulse rifle ready. I followed and Sanchez came after me. We stood in a utility room about two meters square. Tools and a handcart were stacked against the wall to our left. A pair of well-worn pressure suits hung on stanchions anchored to the right. Straight ahead was a simple plastic and aluminum door, half open to reveal a narrow hallway.

I pushed gently on the door, alert for any resistance that might signal another booby trap. Nothing happened. I started to step forward when I heard footsteps pounding up the stairs behind us. Sanchez spun, leveling his pneumatic at the landing, but jerked it upward when Lynch's head appeared above the barricade.

"Trouble, Major," said Lynch. "Half a dozen men on the landing below. They found the first guard and are starting up."

"Right," Sanchez said. "Join us in here; we'll dog the hatch and jam the wheel. It should buy us some time."

"We need to move, LT," Deuce said. "They'll be bringing a cutting torch when they find the dogs locked down. Won't take more'n a few minutes to burn through that hatch."

I followed Deuce into the hallway as Sanchez and Lynch secured the hatch. Lynch took up a position next to the utility room door, covering the sealed hatch. We moved down the hall, past several closed and locked doors. The hallway ended at a large door made of real wood bound with shiny metal strap hinges. Deuce stood off to one side and behind me while Sanchez moved to the left of the door, opposite the hinges and stood with his back to the wall. He nodded.

I reached out and tried the door handle. It moved easily and I pushed the door open with my foot, covering the room beyond with the Huang pneumatic. Sanchez swung low, under my line of fire and rushed into the room, angling off to the right. I followed, angling to the left and Deuce stepped into the doorway, sweeping back and forth with his pulse rifle.

"It's about time you got here, Zack," Cleo said. She sat in a plush armchair on the far side of the room. The floor was covered with a thick carpet, steel gray in color. Recessed glow globes scattered across the overhead cast sharp cones of light on other chairs, a wide desk, and a few holomatrices. Cleo's chair stood apart from the rest of the room's sparse but comfortable furniture. At first she seemed to be lounging comfortably in it, but a second look showed me the shackles on her ankles attached to a heavy bolt set in the floor. She could stand, but her feet had only a few inches of room to move.

I started toward her but stopped at the sound of another voice.

"Not so fast, Mate." Jones emerged from the shadows behind Cleo, a black 9mm Berretta in his hand. Both Deuce and Sanchez moved to cover him, but he barely twitched. He smiled at me and kept the gun leveled at Cleo's head.

CHAPTER THIRTY

I brought my Huang up to cover him. "Drop the gun, Colin. You can't get us all."

"Don't have to," he said. "Just Cleo here. This gun's an antique. Old fashioned cordite and lead shells. It'll make a hole the size of a man's fist. I'd hate to see that happen to your woman here."

"Shoot her and we'll drop you before you can take another breath."

He shrugged. "Maybe. But it won't bring her back. Now I'm thinking that you and Roberto went to a lot of trouble to get at me. You, I can understand. I've got your girl and the notebook. You've got nothing left to trade. So you think you can force me to a bargain for my own safety. But what's in it for Roberto, eh?" He cast a sidelong glance at Sanchez. "How about it, Roberto? You figure to take the notebook and go into business for yourself? Maybe take me out and step into my shoes?"

Sanchez laughed at that. "Just the notebook, Colin. Your boys would never follow me, anyway. Call off your men. My unit will stand down. I take the book and we part ways."

"And Mbele?"

"He knows he's welcome to join me," Sanchez said. "Deuce and Cleo, too."

Jones looked me in the eye. "You trust this bitzer?"

"Not exactly," I said. "But Cleo didn't give me much choice. Alone, I didn't have the firepower to get this far."

Jones chuckled. "He'll cross you, too, Cobber. Maybe better you shoot him and deal with me."

"I can't do that, Colin. Not while you've got that gun jammed in Cleo's ear."

"That's the way of it, isn't it? Martian standoff. I'll tell you what, you drop yours, and I'll promise not to shoot Cleo."

Sanchez laughed again. "How about if I shoot you? I don't give a shit about the woman. You're dead, I get the notebook."

"And I burn your lying head off," Deuce said, his pulse rifle suddenly shifting to cover Sanchez.

"Zack, call off your dog," said Sanchez, keeping his gun on Jones.

"Stand down, Roberto. Everybody just stand down." This was spinning out of control. My nanos tingled and my time sense seemed to slow. Sanchez was shifting his stance, settling his weight to take a shot. Deuce sighted along the pulse rifle, anticipating Sanchez's next move. Jones shifted his gaze from me to Sanchez and back again. I caught Cleo's eye. She smiled and winked at me. I saw the muscles of her legs tense. *Shit, here we go.*

"Colin," I said. "Look, I'm putting up my gun." I raised the Huang to point at the overhead and took my left hand away from the hilt.

"What about your friend?" he asked, jerking his head toward Sanchez.

The movement caused his gun hand to waver. That was the opening Cleo needed. She drove her legs down, pushing the chair backwards into Jones and knocking him slightly off balance. Her hands swept up and grabbed the gun. She twisted it down and away, rolling his wrist outward so that she could shift her right hand up to his elbow. She lurched forward and pulled Jones off his feet and over her shoulder. They ended up on the floor with Cleo on top, pressing the Berretta under Jones' chin.

Meanwhile, I stepped into Sanchez line of fire and swung the Huang down to point at him. "I said, stand down, Roberto." I kept my voice low, just above a whisper.

Sanchez looked me in the eye, then glanced at Deuce. He lowered his gun and eased his weight back on his heels. I nodded to Deuce and he lowered the pulse rifle.

"Cleo," I said, not taking my eyes or my gun off Sanchez. "Where's the notebook?"

"On the desk. Along with the key to these shackles."

I smiled. Even chained to the floor, she was a dangerous woman. "Go get it, Roberto. Take the notebook and get out of here before the Dragons send someone up to check on the Boss. And toss me that key on your way out."

"What about you?"

"We're going to do a little more business with Colin here." I saw him hesitate. "Just take the book and go. Do it! You can still get out the back, but the window's closing."

He looked from me to Jones. Then he crossed quickly to the desk and picked up the notebook. He glanced through it for a second before tucking it into his jacket and snatching up the key to the shackles.

"Come with us, Zack," he said. "The Belt's wide open. Once we get the gems going, these bastards won't be able to touch you."

"Just toss me the key, Roberto," I said. "Then you can go screw yourself."

His face hardened and he flicked the key at me. "You really are a fucking *sangron*. See you in Hell, soldier."

I watched him leave, then motioned for Deuce to cover the door. I walked over to Cleo and Jones, bent down, and unlocked Cleo's shackles. I covered Jones with the Huang as Cleo rubbed her ankles and got to her feet.

"You alright?" I asked her.

"Of course," she said. "You took your own sweet time. I was beginning to think I'd have to take this joker alone."

"Hear that, Jones?" I said. "You're lucky I got here when I did."

"You're dead. You know that, don't you, Cobber?" Jones said in a matter-of-fact tone.

"Aw, now, Colin," I waved him up and into the chair with the muzzle of the pneumatic. "Don't be that way. I just did you a favor."

"Spare me any more favors," he grunted. "That notebook was worth millions."

"In a few days, it'll be worthless. By then, the formula for culturing glowgems will be all over the public nets. You'll just look foolish if it gets out that you spent a lot of money to get that book."

"You're lying."

I shrugged. "Have it your way. The files are with a cop friend of mine. I expect he's already talking to the media."

His eyes narrowed. "Okay, say you're telling the truth. Why? Why would you put the formula out there?"

"Would you have believed me if I told you that I didn't make my own copy of the notebook before giving it to you? That would be stupid of you and I know you're not stupid. You'd have to make sure you had a monopoly on the gems. So there's no way you could leave us alive."

He nodded. "You think I won't kill you now? After you've double-crossed me and shot up my property?"

"You might. But there's no percentage in it for you. There's no secret to protect, so killing us is personal. And, as Cleo is constantly reminding me, vendettas are bad business."

"This isn't just business. I didn't get where I am by letting people make me look weak."

"Maybe," I conceded. "But who knew about the book and

your deal with Cleo? You and Patel for sure. Me, Deuce and Cleo; maybe one or two of your guys who you'd trust not to talk. Nobody else." I paused. He glared at me but didn't argue. "Patel is dead. And from what Roberto told me, you're not exactly broken up about that. You're own guys won't talk or question you. If they did they wouldn't last long. That leaves us. We've got just as much incentive to keep quiet as you have to kill us."

He didn't answer right away, just sat there, tapping his tented fingers against his chin. When he finally spoke, it was in that same matter-of-fact tone. "Patel crossed the line when he took a shot at your ship off Highpoint. It cost me half a million in bribes to keep the *Federales* off my back. He needed to be replaced." He paused for a moment, and then looked at Cleo. "You took him out?"

"He touched me," she said, her voice a low snarl.

Jones held up his hand. "Not my doing, lady. Just confirming what Sanchez told me." He turned back to me. "So I'm supposed to give you a pass on the notebook and and on shooting up my men and my property in return for taking care of Patel? I was only going to pay Sanchez a hundred large for that. Doesn't seem like a fair trade to me."

"Even if I throw in Sanchez?" He cocked his head at me. "Come on, Colin," I said. "You know you can't let him get away. At the least, he knows about your play for the notebook. And he won't be shy about talking, even if the notebook ends up being worthless. If he mentions Pedroia and Samadar, even the Feds might get interested."

"What do you think you're on about? Why should I care about Sanchez?"

I hardened my voice. "Don't try to bullshit me, Colin. You were ready to kill me over the book. And Sanchez knows a lot more about your operation than that."

His eyes narrowed. "And what do you think you know?"

"I know the Dragons made a business of smuggling war

criminals out of Tharsis after Reunification." I saw a slight flicker of alarm in his eyes and made a sudden connection. He'd call my bluff if I was wrong, in which case I'd have to kill him and hope we could shoot our way out of here. But I didn't think I was wrong. "How else did Samadar, Pedroia, and Sanchez end up on a backwater asteroid where the Dragons have a major base of operations? Delilah's mines played out years ago. Someone is keeping the economy propped up out there. Why not you? I think the Feds would pay a lot for that bit of information."

He shifted in his chair and I knew I'd guessed right. "What do you want?" he asked.

"I'll forget what I know about Delilah and guarantee that Sanchez is neutralized. You guarantee my safety. No one comes after me or mine."

"Sanchez is long gone by now. How are you going to get to him?"

I didn't answer him but keyed up my link instead. "Sylvia," I said once the link was open. "Put Rabbit on the comm."

"Yes, Boss."

A second later, Rabbit answered, "Here, Zack. Is everyone okay there?"

"We're golden, Rabbit. Did you get the audio file I uploaded the last time we talked?"

"Sure, Zack. It cleaned up real nice. You can hear everything clearly because I ran it through..."

"Good," I interrupted before he got carried away. "Were you able to slice Sanchez's tactical net?"

"Of course." His tone was smug. "I had it before you hit the dropshaft for Lower Beta."

I should have known. "I want you to broadcast the audio file over his net so all of his troops can hear it. Also send it to a comm locus I'll give you." I looked at Jones. He gave me a string of numbers and I repeated them to Rabbit.

"Will do, Zack. Coming on line in five seconds."

A few seconds later there was a slight hiss as a speaker near the desk activated. Then Sanchez's voice could be heard loud and clear as Rabbit played back our earlier conversation.

"Whoever has it controls the gem market. I mean to have it myself. I'm tired of being Jones' hired hand. Once we control the gems, we'll have all the funds we need to resurrect the Revolution."

"So we're back to that again, are we?" I heard my own voice ask.

"For now. The boys outside think that's what I'm about. I shouldn't have any trouble skimming off enough to live out my days in comfort Earthside. I hear it's easy enough to buy citizenship in the old U.S. of A. Especially after I tell the Feds about a nest of real, live Revenants here on Mars. I'll be long gone by the time they come to roll up this outfit."

The audio cut off and I smiled at Jones. "I don't think Sanchez's men will be very happy with him after this. I'll be surprised if he survives the day."

Jones' sat open-mouthed for a second, and then he howled with laughter and slapped his knee. "I like you, Mbele. You are one devious son of a bitch."

"Just looking out for myself. I'm strong on self-preservation." I folded my arms and held his eye. "And yeah, I can be a real son of a bitch. Do we have a deal?"

"Okay, I agree. You walk away. I let you live and none of my boys will come after you." His tone changed to one of quiet menace. "But don't ever try to play me again, eh?"

"No fear, Colin. You stay away from me and I'll stay out of your business."

He nodded. "You're a smart lad, but you've got too much sand for your own good. It makes you reckless. Another place, another time, I might be able to use that.

"You offering me a job, Colin?" I asked.

"Not bloody likely," he said. "Now get out of here before I forget that we have a deal."

Deuce led the way. Cleo ejected the clip from the Beretta and cleared the chamber before handing it back to Jones. He acknowledged her with a short nod of his head. I handed her my needler and she followed Deuce.

"Call off your men, Colin," I said as we reached the door. "I don't feel like fighting my way out of here."

CHAPTER THIRTY-ONE

We left through the front door this time. True to his word, Jones called off his goons. That didn't stop them from giving us threatening looks as we passed through the gauntlet of armed men near the door.

Sanchez's men were long gone. We crossed the plaza and wound our way through the tunnels to the dropshaft without seeing anyone. Not even a cop. Jones must have had a tight lid on this area to keep a major firefight off the nets.

In spite of Jones' assurance, we kept a sharp watch on the crowds as we made our way across the spaceport and through the Tharsis Docks. I wasn't concerned about the Dragons themselves. Jones would have tight discipline with his soldiers. But for every Dragon, there were a dozen wannabes, and maybe a few who thought they could earn their tattoo by taking us out.

The need to watch our backs limited our talk to a few words here and there, which was fine with me. I was still too angry with Cleo to trust myself not to take her head off. She'd played me again and, damn me for an idiot, I'd let her. She and I would have words when we were safely aboard the *Profit*. And Rabbit would have some answering to do, too.

Either we looked threatening enough to scare away any attackers, or I was being needlessly paranoid. We made it back to the ship unmolested.

I gave Sylvia the release code and she popped open the starboard sally port. Deuce mounted the ladder two steps at a time and disappeared into the ship. I stood aside to let Cleo follow him. Instead, she turned to face me.

"So, Zack," she said quietly. "Where do we go from here?"

"Just get aboard," I said. "I'm too tired to fight with you, right now."

"What do we have to fight about? I just want to know where I stand. Am I your prisoner? Your lover? Something in between?"

"How the hell should I know?" I exploded, the pent up anger and anxiety of a long day spilling out. "You've been playing me like a fiddle since Highpoint. You and Rabbit cook up this vacuum-headed idea that could have gotten us all killed and now you want to know where you stand? That's almost funny."

"I'm not laughing," she said calmly. "I did what I thought I had to do. Maybe I was wrong, but would you have stepped up for me if I hadn't made a play for you?"

I laughed bitterly at that. "So that's the currency you trade in. And I thought I'd earned a little respect, if nothing else." I looked away. "What would you have done if I'd just lifted ship and abandoned you here? Jones had you and the notebook. He would have found out it was worthless soon enough. You'd be dead or worse, and I'd be free and clear."

"I don't believe in anything worse than dead. I've seen too much. I'd find a way to survive."

"I'll bet you would," I muttered.

"And why do you care?" She shrugged. "I'm no good. I know it. You should, too. And yet you did come for me. So I'm asking, what do you want?"

What did I want? I wanted a reason to go on living; something beyond the drive for revenge. For the better part of two years, I'd been fueled by vendetta and regret. Cleo had changed that. She was infuriating, mysterious, and alluring all at the same time. She pushed me and played me and made me do things I knew I'd regret. But I was alive and, for the first time since the Bear, felt something more than guilt and anger. And I knew I wanted that feeling to continue.

"I told you what I wanted once before," I said. "You turned me down. Said I was 'reckless,' worse when I was high." I reached out and took her hand. She didn't pull it away, which I took as a good sign. "I meant what I said then. I still do. No more jolt, no more booze. Just say you'll stay with me."

She flashed those incredible eyes at me and smiled slightly. "I think I can live with that." She squeezed my hand, then turned and climbed the ladder to the sally port leaving me staring after her.

I shook my head and started to follow her. The hard, round business end of a pneumatic being jabbed into the middle of my back stopped me.

"That was sweet," Sanchez said in my ear, his voice full of sarcasm and gloating. "But stupid. You're so hot for that whore that you got careless. There's no way I should be able to get the drop on the great Zack Mbele."

"What do you want, Roberto?"

"I want you dead," he answered. "But that will have to wait. I need you right now. You're going to get me off Mars and take me home to Tycho with you."

"And why would I do that? Especially if you mean to kill me anyway."

The pressure of the muzzle on my back eased and the

nanos shot through my muscles, ready for action. I knew I could turn and deflect the gun before he could pull the trigger.

"Because you owe me," he said. "Without me, you'd never have gotten within fifty meters of Jones. I was ready to offer you and your people sanctuary, and you spat in my face."

I laughed at him. "As if you'd have let us live once we got to the Belt. You're a snake, Roberto."

He nudged me in the back with the pneumatic. "And you're going to get me out of here. Either that, or I shoot you down here and now. I've got nothing left to lose."

I tensed slightly, focusing on the muzzle pressed between my shoulders. Time seemed to slow as my reaction time spiked. I spun to my left, my elbow whipping around to deflect the gun as I lashed out and drove my right fist into his gut just below his breastbone. A pneumatic slug whistled past my ear as he bent almost double with a grunt. I grabbed the gun and twisted it out of his hand.

He slumped to the ground clutching his abdomen and breathing in short wheezing gasps.

I stepped back and covered him with the pneumatic. Call it instinct; call it hyper acute hearing or augmented peripheral vision. Something made me duck just as a plasma rifle bolt crackled over my head and dissipated across the *Profit*'s hull. I crouched, raised the pneumatic, and returned fire as more bolts bracketed me. There were three of them, spread out across the small open space in front of the ship. They'd chosen good cover and had a clear field of fire over the whole area.

"Zack, what's going on out there?" Sylvia's voice was tinny over my link, partly scrambled by the stray microwaves zipping past my head.

"A little help out here," I shouted as I fired the pneumatic at the nearest gunman. A shout of pain told me I'd at least winged him. He sent another bolt my way, just to show he wasn't hurt too badly.

I stood up and hauled Roberto up by his left arm. He was almost dead weight. I cursed as I noticed the blackened cloth and skin at the base of his spine where a bolt had hit him.

"Can't move my legs," he gasped. "The *chingadores*, I can't move my damn legs."

Deuce appeared in the sally port and laid down a rapid barrage of covering fire from his pulse rifle as I hoisted Roberto into a fireman's carry and climbed the ladder. A final shot from behind tugged at my left sleeve and ignited the cloth of my jacket. I ignored it until I had Roberto safely on the deck in the cargo bay and Deuce slammed the sally port closed. Deuce came over and beat out the smoldering sleeve with his hands.

"You okay, LT?" he asked.

"Golden, Deuce. But Sanchez took one in the back. I need you to check the rear hold, make sure everything's buttoned up tight. Then break out weapons and ammo for Cleo and Rabbit." He nodded and headed aft. "Sylvia, open up the autodoc. Major wound protocol."

Cleo slid down the ladder from the upper level and crossed the deck to kneel next to Roberto. She produced a hypospray from her pocket and pressed it to his neck. He stiffened for a second, then his eyes glazed over and he relaxed, breathing more easily.

"Duramorph," said Cleo as she pocketed the hypo. "He'll be out for a few minutes. Where's your autodoc?"

"In the salon, aft bulkhead."

"I'll help get him up there," she said, moving to his feet. "We need to move him while he's still out."

"I can manage," I said, feeling the nanofibers augmenting my muscles. There'd be pain afterwards, but the two of us trying to climb the ladder with Sanchez slung between us would take too long. "Go up and prep the autodoc. You know how to run the setup sequence?"

"I've run major wound protocols before," she said quietly.

"This one doesn't look good."

I nodded and bent to haul the now inert Sanchez into the fireman's carry again. My back protested and my knees creaked as I started up the ladder after Cleo. By the time I reached the salon I was panting.

Cleo had the hatch open and the startup sequence running by then. I laid Sanchez on the contoured treatment bed, stripped off his clothes, and attached the sleep inducer to his forehead.

The 'doc took over at that point, sliding tubes and wires into his body as it beeped and twittered at us. The hatch hissed closed and the tank began to fill with the warm, nutrient-laden fluid that the tissue repair 'bots needed to work their magic.

I watched for a second, but had to turn away as memories of my own time in a biotank flooded through me. I leaned against the bulkhead until the deck stopped spinning and managed to get a grip on the nausea that rose in the back of my throat.

Cleo touched my arm. "Are you all right?"

"Yeah. Just tired," I said. I didn't look at the autodoc as I turned away toward the passageway. "Go down to the main deck and get a weapon for yourself and one for Rabbit. He favors a needler. Deuce will tell you where to set up to cover the forward hatch. I'll check the situation from the cockpit."

She nodded and slid down the ladder to the main deck. I crossed the catwalk to the cockpit.

"What have you got, Sylvia?" I asked.

"Besides the three men who attacked you and Mr. Sanchez, there are three others with high-powered pulse rifles covering the rear of the ship. They're concealed but I can track the energy signatures of the power packs in their weapons."

"Black Ops squad," I muttered. *Who was backing these guys?* I didn't buy Sanchez' story about freelancers looking for a big score; this stank of the Third Directorate. But the Directorate was dead. Reunification and the war crimes trials had driven a stake through its black heart. *So how come a Black Ops death squad was running around loose on Tharsis Docks?*

"Call the Port Authority," I said. "Tell them we're under attack."

"We're being jammed," Sylvia replied. "All networks and comms. I'm trying to bypass it, but it's a high quality jammer."

"Why am I not surprised? Has anyone hailed us yet?"

"No."

"They will. Call me when they do." I left the cockpit and found Rabbit in the salon. Cleo had retrieved a needler for him and he was just sliding the magazine into the grip as I entered.

Cleo stood by the autodoc, checking Sanchez's vitals. She frowned and shook her head at my inquiring look. She had her stun batons tucked into her belt and a pneumatic slung from a shoulder holster next to her left breast. She wore it the way most women would wear a scarf—just another fashion accessory.

"I need you to help Sylvia," I said to Rabbit. "We're being jammed by some high-end equipment and I want you to find a way to cut through it."

"Okay, but who's doing the jamming? Knowing who they are may help figure out what algorithms they use."

I hesitated a second. "Try Third Directorate protocols."

"Revenants," he whispered. "Sanchez led them to us."

"Maybe. I'm tired of arguing with you about them. There's a Black Ops death squad outside covering us with pulse rifles. They can't get in, but we can't get out. And with the jamming, we can't call for help. If they're jamming us, they're probably using gear they salvaged after the war."

He rolled past me toward the cockpit. "Does this mean you'll start believing me?" he asked.

"I'll believe in Santa Clause if it makes you happy. Just cut through the jam."

Before he could reply, Sylvia chimed on my link. "We're being hailed, Boss."

"Put them through." The link chimed again and I said, "This is Zack Mbele. Who are you and why are you jamming my comms?"

"Who I am isn't important. You're holding Roberto Sanchez. We want him."

"He's in no condition to move right now, thanks to you."

"Not your problem. Turn him over now and no one else gets hurt."

I glanced at Cleo. She was only hearing my half of the conversation, but the question was obvious. She shrugged and waggled her hand in an uncertain gesture.

"Sanchez isn't going anywhere," I said. "As long as he's wounded and aboard my ship, he's under my protection. If you want him, come and get him."

The connection went dead. Not a good sign. But buttoned up like we were, I didn't see how they could get at us without a laser torch, or some really heavy artillery.

"Monitor the troops outside, Sylvia," I said. "Any luck with the jam?"

Rabbit came on the link. "Not yet. You were right. They're using a Third Directorate algorithm, but they changed it just enough that I don't recognize it. This could take a while."

His voice trailed off, the first time I'd ever heard Rabbit be brief. With a difficult enough problem to solve, he might even be mute.

"Keep an eye on our patient," I said to Cleo. "I'm going down to back up Deuce and make sure the rear hold is secure."

"I still don't get you, Zack Mbele," she said. "You could drop Sanchez out the forward hatch and be off to Tycho within the hour. Instead you get a sudden fit of honor? 'As long as he's aboard my ship he's under my protection,'" she intoned. "Where did that come from?"

"I wouldn't turn a dog over to the Black Ops. And I hate dogs." I shrugged. "Until he can speak for himself, he's my responsibility. Burden of command; you wouldn't understand."

She touched my arm as I turned to leave the salon, stopping me. "I do understand. And it suits you."

Before I could say anything, the alarm claxons sounded. I turned and dashed to the catwalk above the cargo hold. The bow ramp was slowly descending toward the ground and the cargo lock was wide open.

"Sylvia, what the hell are you doing?" I shouted.

"It's not me, Boss. They have some kind of override program. I can't stop it."

"Shit." *Profit* had started her life as a warship. It figured that there was some sort of override hardwired into her systems and that the Directorate would know it.

Deuce stuck his head out from behind a barricade of cargo boxes under the ladder from the main deck. "I dogged the emergency hatches to the aft hold, LT. They'll need a cutting torch and a couple of hours to cut through from back there."

"Good job, Deuce," I said as I drew my pneumatic and checked the magazine. "Cleo! We need some cover out here." No answer. "Cleo?"

Rabbit rolled out of the cockpit. "The override is hardwired, Zack," he said. "I can't slice it fast enough to stop them."

"Never mind. Go to the salon and relieve Cleo. Keep an eye on Sanchez in the autodoc and sent her out here to cover Deuce and me."

He nodded and rolled across the catwalk. I hooked my arms and feet around the handrails and slid down the ladder to the main deck. The forward ramp was almost level with the deck and descending slowly toward the ground. I didn't see anyone outside waiting to rush us, but didn't doubt they would as soon as the ramp touched down. I moved to the port side of the hold, opposite Deuce, and dragged a couple of cargo boxes away from the bulkhead to form a firing position.

"Zack, she's gone," Rabbit shouted from the catwalk behind me. "She's not in the salon."

Damn! What the hell was she playing at now? "Never mind," I called. "Get back to the salon and keep an eye on the autodoc."

His reply was drowned out by the sizzling crackle of pulse rifle bolts striking the bulkhead just above my head. Deuce returned fire from my right. I fired blindly over the top of my makeshift barricade hoping to force someone to move and give Deuce a target. More bolts hummed and sent lightning dancing across the cargo box in front of me. Electric ice shot up my arm where my bare flesh had touched the metal. I jerked back and shifted the pneumatic to my left hand.

My vision shifted to infrared as the nanos augmented my optic nerve. A bloom of body heat off to my right caught my eye. I raised the pneumatic and fired. The slugs punched through the thin plastic packing crate the gunner was using for cover. He dropped with a shout of pain; whether dead or wounded, I couldn't say.

I heard a dull thump followed by the clatter of metal on the deck. Green vapor gushed from the small round grenade that had landed in the middle of the cargo bay.

"Sylvia," I shouted. "Purge the lower deck, now!"

The gas crept along the deck toward me and billowed up in the center of the hold. A whiff was enough to bring burning tears to my eyes and churn my stomach up with violent nausea. Any more and I'd be on the deck vomiting my guts out.

"Sylvia," I croaked. She didn't answer, but I could hear the rush of air from the vents above me and felt the pop in my ears as the pressure rose in the hold. The gas began to thin and flow out toward the open airlock. A dark figure wearing a gas mask loomed out of the greenish mist and swung the business end of a pulse rifle toward me. I brought up the Huang, but even with my augmented reflexes I knew it was too late.

Deuce's rifle crackled and the dark figure went down and disappeared into the greenish fog.

The gas gradually cleared and we could breathe easier.

"Everything Jake with you, LT?" Deuce called.

"Golden, Deuce. You okay?"

"Got a whiff of gas. My guts are in a knot but no real damage done. What's our next move?"

I considered that for half a second. "I figure they're down by two. That still makes it four to two, and they may have more gas to toss at us." The tactical situation hadn't changed all that much. We may have taken two of their guys out of action, or maybe not. If we could button up the ship, they couldn't get in without heavy artillery. But with the forward lock open, they could hit us in force or try to pick us off piecemeal.

"Sylvia," I said over my link. "Can you still track their positions?"

"Yes, Boss. At least within ten meters of the ship. There are four that I can detect, all of them just beyond the forward ramp."

"Download the image to my eye camera."

A second later, the heads up display in the camera in my left eye lit up. Four green spots glowed against a schematic image of the bow of the ship. Two of them flanked the ramp, just out of sight from where Deuce and I covered the airlock. The other two were about five meters away, flanking and covering their counterparts. We were bottled up. If we tried to rush the two closest to us, the other ones would get us.

The guys outside would have to make a move soon. The authorities tended to ignore what happened on the Docks, but a serious firefight was bound to attract attention, even from the Tharsis cops. It might take a while, but eventually they'd show up with a combat team to restore the status quo. The problem was, they wouldn't make much distinction between the Black Ops squad and us.

"Sit tight a second, Deuce," I said. "They've got two on either side of the ramp, and two more in covering positions. That leaves two more. We may have gotten them already, or they may be hiding out of Sylvia's range."

"Can't sit still, LT. Gives them all the advantage."

"I know that, damn it." I measured the distance to the ramp in my head. Then I gauged the distance to the second pair of gunmen. The geometry didn't work. We'd be dead before we could get a shot at either of them.

"Sylvia," I said. "Is there anyone at the aft airlock?"

"Not with active pulse rifles. And I don't see anyone on any of my external sensors."

Deuce grunted, his way of pushing me to make a decision.

"Undog the emergency hatches and go through the aft hold," I told him. "See if you can flank them on the right. I'll cover things from here until you're in position."

He didn't answer, but I could hear the metal grating of the hatch dogs as he turned the wheel to release them. I rechecked the positions of the four men outside. The green dots marking their pulse rifles hadn't moved. I heard a dull *thunk* as the dogs released and the hatch unsealed. Suddenly the green glow of the far right flanker swung violently back and forth, then winked out.

"Deuce, hold on!" I shouted. As I watched, the left flanker jerked sharply to the right and down, then became very still. "It's Cleo. She took out their cover. We rush the other two on three. One, two, three!" I dashed forward and to the left. Deuce was a half-step behind and angling to the right.

A pulse rifle crackled somewhere in front of me. Time seemed to slow as the nanos kicked my muscles into overdrive. I dove through the airlock, turning my body to the left and bringing the pneumatic up to center on the man crouched next to the ramp. I fired twice, hitting him in the chest. I tucked my shoulder and rolled. As I hit the ground, I realized that the man I'd shot hadn't been looking my way. His attention had been on something behind him.

I came out of my roll onto one knee and swung to cover the other side. The gunman there was already down, sprawled across his pulse rifle.

Deuce skidded to a stop at the top of the ramp, taking in the two downed men with a puzzled look. Then his eye caught something behind me, and he grinned as he lowered his weapon.

I turned and saw Cleo walking calmly toward me. She held her stun batons in one hand and the butt of a pulse rifle propped on her hip with the other.

"You boys need some help?" she asked.

"Thanks," I said. "But you could have told me what you were up to."

"No time. I realized what was happening as soon as the alarm sounded and got out through the aft hold just before Deuce locked the hatches down. I figured they'd try to mass their guns in the front and either force their way in or draw you out. I marked the two guys they held back for covering fire. As soon as you took out the first two, I decided to make a move."

I nodded. "I figured it was you when I saw the first pulse rifle shut down. How'd you take him out without alerting his buddies."

She held up a stun baton. "I got behind him and hit him with this. I powered down his rifle and hoped Sylvia was monitoring the power packs. The second guy was an easy shot with a needler. Then all I had to do was stroll over and pick up his rifle and take out the last one while you were doing acrobatics. Very impressive, by the way, but the guy on the right had you in his sights and would have dropped you if I hadn't fired first."

"I said thank you," I muttered.

She smiled and touched my cheek. "I know," she said. Deuce laughed out loud.

I shot him a look, but he just laughed more.

He walked down the ramp and checked the man I'd shot. "Dead." He hefted the man's pulse rifle.

I saw the gleam in his eye and shrugged. "Spoils of war," I said. He'd always wanted a Nakajima.

The man Cleo had shot was dead as well, hit in the center of mass with a pulse bolt that must have stopped his heart instantly. I searched him but found no identification other than a black teardrop tattooed on his left wrist.

"How about the other two?" I asked Cleo.

"The one I got with my needles is dead. I'm carrying cyanide, not sleepers. The one who got stunned is still out, but should wake up in an hour or so. The two you shot earlier were still alive but hurt badly enough to need attention. They left with a seventh guy in a ground car just before I used my stun batons."

"Then we haven't got much time," I said. "They'll have backup somewhere nearby. Either that, or this little firefight will attract official attention."

"On Tharsis Docks?" Cleo scoffed. "Not unless somebody goes nuclear."

"These guys are tied in with the cops somehow. They breezed past security when we first met them on the way to get you. Sooner or later, they'll be back with help."

"So what do we do?"

Instead of answering her directly, I called Sylvia. "Get in touch with the Port Authority. Tell them to get us a tractor for immediate departure. We'll pay the priority fee, but I want to lift ship in twenty minutes."

"Yes, Boss. Edward needs to speak to you urgently, too."

"Put him through."

"Zack," Rabbit said. "I did everything I could. I'm a slicer not a med tech. I could only do what the autodoc said to do, but it wasn't enough."

"What wasn't enough?"

Rabbit took a deep breath and held it for a second before speaking. "He's dead, Zack. Sanchez, I mean. The autodoc started alarming just after the gas attack. I ran the resuscitation protocols, but it didn't work. Then the 'doc started calling for human intervention. I didn't know what to do."

"Calm down, Rabbit. There's nothing any of us could have done."

He started to go on again about how primitive the autodoc programming was. I shut him off and turned to Deuce. "Grab the guy Cleo stunned and bring him aboard. Then get these bodies out of sight. The tractor should be here in a few minutes. We'll lift and run for Tycho as soon as we clear the dome."

Deuce nodded and tossed me his new pulse rifle. I slung it over my shoulder as he trotted off toward where the stunned gunman lay. Cleo and I moved the man I'd shot behind some rubbish near a recycling bin. By the time we finished, Deuce was making his way up the loading ramp with the inert body in a fireman's carry. He lowered the man to the deck, none too gently, then trotted back down the ramp to help me move the guy Cleo had taken out with the pulse rifle.

Cleo had stowed her captured rifle in the weapons locker along with her batons. She kept the needler in a clip holster at her waist. Deuce took my weapons as well as his own and stowed them away while I closed the ramp and resealed the airlock.

"We're cleared for departure, Zack," said Sylvia. "The tractor will be here in five minutes."

"Okay. Ask Rabbit to join us in the salon, please."

The man Deuce had dropped on the deck stirred and moaned softly.

I opened the first-aid kit on the bulkhead next to the weapons locker and took out a hypospray. I pressed it to his arm and shot him up with a jolt of anti-inflammatories and a bit of adrenalin.

His eyes popped open and he sat up, rubbing his neck.

Cleo stood nearby and covered him with her needler. His startled look faded quickly, replaced by a bland, neutral expression as he looked from me to Cleo and back again.

"My men?" he asked.

"Three dead, two wounded. Not a very good day for you."

His expression didn't change. "Sanchez?"

I considered for a second. If Sanchez were still alive, we'd continue to be a target for him or whomever he was working for. Dead men aren't usually of interest to anyone. "Sanchez is dead. His wound was too much for our autodoc."

"I need to see his body."

I laughed at him. "You're in no position to make demands. Cleo's needler is loaded with cyanide. You could be dead right now if she'd wanted it that way."

He glanced toward her, then returned to look straight into my eyes. He was a cool one; a hard-core Black Ops commando, probably a First Sergeant. Even with my nano-augmented senses, I couldn't detect a flicker of alarm in him. "My superiors need proof."

"And who are they? Who's behind all this?"

He stared straight ahead but said nothing. I knew the look and the training behind it. I'd been through that training myself. He could be broken; hell, anyone could be broken. But it wouldn't be fast or easy and there wouldn't be much left of him afterwards.

"Boss, the tractor is here," Sylvia announced over my link.

"Give me a second." I looked down at the man sitting on the floor in front of me. "Time's up, Sergeant," I said softly.

A flicker of surprise crossed his face.

"I know you. I know where and how you were trained. I knew most of your instructors. I know you're ready to die for the cause, but I'm not going to oblige you. Not today, anyway."

He resumed his bland stare, but his heart rate bumped up slightly.

"I don't know the names of your 'superiors,' but I know them, too. I used to be one of them; a true believer in Metternich and his Glorious Revolution." I leaned down close to his face, my voice a harsh growl. "You're going to take them a message. Tell them Sanchez is dead. Pedroia is dead. Samadar is dead. Tell them First Lieutenant Zachariah Mbele is dead. That person no longer exists. My war is over. Leave me and mine alone or I'll track your 'superiors' down and kill them, too."

I straightened up and waved Cleo back. "Let him go."

"Is that a good idea?" she asked.

"No, but I've had enough killing." I hauled the man to his feet and gave him a shove toward the sally port. "Get out of here and see to your men. Then deliver my message to your bosses. They'll know who I am and what I can do. The next move is theirs."

He staggered a little as he took his first steps, then straightened his back, and walked slowly to the starboard airlock. It hissed open for him. He turned to face me, and snapped a salute my way. "*Non sibi sed Mars.*" Then he stepped through the hatch and was gone.

I sighed, suddenly very tired. "Seal the ship, Sylvia," I said. "Tell the tractor we're ready to move."

Cleo holstered her needler, removed the clip-on holster, and walked over to the weapons locker. "Can you open it for me? I don't think I need a weapon under my pillow tonight."

I thumbed the lock and it popped open. "I'll have Deuce key it to your print once we're underway."

She stowed the holster on a shelf and closed the locker. She stood with her back to me. "Did you mean what you said, Zack? No more jolt, no more booze. I need to know you're serious." She turned to face me, looking into my eyes. "I can't imagine what it must have cost you; the war, prison, torture, all of it. But I see it in your eyes and in the way you react to men like Sanchez. You've been damaged in ways most people don't even survive."

I tried to speak but she touched a hand to my lips, her eyes tearing. "You've got to understand, I'm damaged goods, too. I can't be the one to save you. It's all I can do to keep my own head on straight."

I put my arms around her. "I'm not asking you to save me. Just to stay with me. I'll do whatever it takes."

She leaned into me. "This will end badly, you know. It always does with me."

"Maybe. But right now, I'm just looking for a beginning. The ending will take care of itself."

She looked up at me and smiled. "Then I'll stay. At least as far as Tycho." Then she kissed me. It wasn't long or passionate, but was full of promise. She pulled away and climbed the ladder to the upper deck.

I watched her climb, savoring every move.

I hadn't heard Deuce approach until he stood at my elbow, watching her disappear toward the salon.

"You offer her a share?" he asked.

I nodded.

"She said, 'yes'?"

I nodded again. "At least as far as Tycho. Then we'll see."

He laughed, softly. "Better hang on tight, LT. It's gonna be a wild ride."

We lifted from the Tharsis launch pad a few minutes later. Sylvia took us smoothly up through the thin atmosphere on the impulse engines and engaged the Moss drive once we cleared Phobos traffic control.

Rabbit rolled out of the salon as soon as the gravity was turned back on to tell me that Malloy's process for culturing glowgems was all over the public nets.

I smiled. Kensai hadn't let me down. He could have become a rich man, but I knew his sense of justice wouldn't let him keep the process secret. Before long, the market would be flooded with cultured gems and a potential source of funds for whoever was behind the Black Ops operation would be gone.

Sanchez had said there were still pockets of Martian Way faithful out in the Belt. Maybe even some of Metternich's inner circle. If so, many of them would know my name. I didn't care. I had settled my personal scores and found that revenge wasn't a satisfying dish, even when served cold. If someone out there thought they had issues with me, let them come.

We sent Sanchez's body into space with as much military honor as we could muster. He may have been a snake and a traitor, but he had once been a fellow soldier. I chose to honor that memory, rather than think about what he'd become.

Sylvia played a few bars from the old Martian Anthem and Deuce and I stood at attention as Rabbit purged Roberto's body from the starboard lock. Cleo stood quietly nearby, watching me.

"*Non sibi sed Mars,*" I said softly as the lock cycled closed.

Cleo came to my cabin later that night. She didn't speak, just slid into my bed next to me. I held her close as the *Profit* sped through the black, heading home.

About the Author

Bruce Davis is a Mesa AZ based general and trauma surgeon. He finished medical school at the University of Illinois College of Medicine in Chicago way back in the 1970's and did his surgical residency at Bethesda Naval Hospital. After 14 years on active duty that included overseas duty with the Seabees, time on large gray boats and a tour with the Marines during the First Gulf War, he went into private practice near Phoenix. He is part of that dying breed of dinosaurs, the solo general surgeon. He also is a writer of science fiction and fantasy novels. His independently published works include the YA novel *Queen Mab Courtesy*, and his military science fiction novel *That Which Is Human*. His nonfiction memoir, *Dancing in the Operating Room*, is a glimpse into the life and training of a Trauma Surgeon. *Glowgems for Profit* and *Thieves Profit* are parts of a continuing series of stand-alone novels about Zach Mbele, former Republic of Mars commando and captain of the fast freighter, Profit. They and his latest work, *Platinum Magic*, his first foray into the world of fantasy, are published by Brick Cave Media. *Platinum Magic* represents the start of an exciting new series set in a surprising modern world, like our own, only different.